HENRY'S WOMEN

*Pamela Oldfield titles available from
Severn House Large Print*

HENRY'S WOMEN

Pamela Oldfield

Severn House Large Print
London & New York

This first large print edition published in Great Britain 2007 by
SEVERN HOUSE LARGE PRINT BOOKS LTD of
9-15 High Street, Sutton, Surrey, SM1 1DF.
First world regular print edition published 2005 by
Severn House Publishers, London and New York.
This first large print edition published in the USA 2007 by
SEVERN HOUSE PUBLISHERS INC., of
595 Madison Avenue, New York, NY 10022.

British Library Cataloguing in Publication Data

Oldfield, Pamela
  Henry's women. - Large print ed.
  1. Sisters - Fiction 2. Politicians - England - Fiction
  3. Great Britain - Social conditions - 19th century -
  Fiction 4. Love stories 5. Large type books
  I. Title
  823.9'14[F]

ISBN-13: 9780727875822

Printed and bound in Great Britain by
MPG Books Ltd, Bodmin, Cornwall.

One

As the music from the organ rose and fell, Millie ignored the occasional wrong note and kept her gaze on the large flower arrangement on the altar. Her eyes were already red from weeping and she was struggling to prevent further tears. She refused to look at the elaborate coffin, which had been decreed years earlier when her father had begun putting money aside for his funeral. Instead of considering her loss, she forced herself to think about those who remained – the people who shared the front pew with her. The closest family member was her sister Esme, who sat beside her. Leo Walmsley, her brother-in-law, looking drawn and older than his thirty-five years, sat on the far side of Esme. Millie had no need to look at him, for the familiar dark hair and fine grey eyes were rarely far from her thoughts. She sighed.

Esme, three years younger than her husband, looked wonderful in an expensive black skirt and matching jacket, and her delicate

5

features and soft fair hair were enhanced by the fine black lace of her mourning veil. Her complexion, Millie knew, was unravaged by tears. Yet the man they were here to bury was her father, too, thought Millie, with a tightening of her lips.

Esme leaned towards her. 'Did you notice Aunt Flora's hat? What a joke!'

Millie *had* noticed, but she shook her head silently and closed her eyes as if in private prayer. Still, the roar of the London traffic was a constant hum, reminding her of the outside world, and she thought back over the years to a happier time, when they had been a complete family. As children, separated in age by a gap of eight years, they had never been exactly close, but Millie remembered the relationship as reasonably friendly. She had looked up to Esme as the older sister, but with hindsight Millie realized that Esme must have found a younger sister an annoying addition to the family. It was the later events, however, that had brought about a distinct rift in their relationship. Esme had married Leo, leaving Millie to care for their ailing parents. Six months ago the mother Millie adored had died after a fall from a horse-bus and their father, always a morose man, seemed to have lost the will to live. He had always found it hard to show affection to anyone, including his wife, and Millie was surprised by the extent of her grief.

From a doorway near the altar the vicar appeared.

6

Esme nudged her. 'About time too! I'm half frozen!'

The organist brought his rendition of soothing music to a close and Millie drew her coat about her. It was September and the weather had taken a turn for the worse with a strong, cool wind that was bringing down the first of the autumn leaves outside in the churchyard. Inside the church the only warmth came from the sunlight which shone sporadically through the stained-glass windows. The congregation rose for the first hymn and Millie sang distractedly, her mind on the manner of her father's death, which she had shared with no one. She had found him dead in bed, a glass beside him on the bedside table. Shocked and puzzled, she had dipped her finger into the sediment and found it to be laudanum. In fact it was a very strong mixture of opium and wine. Her father had killed himself, leaving a note, which read: 'Cannot go on. Forgive me, Millie.' Alone, unable to face the post-mortem which always followed a suicide, Millie had thrown away the note and washed out the incriminating glass, but she had not forgiven her father for what she considered his cowardice. He had given no thought to his daughter or the stigma that would follow if she allowed the truth to emerge.

The hymn ended and the congregation knelt for the prayers; Millie made her responses automatically, still deeply troubled by her own behaviour. Too late now to tell the doctor or the police and to have done so earlier would not have brought her father back to life. He had made his choice and so had she, and now she must live with her conscience. A second hymn followed and then a sermon that seemed to last for ever, as though it was all happening in slow motion; but at last the bearers moved to carry the flower-laden coffin outside for burial. As they walked back up the aisle, the tattered black rose on her aunt's ancient hat bobbed disconcertingly.

Leo caught up with her and laid a hand on her arm. 'You did all you could for him,' he told her. 'You have nothing with which to reproach yourself.'

His grey eyes were kind and for a moment she was reassured by his words, but then realized that the words were a platitude in the circumstances. She forced a smile, but before she could reply Esme had moved between them and now slipped her arm through Millie's.

'This should bring us closer,' she whispered. 'A death always unites a family.'

Millie ignored the words, certain that nothing could ever bring her closer to Esme.

They stood at the grave side in the sunshine while the last words were spoken over the coffin and Millie watched as it was lowered into the ground. She had a sudden vision of her father one Christmas, sitting at the head of the table, a white table napkin tucked into his collar to protect the gold paisley waistcoat that he wore for high days and holidays. He was carving the goose with familiar, slow precision while her mother watched anxiously for fear he found any fault with the way she had cooked it...

A cough from the vicar brought her back to the present and hastily she sprinkled a handful of earth over the coffin. Suddenly Esme began to sob loudly – as well she might, thought Millie, for her sister had been their father's favourite. From photographs, Millie knew that Esme had been a beautiful child with golden ringlets and bright-blue eys and a pert, elfin face that melted most hearts. Millie, who took after her father, was plainer, her face rounder, her hair a soft mouse-brown, her mouth a little too generous – her appearance saved only by her large dark-brown eyes.

Leo put his arm around Esme and, still sobbing, she leaned her head against his shoulder. Millie almost winced. She had never reconciled herself to the marriage, nor had she forgiven Esme for taking Leo Walmsley from her. Forcing back her feelings, Millie tried to concentrate, but the service had finally ended and the vicar was shaking her hand.

'Your father will be sadly missed,' he said.

'Thank you,' she murmured. 'A beautiful service.'

Had it been beautiful? she wondered. It had passed in a daze and for that she was grateful. She had other things to worry about now that

9

her father was gone.

Aunt Flora rushed towards her and threw her plump arms around her in a bear hug. She smelled of musty garments and the violet cachous she always sucked, but she was good-hearted and Millie liked her mother's only sister.

'You poor dear!' Flora said. 'What a burden for you all these years, but your poor mother was most appreciative of your efforts. She told me that before she died – that you were a wonderful daughter. Such a tragedy, too, to lose your father, God rest his soul. Fifty-five is no age. Poor Horace. Whatever will you do now, my dear? You will be all alone in that gloomy house. All that dark panelling and your mother's heavy curtains. Not to mention all those aspidistras! I've never understood why they are so popular.'

'Father liked them.'

'Did he? Well, there's no accounting for taste. It was more like a jungle than a drawing room. I never did know why they chose to live in Lambourne Street except that it *is* handy for the buses and trains. Not that they ever used public transport. Your father hated mingling with what he called "the proletariat".' She sighed and clasped Millie to her once more. 'You poor, *poor* dear!'

Millie managed to disengage herself. Being a poor, *poor* dear held no appeal. She wanted no one's pity. She smiled. 'Thank you for being with us today, Aunt Flora. You are coming back to the house, I hope, for some refreshments.'

'Most certainly I am. And if I may, I will stay overnight. I find travelling so disagreeable. Whenever I go by horse-bus the drivers whip the horses along with no regard for the passengers, who are thrown about all over the place! They race other drivers although they never admit it! And as for the trains! Nasty, noisy and smelly – and I always seem to get grit in my eye from the engine.'

'I'll make up a bed, Aunt. You must stay as long as you wish. I shall appreciate your company.'

Flora leaned closer. 'Don't put me in your parents' bed, will you, dear,' she whispered. 'It's bad luck.'

Millie promised, but at that moment a tap on her shoulder made her turn and she came face to face with Leo. Hoping that her eyes gave nothing away, she managed to smile.

He said 'Is there anything I can do to help, Millie? Anything at all.' As Flora drifted away, he added in a lower voice, 'You know I'd do anything for you.'

She stared at him, taken aback by his tone and the look in his eyes. Did she know that? Would he do anything for her? Ridiculously her heart leaped at the thought. 'Thank you, Leo. I think all goes well at present.'

'The service was very suitable,' he said.

'I hope so.' She smiled faintly. 'I thought the organist needed a few more lessons.'

'He did stumble rather.'

Esme materialized at Leo's side and gave

11

her husband a suspicious glance. 'I wondered where you were,' she said accusingly, then turning immediately to Millie said, 'I expect you would like a say in the choice of Papa's tombstone.'

'You may make the choice alone if you wish.'

'Perhaps I should.'

Leo said, 'Won't he be buried with his wife?'

Esme shook her head. 'Mama was buried with her parents. It was her last wish.'

Ellen, the hired help, arrived with a tray of cheese straws and they helped themselves. The table in the dining room was laid with cold ham, tomatoes and potato salad, and wine was offered as well as home-made lemon barley water. Quickly the mourners seated themselves around the long table and gradually the conversation moved from the earlier respectful murmurs to happier reminiscences of times past. Flora, flushed and excited by the occasion, remembered their father as a young man who had played golf with her husband.

'And now they have both gone,' she said, 'to the great golf links in the sky!'

Everyone laughed and Millie smiled to herself. Flora was a little too keen on her wine and it always made her merry. Her husband had been a pompous man but, being childless, he had always been kind to the two nieces. Millie caught Leo's eye and they both laughed.

'What's so funny?' Esme demanded.

12

Leo said, 'The golf links in the sky! Don't you think it's funny?'

Flora gave Esme a pitying glance. 'You never did have much of a sense of humour, Esme. You take after your father.'

Esme flushed. 'At least he could play golf!'

Millie intervened quickly by offering her sister another helping of ham. 'But save some room for the dessert, Esme. It's plum pie – your favourite. I made it especially for you.'

Mollified, Esme was neatly distracted and the awkward moment passed. Eventually Ellen removed the plates and the pie was served with warm custard.

Time passed; eventually the guests wandered away homeward and what remained of the family gathered in the lounge while Ellen cleared the dining-room table and washed up. They had discovered no last will and testament and Esme explained why.

'About ten years ago Papa found himself in a bit of a muddle financially,' she told them. 'It never was properly explained to me but Mama insisted that it was not his fault. Something about a partner in the firm who embezzled money; but it was never proved to the satisfaction of the law so nothing could be done.'

Millie looked at Leo. 'Did you know about this?'

'Not until a few days ago.'

Esme said sharply, 'It has nothing to do with Leo, Millie. Please address your questions to me.'

Flora frowned. 'You mean your father lost some money?'

'Worse than that. He lost all his money and began to fall into debt.'

Millie felt a spurt of anger. 'He told you all this? Why was I left in the dark?'

'Because I am older by eight years, married to a an assistant bank manager and one of us had to know what the future held for you.' Try as she might, Esme's eyes could not hide a glint of triumph.

'Also Papa considered me, as a married woman, the more worldly. I'm afraid there was nothing to leave any of us, Millie. No inheritance at all.'

Millie gasped but almost immediately said, 'Except the house!'

They all stared expectantly at Esme, who slowly shook her head. 'I'm afraid the house was sold to pay off debts. Two years back, to be exact. Since then it has been rented from the new owner, a Mr Douglas Beam, who is anxious to recover it. I'm sorry, Millie, but you will have to leave.'

Flora's plump face crumpled. 'Leave? How can she leave? She's got nowhere else to live. That's outrageous.'

Leo said quietly, 'I, too, am appalled. I have been wondering what should be done.'

Esme glared at him. 'You are not family, Leo. Please don't interfere.' She turned to Flora. 'Why can't she live with you, Aunt Flora?'

There was an awkward silence and Millie

14

closed her eyes, utterly humiliated by the row that was developing. She avoided Leo's eyes, knowing that she would see nothing but pity for her awful predicament; but before Flora could reply a knock at the door interrupted them. Ellen reported that she had finished her work and Millie hurried to pay her. When she had gone, the silence continued until Flora spoke.

'You know very well that my mother-in-law lives with me and we only have two bedrooms.'

Millie felt her cheeks burning. 'None of you need bother about me. I can look after myself. I shall find a job ... a position of some kind. I could be a companion or – or a governess. I could—'

Leo thumped a fist on the table, making them all jump. 'You will do nothing of the kind, Millie. You will come and live with us. We have a spare room and the least we—'

'Stay with us?' Esme's voice rose angrily. 'I shall decide who—'

'No, Esme!' He glared at her. 'I have already decided. Your sister will stay with us. How could you even consider allowing her to become a governess or a companion.'

'That was *her* idea, not mine!' Esme's eyes flashed. 'She is my sister and I will decide what—'

'I pay the rent, Esme, and it is decided.'

Flora was staring at them, her mouth agape. 'Really, Esme, I can't believe this of you. Your own poor dear sister!'

15

Millie wanted to crawl under the table and hide, but Leo reached across the table to pat her hand in a kindly gesture of reassurance. At once Esme slapped his hand away, her face chalk-white. 'I'm sure Millie doesn't want to be a burden on anyone,' she said.

'Indeed I don't!' Her heart was racing with a mixture of fear and anger.

Flora tutted. 'How could your own sister ever be a burden? That's a most un-Christain thing to say, Esme!'

Leo's jaw tightened. 'I insist that Millie is allowed to live with us. She is not to blame for this predicament. She has never been able to follow a career of any kind and your mother and father had need of her in their latter years. She devoted her life to them and that released you, Esme. For heaven's sake! You must see...'

'Must I? Well, I don't!' Esme jumped to her feet, pushed back the chair and ran from the room.

Unrepentant, Flora said, 'Well! I never expected to hear such words from my sister's child! Your mother must be turning in her grave!'

Leo sighed heavily. He looked understandably troubled and for the first time Millie realized that the relationship he shared with Esme was far from the marital bliss that she had imagined.

Leo turned to Millie and looked directly into her eyes. 'Please say you will come, Millie. I could not bear to see you in service.

A companion would be bad enough but a governess! ... Those poor souls are always despised and utterly undervalued. Your sister will recover her good sense in time, you'll see. It has all come as quite a shock.'

'A *shock*?' Flora said. 'But Esme says she *knew* the situation. She has had plenty of time to think of a solution. I'm disappointed in that young woman and that's the truth.'

Haunted by Leo's apparent desperation, Millie came to an abrupt decision. She said, 'If Esme is willing, I will come for a few months, perhaps, but only on one condition: that I come as your housekeeper. I cannot come as an equal and I will not intrude. If I could have a little sitting room instead of a bedroom I can keep to myself in the evenings with a book or some sewing.'

Leo protested, but Millie stood firm. They sought out Esme, who reluctantly agreed. Perhaps, thought Millie, Esme's idea of her younger sister as little more than a servant appealed to her. Before the day was out the details had been arranged. Millie would receive bed and board and a small sum weekly in exchange for work around the house, which included cooking. It wasn't ideal but what choice had she?

As Millie lay in bed that night, she wondered why she had put up so little resistance to the idea and hoped she wouldn't live to regret her decision. Slowly, unwillingly, she accepted the truth. The prospect of being near to Leo had swayed her judgement.

17

The next morning she awoke early, before it was light, and lay thinking about her father. Now she understood the reason he had chosen to die. He had known that at any moment the money for rent and other living expenses would run out and he couldn't face the shame. Millie had imagined that they were comfortably off, but obviously they had been living on borrowed money. She could see now why he had summarily dismissed Izzie, their cook-housekeeper, and she wondered if the charge of theft had been trumped up to avoid telling anyone the truth. And they had changed their butcher when her father claimed he had been impertinent. Perhaps poor Mr Lettworth had merely asked for the money that was owing to him.

'Papa! You should have confided in me,' she muttered.

She sat up suddenly. She would go to the bank manager and ask for details of their situation. Perhaps there would be enough money left to pay the tradesmen ... and maybe Mr Beam would grant her two weeks' grace while she made arrangements to put some of the furniture into store and sell the rest. She wanted to keep a few pieces of furniture in the hope that one day (the sooner, the better) she might be independent of her sister and Leo.

Padding across the floor, she found her slippers and a robe and made her way downstairs. The house was silent, but it had never been a bustling place and during the past months her father had taken to rising late from his bed. Now she understood that he had been unable to face his diminished circumstances.

She raked up the embers of the stove and heated water for a wash. Later, dressed, she was eating her porridge when there was a knock at the front door.

'Morning to you, ma'am.' A young man stood on the threshold, hat in hand. He was dressed in a faded brown suit, and a well-worn bowler hat crushed a tangle of dark curls. His round face was cheerful and blue eyes smiled down into hers.

'Would you be Millicent Bayley, daughter of Mr Bayley?'

'That'right, but what...?'

'Compliments of Mr Beam and will you be needing help with the move? If so I'm your man – me and my pa. We can move almost anything and store it too. We charge reasonable rates.'

'You're Mr Beam? The owner...' Millie stared at him, disconcerted by the haste with which her life was changing. 'I – Mr Beam, I need a little time.'

'No, no!' He laughed. 'Hardly, miss. I'm not the owner of the property. I'm the bailiff but...'

Millie shrank back. 'A *bailiff*! What – what does a bailiff do ... exactly?'

His smile was reassuring. 'Well, I'm not here to throw you out into the street, if that's

19

what you think? Do I *look* that sort of a man?'

'No-o, but what *do* you do?'

'I throw folk out into the street!' He grinned. 'Sometimes I bring a van and we seize the furniture or maybe only some of the goods and chattels – stuff to the value of the debt.'

If his grin was supposed to reassure her, it failed dismally.

He went on: 'But only when they've refused to go and we've given them fair warning. Like now.'

'This is fair warning?' Millie was shocked. 'So how long have I got?'

'A week. Mr Beam reckons that's fair because the tenant knew the date weeks ago when I served the summons.'

'But I didn't know anything about it!' she protested. 'The tenant was my father. We buried him yesterday.'

'There you are then.'

His logic escaped her, but Millie's immediate panic subsided and she looked at him thoughtfully. He looked very young – about twenty, she decided. He had a boyish, innocent air, but that might be deceptive. Millie had very little experience of men. Leo had been her one and only suitor. She had trusted him and he had betrayed her. 'What's your name?' she asked cautiously.

'Ned Warren at your service.' He gave a mock bow. 'I work for Betts and Company. Bailiffs – and highly respected too.' He leaned forward, lowering his voice. 'I'm gasping for a cuppa tea, if it wouldn't be too much trouble. Get me out of sight of the neighbours too, if you know what I mean.' She could smell the oil he wore on his hair.

'Oh!' She gave a nervous glance up and down the road. Lambourne Street was where she and Esme had been born. Number thirty-three was the only home she had ever known and the plane trees and the red pillar box on the corner were her earliest memories of the world outside. Incredibly the street was only a Bayley's throw from London's centre and the sound of the city's traffic was a permanent low roar in the background of their lives. A few streets away were the bus routes and the intrusion of other cultures which made up the rapidly growing city with its new cosmopolitan atmosphere.

Frowning, she wondered what Leo would say if he knew she was inviting a strange man into the house. He would most definitely advise against it. The thought fortified her.

'You'd better come in,' she told the bailiff. If any of the neighbours *were* watching, they might think he was a normal visitor. As far as she knew no one else in Lambourne Street had ever had a visit from a bailiff. Why hadn't her father prepared her for this predicament? Maybe he had been trying to tell her and never quite plucked up the courage. Another thought occurred. Did Esme know the bailiffs would be sent in? If so, why hadn't Millie been warned?

As she poured a mug of tea and passed it to

21

him, Ned Warren settled himself comfortably on a chair at the kitchen table and looked around the room with interest.

She stirred her tea, busy with her own thoughts. She should at once make a list of furniture she might need, but how could she pay for the storage? Would the little pocket money Esme paid her be enough to cover the costs – and did she need to ask her sister's permission? Leo would allow it but, as Esme repeatedly told him, he was not strictly family. She glanced up and saw that Ned was watching her. Something in his gaze made her blush.

'So,' he asked, 'where you going to from here?'

Millie hesitated. She was not prepared to discuss her impoverished state with this cheeky young man. 'I have somewhere ... arranged. A rather nice first-floor flat, if you must know, in Allbrin Street.'

He looked at her quizzically and she realized how unlikely that might seem.

'I have money of my own, if you must know,' she said, secretly appalled at the lie. What on earth had possessed her to pretend? Trying to impress the bailiff! Ridiculous.

'Allbrin Street,' he said. 'Nice area, that. Mind you, I served a summons on a chap there not long ago. Locked himself in and wouldn't leave. Threatened to hang himself. Had to bring in the police in the end. It sometimes happens.' He shrugged. 'And you know what? He was a doctor. Respectable, wouldn't you say?' He shook his head. 'I could tell you some tales.'

Not trusting herself to speak, Millie nodded. He was staring at her.

'So you're off to Allbrin Street.'

'Yes. I shall be very comfortable.' Did that sound convincing? It would explain why she was getting rid of some of the furniture. She wondered exactly how much the bailiff would have been told.

As if reading her thoughts, he said, 'If you want to store a few bits and pieces, my pa's got a workshop in Haddon Yard with a lot of space over it. Stanley Warren – that's his name. I could get it for you cheap.' He drank the tea noisily then glanced up as the nearby church struck the half-hour. 'I'll have to be going when I've got this tea down me. Plenty more calls to make. Some not as pleasant as this, I can tell you.' Seeing her interest, he elaborated. 'Sometimes I'm threatened with violence. Once I got whacked over the head with a saucepan by an old woman. Saw stars, I did...' He rolled his eyes. 'Usually the wife cries, but I have to ignore tears. "I'm only the messenger," I tell them; but of course they blame me. Only you didn't.' He grinned. 'So that's one to chalk up.'

Millie smiled. 'I do have a heavy saucepan!'

He emptied the mug and stood up. 'Not you. Not a pretty woman like you. I can always tell. I can size people up.' He followed her along the passage and said, 'How come you're not married? You should have been

23

snapped up years ago.'

Millie's hand fumbled for the latch and she felt the colour rush into her face. 'Maybe I didn't want to be snapped up,' she stammered.

'You must have had admirers.' Grinning at her embarrassment, he stepped past her on to the pavement, then turned and gave her a long look. Shaking his head he said, 'You're the dutiful type. Tell me if I'm wrong. Turned down the offer of marriage to stay at home and look after the parents.'

His careless words had touched a nerve. If only he knew. 'It's no business of yours!'

'It's not, is it?' he agreed with a conciliatory grin. 'Me – I just hate to see a lovely woman go to waste.'

Before Millie realized what he was doing, he lifted her right hand to his lips and kissed it. 'Thanks for the tea, Miss Bayley!' he said and was away, hands in his pockets, walking jauntily down the road. At the corner he turned and waved as if he knew Millie would still be watching.

'The cheek of the wretch!' she muttered as she closed the door. For a moment she stared at her right hand, then quickly rubbed away the kiss. Leo had been the last man to show her any kindness or affection and she didn't care to remember how long ago that had been. But with a faint smile she admitted to herself that Ned Warren's visit had cheered her and she felt that, because of his breezy compliments, she would somehow get

24

through the rest of the day.

First, though, she must see to her aunt's needs and send her on her way.

Less than a mile away Esme awoke and saw that her husband was already gone from the room. He liked to eat an early breakfast, whereas she liked to sleep late and rise about nine, when the daily woman had finished most of her chores. Forty minutes later, washed and dressed, she made her way downstairs and into the dining room. It was obvious that Leo had breakfasted and she helped herself to stewed apple and rang the bell for a fresh pot of tea.

'Where is Mr Walmsley?' she asked.

Mrs Wetton paused halfway to the door. 'He said he was going to your sister to see what he could do to help. Sorting out and suchlike. Said to tell you they could do it between them and you was not to miss your trip to the chiropodist.'

'He did, did he?' Esme looked at the woman with distaste. Mrs Wetton was a large, lumpy woman with a plain face hardened by ill luck and a bad-tempered husband, but she was very strong and hard-working and had been scrubbing floors and cooking breakfast for the Walmsleys ever since their marriage. 'Thank you, Mrs Wetton. Scramble me an egg and then you can go.'

In the dining room, Esme took a spoonful of apple and thought about her husband's message. Did she care that he had gone to see

25

Millie? She was tempted to follow him and make a scene, but her feet were troublesome and she valued the visits to the chiropodist. She also had an agenda of her own for the afternoon and with Leo out of the way she would find it easier to accomplish it. As she thought about her husband, her face assumed a martyred expression. He had not turned into the great catch she had anticipated when Millie first brought him home to meet her parents. At the time she had been piqued that her younger sister had met a man who found her interesting. She, Esme, was the beautiful daughter and she expected to make a good marriage. Leo Walmsley was a bank teller and her father had talked enthusiastically of his potential career. 'The man's got the ability,' he had enthused, 'but has he got the drive?'

Leo, then, had been an immature thirty-year-old and Esme had been twenty-seven. Millie, only just nineteen, had been deeply in love and believed that he loved her in return.

'Millie is not the right wife for a man like that,' Esme had told herself. 'She is too shy and would do him no credit. A man who might one day become a bank manager needs a suitable wife – a strong woman with poise and flair who is a good conversationalist.'

In this way she had convinced herself that she must save Leo Walmsley from himself and, after convincing him that Millie was merely infatuated, she had set about en-snaring him for herself. Confused and over-whelmed by her attentions, Leo had sur-

26

rendered and they had been married before the year was out.

Since then, however, Esme had admitted to herself that Leo's career had not thrived, nor had the relationship blossomed. True, they rented a pleasant house in Allbrin Street, known as 'a good neighbourhood', and Leo had recently been made assistant manager at a smaller branch, but Esme now felt that she had been cheated of the wonderful life she had been led to expect and blamed Leo. Had they been blessed with a child she felt sure things might have been different, but they remained childless and she also laid the blame for this squarely at her husband's door.

Now she sighed heavily and poured another cup of tea, which she drank distractedly; then, with an effort, she squared her shoulders and forced the unhappy thoughts from her mind. Mrs Wetton brought in the scrambled egg and Esme nodded her thanks.

'Let him go to his precious Millie,' she muttered as Mrs Wetton departed. 'If he wants to play Sir Galahad, I won't stop him.' The day ahead held greater pleasures for her and she would allow nothing and no one to spoil it for her.

Less than a mile separated the Walmsleys' home from the house from which Millie was soon to be evicted and Leo, walking at a brisk pace, covered the distance in twenty minutes. He stood on the doorstep, his heart beating, and when Millie opened the door his face

27

broke into a restrained smile at the sight of her.

'Leo! Do come in. I was just sorting out Papa's clothes. They are too good to throw away. I don't suppose any of them would fit you, would they?' She closed the door and led the way into the drawing room, where a table was piled with jackets and trousers. Waistcoats were folded on a nearby chair and hats covered the sofa.

'Ah! You've been busy,' he said. 'I've come to offer my services. I thought you'd need some help.'

'Does Esme know? I mean, does she ... approve?' She clasped her hands nervously.

'Of course she does. Why shouldn't she? Closing up a house involves a great deal of work.'

They stared at each other and Leo wondered if this was a suitable time to deliver his own message. Before he could waver he said, 'I wanted to see you alone to tell you ... that you will be more than welcome in our home and must stay as long as you wish.' He wanted to add that he hoped it would be for ever, but that was much too dangerous. She might well have recovered from her earlier infatuation and his own feelings must remain hidden from both sisters.

Millie nodded. 'Thank you, but I shall certainly not outstay my welcome. I can see that Esme might find it awkward, having another woman in the house. It rarely works satisfactorily, but I shall do my best to fit in.'

She was wearing a dress of pale lavender with a large apron over it and already she looked like a servant. It was unbearable that she should have come to this, he thought bitterly. She deserved so much more. Millie deserved all that Esme had gained in her stead and he was to blame for that. He would never forgive himself. He said, 'The two attic rooms are quite pleasant. You could have them both and bring whatever you wish in the way of furniture. You would be very snug up there if you don't mind the extra stairs.'

'Two rooms of my own? That is very generous, Leo. I'm sure I shall be very comfortable and hopefully it won't be for ever.' She smiled. 'I haven't quite given up the idea of marriage, if the right person comes along.'

'Marriage?' He struggled to hide his sense of shock and cursed himself for his stupidity. Why should he imagine that Millie would remain a spinster just because he had not married her? 'You're an arrogant fool!' he told himself.

To Millie he said, 'All I want is for you to be happy.'

'As you are.' Millie gave him a searching look.

'Me? Of course.' Did he sound convincing? he wondered, and was relieved when she changed the subject.

'A bailiff called here about an hour ago,' she said, and went on to describe his visit.

Leo frowned. 'Sometimes they can become violent towards the tenants,' he warned.

'Maybe you should keep him on the doorstep if he calls again.'

'He will call again. He's going to move my furniture. There's nothing to worry about, Leo, I can assure you.'

Minutes later they were engrossed in the work of sorting clothes and other items into categories – some to be taken to the Salvation Army for the poor and others to be considered by an antiques expert, for sale. Leo, happy to be in Millie's company, was secretly glad that in a day or two she would be safe under his roof.

Two

A month passed – a month in which the Bayleys' family home was handed over to the new owner and Millie moved into the two attic rooms in her sister's house. She took enough furniture with her to create a sense of familiarity and, with Ned Warren's help, put some more into the space above the workshop in Haddon Yard. She met Ned Warren's father, Stanley, who bore little resemblance to his attractive son and who smelled of sawdust and cheap pipe tobacco. He seemed friendly enough, though, and for the use of the attic he charged the very reasonable sum of sixpence per week.

It had been arranged that her 'pocket money' would be three shillings a week, and this money was given to her every Saturday morning by Esme, who counted the coins carefully into Millie's outstretched hand. The work was not arduous, but being under her sister's supervision was irksome in the extreme. Millie bore it philosophically, however, determined that the situation was only temporary and that she would somehow find a way to gain her independence.

Being under the same roof as Leo was a

31

two-edged sword. She relished the fact that she could see him regularly but could not reconcile herself to the sight of her sister with a hand linked through his arm or sitting close with her head on his shoulder. Millie sensed Leo's discomfort when Esme's show of exaggerated affection became too embarrassing. On these occasions Millie left the room on some pretext or other. Life was far from perfect, but she told herself it was bearable.

On Friday, 24 October, Millie set off to the nearby market in Ledbury Way with Esme's shopping list and a purseful of money. She was choosing plums when a shout nearby turned all heads towards the sound.

'Come back, you wretch! Stop him, someone! He's taken my purse!'

Millie saw a young man dashing through the crowd towards her and, without stopping to think, she reached out with her foot and tripped him up. With a cry of fury he fell headlong, the small purse still clutched firmly in his right hand. At once the crowd descended on him and the purse was retrieved. The young pickpocket, dishevelled and unwashed, was set roughly on his feet by a passing coster, who held firmly on to the collar of his faded shirt.

'Thank the Lord!' An elegant woman had pushed her way forward and was now handed her property. 'What's the world coming to? Robbed on my own doorstep!'

An elderly woman jerked a thumb in Millie's direction. 'You've got 'er to thank for your purse, missus. Tripped him up good and proper. Went flying, 'e did.'

The pickpocket mumbled something unflattering and spat in Millie's direction. She stepped back smartly, eyeing him with distaste. His captor snapped, 'Watch yer manners, you little tyke!' and gave him a sound shaking.

The owner of the purse seized Millie's hand enthusiastically. 'Thank you so much!' She was well dressed in a matching grey skirt and jacket, both of which were edged in a bright yellow, a colour that was echoed in the buttons. A colourful feathered hat was set at a jaunty angle on auburn curls. Millie noticed her eyes with envy: they were a deep green with gold flecks, surrounded by dark lashes, and below them her cheeks were suspiciously rosy and her lips scarlet. Millie realized she was staring. The effect was dramatic, but was her complexion real?

The woman smiled. 'Quick thinking on your part. Well done!'

There were approving murmurs from the crowd and Millie felt herself blushing. 'Please!' she stammered. 'It was nothing. I didn't stop to think.'

A man said, 'What about the young roustabout? Want us to fetch a p'liceman, do you? Gonna charge 'im?'

The woman hesitated. 'Perhaps...'

Her indecision gave him his chance and with a quick twist of his scrawny shoulders he jerked himself free and dashed away through the crowd.

The coster looked apologetic. 'Little perisher! Like a ruddy eel!'

'It doesn't matter.'

The man tutted. ' 'Cept now 'e'll go and pinch somefing else off some other poor soul! Pickpockets! Breed like bloomin' rabbits, they do!' With a shrug he lost interest and wandered away and within seconds the rest of the little crowd followed suit. The woman remained, smiling at Millie.

'My name's Prunella Gayford but I'm better known as Poppy. You may have heard of me.' Her voice held a hint of smothered cockney vowels, but she remembered her aitches.

'Poppy Gayford?' Millie shook her head.

The woman looked disappointed. 'I'm an artiste,' she told Millie. 'A theatrical artiste. I appear on stage at Tapper's Supper Room.'

Millie looked blank. 'You must have heard of Tapper's.' Poppy was astonished. 'It's a supper room. A meal and a bit of entertainment. There aren't many of them left now. People prefer the music halls, but we do all right.'

'A supper room.' Millie was intrigued by her new friend. A theatrical artiste. So the rosy cheeks *were* helped by a little rouge. Never in her life had she met such a colourful person. 'Are you a singer?'

'Better than that: I *pose*! In the "altogether".' She laughed at Millie's expression. 'So called. We don't even wear sandals, although

34

the Greeks did, naturally, because they had to walk about. We don't. We have to stand very still like statues in a temple. We're draped, you see, in silk. They call it the Grecian Temple Scene. The men go wild for it.' She shrugged. 'I know some people think it's old-fashioned nowadays, but our clients love it.'

'It sounds very–' Millie searched for a suitable adjective – 'very high class.'

'Oh it is high class.' Poppy patted her curls. 'It's educational in a way. The audience gets to know what life was like in Grecian times long ago.'

'So ... didn't Grecian women wear very much?'

'I suppose not, although it is called a–' she frowned – 'a dramatic representation. That could mean anything.'

Millie tried to hide her astonishment. 'So it's rather like acting.'

'Of course it is. Only we don't act. And you do have to have a good body that stands up to scrutiny. I've got some photographs. Want to see them?' She pointed upwards. 'My flat's up there. Come and have a drop of something and I'll show you the scrapbook.'

'Oh no!' Millie cried instinctively, taken aback by the unexpected suggestion.

Poppy blinked. 'Why not? I just want to say thank you for getting my purse back. A little drink never did anybody any harm. Why should the men have all the fun?'

Millie meant to refuse, but she was suddenly tempted. Poppy had fluttered into her

35

life like an exotic bird and Millie was reluctant to let her go. It was an exciting offer, she told herself, maybe even a little dangerous; but what had her life had to offer so far in the way of a challenge? The past years had held nothing but duty and now she had next to nothing and was forced to accept charity from her sister. Dare she accept Poppy's invitation?

She heard herself say, 'Well, just for ten minutes then, but I have to finish the shopping.'

'Oh blow the shopping!' Poppy slipped an arm through hers.

With her heart thumping Millie accompanied her new friend up three flights of gloomy stairs. By the time they reached the top she was already regretting the impulse that had made her accept the invitation. They stopped outside a newly painted door; Poppy found her key and led the way inside.

Millie was astonished. 'It's *beautiful*!' she gasped.

The flat was furnished with style and no expense had been spared. There were thick rugs on the polished floor, a suite upholstered in green damask, polished wooden chairs and tables, and large pictures on the wall.

Poppy watched her, a smile on her face. 'I have a rather fond gentleman friend,' she said proudly.

'A gentleman friend?' Millie was trying to make sense of it all. 'Doesn't he mind you posing ... the way you do?'

Laughing at the absurdity of this suggestion, Poppy shook her head. 'He's proud of me. He'd like to marry me, but he's already got a wife tucked away in Somerset. So he set me up here seven years ago. Our little love nest.' She laughed gaily as she drew out the hatpin and removed the feathered hat. 'But first a little drink and then the photographs.'

Crossing to a cabinet on the far side of the room, she opened it up to reveal a row of bottles. 'What's your tipple,' she asked. 'And what's your name?'

'I'm Millicent Bayley – known as Millie.' To ward off the next question Millie said hastily, 'I do nothing artistic, I'm afraid. Just house-keeper to my married sister. I – I don't usually drink.'

'Don't drink? Good Lord! You'd better start now then. A small sweet sherry. Can't go wrong with that.' She handled bottle and glass deftly and Millie could see that she was practised in the art. 'And thanks again for saving my purse. *And* my reputation.' She handed Millie a glass, which seemed anything but small. 'My gentleman friend already thinks me the world's biggest scatterbrain! If I'd lost my purse he'd *know* I am!'

Moments later the sherry was warming Millie's stomach and the two women were deep in conversation as they turned the pages of Poppy's scrapbook. This contained a mixture of programmes, newspaper cuttings and photographs, some professional, others obviously amateur. The name 'Tapper's Supper

Room' appeared on every page, heading lists of various theatrical acts or menus.

'Tapper's do good food,' Poppy told her. 'The sort of food men like. Hearty, meaty pies, puddings, lashings of gravy. Some come for the food, others for the thrills, if you know what I mean.'

The photographs of Poppy on stage were, to Millie's untutored eyes, rather shocking. Millie had never seen women posing in such flimsy wisps of silk. These were draped with the utmost cunning to suggest nudity while revealing nothing and she wondered curiously what would happen if one of the women sneezed. In most of the photographs Poppy was leaning against a false marble column. In others she was seated on a curve of steps, always surrounded by women similarly dressed. There was not a man to be seen, for which Millie was thankful. A scantily clad man would have been too great a shock for her system. It was all elegantly done and presumably legal. Millie didn't want to ask.

'You should come to the show one evening,' Poppy urged. 'Get your sister and her husband to bring you along. You can have a bit of supper and a drink. You'd enjoy it. It's not just for roughs, you know. Tapper's is a respectable business. Lots of wealthy people pop in, specially the young blades! Not to mention the military men home on leave.' She laughed. 'When we close, they're all out there, waiting by the stage door. That's how I met my gentleman. Not that he's a young blade. He's nearer fifty, but I don't care. He's got plenty of money and a good job – if you can call it a job.' She lowered her voice, leaning closer. 'He's an MP! What d'you think about that, eh?' and laughed as Millie's eyes widened.

'A Member of Parliament!' Nearly halfway through the last mouthful of sherry, Millie began to splutter.

Poppy patted her on the back and then hauled her to her feet. 'Come on. I mustn't keep you from your shopping. Don't want to get you into trouble with that sister of yours. Where does she live? Is it far?'

Millie explained.

'Allbrin Street? I know it. Had an aunt lived there once but she's dead now. She married a man who had a big grocery shop and I do mean big. Nice street. You'll be all right there.'

She escorted Millie to the top of the stairs and shook her hand again. 'Come and see me one afternoon if you like. I'm mostly in.'

'But suppose your gentleman friend arrived. He wouldn't want to be seen, surely.'

'Don't worry your head about that. I'd introduce you but not mention his name and then you'd say you were on your way out. It's no problem, I promise you.'

Millie made her way down the stairs, carefully clutching the banister rail. Her head felt strangely light, but she had enjoyed the sherry. In fact, she thought, making her way home later with the shopping, she had actually enjoyed the whole adventure. It had been something of a revelation. There was a whole different world out there and she had only just discovered it. Hugging her secret close, she returned to the house and her housekeeperly duties. If Esme noticed a change in her, she did not comment.

In bed that night Millie reviewed the situation and saw no dangers. Why shouldn't she have a friend? Neither Leo nor Esme would approve of such a friendship, but Millie made up her mind that she most certainly *would* see Poppy again. Unaware that the day's events were about to change her life, Millie slept peacefully through the night with the hint of a smile on her face.

It had been agreed that Leo, Esme and Millie should eat breakfast together and that Esme and Millie would share a meal at lunch time. Leo would continue to dine in a small restaurant close to the bank but he would eat supper alone with Esme while Millie dined in the kitchen, or upstairs if she chose. That way they would keep their lives reasonably separate. Although Leo was unhappy about the arrangement, Esme was determined on this point and Millie was glad enough to agree. She welcomed the time she spent in her own rooms when, for the first time in her life, she was able to be alone. It was an unaccustomed luxury.

The day after her visit to the market Millie and Esme were still at the breakfast table but

Leo had hurried off to walk to his office – a twenty-minute walk which he referred to as his 'constitutional'. Esme was wearing a heavy silk robe over her nightdress, for she liked to take her time first thing in the morning. She looked up from her toast and marmalade and smiled at Millie.

'We have two friends coming this evening to play whist,' she told her. 'I can't ask you to join us, but perhaps you would serve us some biscuits and a plate of cakes and a pot of tea around seven. They aren't late birds so will be leaving around nine.'

'Of course I will,' Millie said, hiding her elation. She had never liked cards, though she had sometimes partnered her father when they were invited to play with their neighbours.

Esme gave her a searching look. 'You seemed a little flustered yesterday, when you came back from the market. I didn't ask because Mrs Bray was here, but I was puzzled. Did something happen?'

'Nothing much.' (She hoped God would forgive the lie.) 'A woman had her purse stolen by a pickpocket and as he ran past me I tripped him up and we recovered the purse.'

'And you didn't tell me?'

'Why should I?'

Esme's expression hardened. 'Because we give you shelter and you owe it to us to...'

Millie bridled at her sister's tone. 'I am not a child, Esme, and you are not my employer in the true sense of the word. I don't see why

41

I should have to report back to you if I choose not to. It was hardly earth-shattering. I suppose I forgot about it.'

For a moment Esme was silent; then she asked, 'Who is this woman?'

'Her name's Prunella Gayford.' Something made Millie hold back the rest of the story – firstly because she knew Esme would be scandalized and secondly because she liked the idea of a secret. There was no way Esme would ever find out the truth.

'A *decent* woman?'

'Yes – but would it matter to you if she were not?'

Esme's eyes narrowed suspiciously. 'I don't much like your attitude, Millie. What on earth has got into you?'

'I don't much like the interrogation, Esme. I don't enquire into your every move or question you about your friends. I have never asked who you visit on your Friday afternoon outings nor do I...' She stopped in surprise, because Esme's face had coloured slightly and there was a startled look in her eyes.

Esme rose abruptly to her feet and pushed back her chair. 'I should think not!' she stammered. 'You should remember that you are only here on sufferance, Millie, so you'd be wise not to upset me.'

'How have I upset you? I had no idea that the mention of your Fridays was going to—'

'That's enough!' Esme's voice rose sharply. 'What I do with my time is not your affair. You are not here to spy on me, Millie.'

'Nor you on me.'

It was Millie's turn to be suspicious. Where did her sister go each Friday?

As if reading her thoughts Esme's expression changed again. 'Has Leo asked you to check up on me? Is that it?'

To Millie's surprise she saw fear in her sister's eyes. 'Of course he hasn't. How could you think him so low? If he wants to know something, surely he has only to ask you. He trusts you, doesn't he?'

While the silence lengthened, Millie felt a coldness within her as the suspicion grew. Her sister was deceiving Leo. But why? A terrible thought entered her mind: she was visiting the doctor.

'Oh Esme! It's not – I mean, you're not ill, are you?'

Esme hesitated and another thought jostled its way in. Perhaps Esme was expecting a child. Shocked, Millie considered the implications. Leo would presumably be pleased to become a father. In those far off days with Millie, Leo had talked about the children they would have when they were married. It had been a joke between them. Hopefully two boys and two girls.

'Or three of each!' Millie had laughed.

'Or four! The sky's the limit!'

That day was still etched clearly in Millie's memory. High hopes so quickly dashed when Esme had made up her mind to become Leo's wife. Now it seemed Leo's plans had come to naught. Even if Esme should die,

Millie could never become Leo's wife, so in no circumstances could she ever give Leo a child. Victorian law did not allow marriages 'within the family', and Millie was now Leo's sister-in-law.

Now Esme said, 'No, I'm not ill and I'll thank you not to ask any more questions about my private life. But if Leo should ask you about...'

'He never does and I'm sure he never will. You should know him better than I do and even *I* know that.'

'You think you know him, do you? You silly creature!' Esme turned and walked quickly to the door. There she turned again. 'If you must know, there are times when I wish I had never married him!'

She slammed the door behind her, leaving Millie staring in shock, her mind reeling.

The following Monday Mrs Wetton was down on her knees scrubbing the kitchen floor and muttering to herself about her good-for-nothing husband, who frittered away her hard-earned wages whenever he got the chance. She had long since learned to hide the money in various nooks and crannies around the flat they shared with her parents. Her remaining son, she suspected, was going the way of his father.

The front-door bell disturbed her and she struggled upright and made her way along the passage.

'What now?' she demanded.

44

The young man smiled and gave a small nod which was almost a bow. 'The mistress in?' he asked.

He had a cheerful, good-natured face and dark curls and she almost returned his smile. But not quite. Just in time she remembered that he was one of 'them': the enemy – men.

'Who wants to know?' she demanded, wiping her wet hands on her apron.

'Ned Warren. I'm a friend of hers.'

'If you want the mistress, she's out.' She narrowed her eyes. 'You sure you come to the right house?'

'Pretty, with a lovely smile.'

'That's her, but I've told you: there's only me in and I'm busy so...'

'D'you know when she'll be back?'

' 'Fraid not. They don't tell stuff like that to the likes of me.'

He rolled his eyes, pondering her answer. 'You wouldn't do me a great favour, would you? Give her a message?'

'Why should I?' She regarded him curiously. He didn't seem the type of man who would know someone like Mrs Walmsley. He looked suspiciously like a tradesman of some kind. Up to no good, probably. But if she refused she would never find out what the message was and that might be interesting.

She said, 'You a money-lender?'

'Certainly not!'

'Friend of the family, then?'

'Something like that.' He smiled. 'I'll make it worth your while. A sixpence, say?'

45

'I'd rather say a shilling!'

'A sixpence or nothing.' She nodded and he clapped a hand to his thigh to seal the arrangement. 'Tell her I'll be at the end of the road–' he pointed – 'tomorrow at four, with a proposition she can't refuse.' He grinned.

Now Mrs Wetton was thoroughly intrigued. Her mistress was going to meet a good-looking young man at the end of the road. She would have given that particular message free of charge, but the sixpence was already agreed and she held out her hand.

She sighed as he sauntered away, full of youth and confidence. If only her own son could be like that, but he was a useless lad like his father, with no redeeming graces. She resumed her position on the kitchen floor and reached for the scrubbing brush. When the good Lord had been handing out favours, she had obviously been elsewhere.

While Mrs Wetton was talking to Ned Warren, Millie had been wandering up and down Signet Street, sizing up Tapper's Supper Room in what she hoped was an inconspicuous way. From the outside it looked like an overgrown tavern in the middle of an undistinguished street of tall brick houses smoked a dark grey by the soot from the surrounding chimneys. The double doors were painted dark green and opened inwards when she gave them a tentative push. There was a window of frosted glass through which she could make out a red curtain, which

46

covered the glass and hid the interior. Millie stopped several times as she passed it, pretending to attend to her buttoned boots, and watched as people went in and out. She didn't see Poppy Gayford and, to her disappointment, no one who entered looked at all theatrical. One man carried a tray of pies on his head and another came out to paste a large notice on the display board. This was to the effect that Lennard Hornby, 'the Toast of the Halls', would be appearing that evening with a fully supporting cast.

'Lennard Hornby?' Millie didn't know the name. While the street was comparatively empty she ran to the window and peered in but saw nothing through the curtain except a few shadowy shapes and one glittering light.

'Still, it is the middle of the afternoon,' she told herself.

The place probably came alive at night with all manner of excitements. Recrossing the road she took a last look at the place where Poppy was employed. Above the window a rectangular painted board bore the words 'Tapper's Supper Room' in large capital letters in black and gold. An old woman approached, shuffling along in worn slippers. 'That's not for the likes of you, my duck!' she wheezed. 'A bit saucy, that is!'

'Oh!' Millie felt absurdly guilty. 'I was just wondering ... I've never been to a supper room.'

'Nor never should, a young lady like you. Mind you, it's not all naughty nudery. There's a few ditties and a comedian. And Lennard Hornby – now he's a singer. My Bert used to go with his brother before the lungs took him. Coughed himself to death, he did, poor old sod; but he used to like the odd evening out. Pint of ale and a chunk of meat pie and a bit of entertainment. Harmless enough.'

Millie took a chance. 'I know one of the – the theatricals. She's in the Grecian tableau. Poppy Gayford.'

'Never heard of her, my duck!'

She shuffled on her way and Millie decided on one further foray. She walked up to the green doors and pushed her way in. Inside it was gloomy, but her eyes quickly accustomed themselves to the difference in light. She found herself in a thickly carpeted area with a bar along the left side. Behind it the wall was hung with an array of bottles and a mirror reflected the room. On the opposite side of this there was a counter, behind which she noted a row of coat hangers on a stand. So this, she thought, was where the patrons left their coats.

Millie took a few steps further into the room, which appeared to be empty, and for a moment it was enough for her simply to relish the sense of forbidden fruit. She smiled as she drew in the heady mix of stale cigar smoke, patchouli hair oil and perfume. Ahead of her the room widened and in the far wall she saw large double doors; these were propped open, but the way forward was barred by a thick red silk rope with tasselled ends.

48

Beyond the rope a vast room was dimly lit, but she could just make out tables and chairs and a raised platform at the far end. Presumably this area was the stage and this was where Poppy took part in her Grecian tableau. She tried to imagine the place teeming with people, some of whom were Members of Parliament. Who was Poppy's mystery man?

'Can I help you, miss?'

She jumped as a small muscular man appeared beside her. He was frowning and looked as though he would actually be most unwilling to offer any help of any kind. His head was bald and small bulbous eyes did nothing to improve his fleshy face.

'I'm – I was hoping to see Miss Gayford,' she lied.

'Too early, miss. Come back tonight after eleven. You can see them all at the stage door through the alley.' He jerked a thumb.

'Where do they sell the tickets?' Millie had no idea why she asked such a question.

His frown deepened. 'Not thinking of coming to the show, I hope. Not unaccompanied, at any rate. It might be a bit – a bit near the knuckle for the likes of you.'

'Oh. I see ... After eleven then, at the stage door. Thank you.' She retreated, heart thumping, to the safety of the street. Staring up and down, she felt disappointed by its mundane appearance and the ordinariness of the people. There had been a certain element of faded glamour about the interior of Tapper's

49

Supper Room that had excited her. With a sigh of regret Millie turned and made her way back in the direction of Allbrin Street.

The trip had pleased her. Another little secret to keep from Leo and Esme, she thought defiantly. It wasn't much but it was a step in the right direction.

Mrs Wetton was on the point of leaving when Millie arrived back and she mumbled the message through the large hatpin she held between her teeth.

'What was that?' Millie asked.

Mrs Wetton removed the hatpin and stabbed it through the ancient hat that covered her straggling hair. 'Message for your sister from a young man. To meet him tomorrow at four at the end of the road. That end.' She pointed.

Millie stared at her. 'Are you sure it was for Esme? I don't think she knows any young men.'

Mrs Wetton shrugged. 'Said she was pretty with a nice smile. His name was Ed Something. Made out like she'd be pleased with the message.'

Millie frowned. 'Maybe he came to the wrong house.'

'He said he had a proposition for her.' She picked up her umbrella and stared out of the window. 'Not raining, is it?'

Millie hid a smile. 'No, it's still a fine day.'

Mrs Wetton, she had learned, was obsessed with the weather and carried an umbrella from January to December, even though she lived less than half a mile away from Allbrin Street.

'He gave me a sixpence to pass on the message. I've done my bit.' Mrs Wetton pushed past Millie and lumbered towards the front door, and Millie, still full of her investigation of Tapper's Supper Room, put the conversation out of her mind.

As part of Millie's duties, she prepared supper on alternate days and she was carrying a tray of fruit jelly into the dining room that evening when she saw a shape at the front door and an envelope was pushed through the letter box. Assuming it was a letter for Esme and Leo, she paid it no heed until the meal was over. It was Leo who picked it up and carried it into the kitchen, where Millie was washing up.

'This came for you by hand,' he said, not bothering to hide his curiosity.

'For me?' Wiping her hands on her apron, Millie opened the envelope and found three tickets for Tapper's Supper Room. Obviously they had been sent by Poppy. Millie's cheeks flushed. It was so kind, but how was she to explain them to Esme and Leo? Poppy had put her in a very awkward position. Agitated, she thrust the tickets back into the envelope and stuffed it into the pocket of her apron. 'It's nothing,' she told Leo and plunged her hands back into the soapy water.

Leo watched her, puzzled. 'What is it, Millie? Has someone frightened you?'

'No! I told you. It's nothing. Something personal, that's all. Something private.'

He came closer so that he could look into her face. 'Millie, you can trust me with anything that happens to you. If someone is – is upsetting you, I'll take care of it for you. It's not that we want to pry, but I have to consider the security of the house and our safety. If some wretch is trying to worm his way into your confidence, I should know. We don't want to be robbed, or worse.'

Millie groaned inwardly. Perhaps she should confide in him – but he would almost certainly try to prevent her from meeting Poppy again. And if he told Esme...

'It's nothing to concern you or Esme,' she told him. Unless ...Would it be proper, Millie wondered, for a man to escort his wife and sister-in-law to Tapper's Supper Room? Suddenly she decided to take a chance. But she would put a new slant on the incident. 'If you must know, Leo, a woman – I mean a man, was giving out tickets in the streets for a supper-room show. Lennard Hornby is performing.'

'A supper room! How very odd. Business must be bad.'

'I suppose so. They were offering free tickets to encourage people to go along. It looks as if they are pushing free tickets through letter boxes now.'

'Complimentary tickets? Show them to me, Millie, please.'

'Hardly suitable for such as us,' he told her,

handing them back. 'They get a mixed audience in those places. Working-class most of them, plus a fair sprinkling of young toffs out for a bit of low life. Not really our kind of thing.'

'I thought not,' Millie said hastily. 'I'll give them to Mrs Wetton. She might care to go along with some of her family.'

Satisfied, Leo returned the tickets and made his way back to the drawing room to rejoin his wife, and Millie let out a long sigh of relief. She had escaped censure by a whisker; but the idea of the lost opportunity rankled. It would have been wonderful to make use of the tickets, but it was obviously out of the question.

Three

The following afternoon found Ned Warren waiting at the end of the street in the appointed place at the appointed time, but the minutes ticked by and there was no sign of the young woman he was hoping to see. The church clock struck the first quarter and then the half-hour and Ned knew she wasn't coming. He leaned back against the area railings of the nearest house and pondered his next move. Quarter to five. A young nursemaid came by wheeling a large perambulator containing twins. Catching sight of him, she fussed with her collar and beamed.

'Ned! Where have you been these past few days? I missed you. We all did. The Duke's Head's not the same without you.'

Grinning, Ned leaned over the pram. 'What. Both asleep? What d'you do to them? Drop of mother's ruin?'

'What? Give the babies gin?' She straightened her hat, which was already straight. 'You saucy devil! I'd do no such thing. Get my cards, I would, if I ever did. The mistress would go mad!' She gave him a provocative smile.

54

Once it would have turned Ned's knees to jelly, but today he barely registered it.

She said, 'So where *have* you been?'

He shrugged. 'Here and there! You know.'

'Coming down tonight? I'll be there around seven or just after. Just for half an hour. I offer to walk their stupid dog and that gives me an excuse.' She bent over the pram and fidgeted with the blanket, giving him a tantalizing view of her slim back and pert bottom seductively hidden by the dark serge uniform.

Ned rolled his eyes. 'Might be. I don't know. We're pretty busy right now, me and Pa. I'm giving him a hand some evenings.'

Hearing the clock strike five, she made her farewells, threw him a kiss and reluctantly resumed her journey. Ned watched her trim figure with some regret. Nice little thing. He sighed, but soon forgot her and suddenly decided to call again at Miss Bayley's flat. He was not used to being stood up.

Minutes later the door opened and there she was, but after the first smile of recognition, she glanced hastily up and down the road.

'What on earth are you doing here?' she demanded anxiously.

'I've been waiting for you like I said in the message. At the end of the road at four o'clock. I gave it to your daily woman.'

She stared at him. 'That message was from you? But Mrs Wetton said it was for the mistress.'

'Isn't that you? Isn't it your flat?'

'No … That is, yes but…' She looked flustered. 'She said it was from someone called Ed.'

'It was from me: Ned. I gave the woman a
sixpence!' He scowled briefly. 'She should
have got it right.' Then he brightened. 'So
now that's sorted out d'you want to hear the
proposition?' He grinned disarmingly. His
smile had never been known to fail with the
young nursemaids, and the barmaid couldn't
resist it either; but now the smile seemed to
have lost its power.

She shook her head. 'Proposition? Certainly
not!'

'You don't know what it is yet! I want to
take you for a walk in the park. That's it in a
nutshell. No harm in that. Sunday morning at
ten? I'll be wearing my best bib and tucker! I
dress up a treat when I put my mind to it.
You'll be perfectly safe with me, I promise. A
walk in the park in broad daylight. Bit of fresh
air and a few laughs.' She still looked
doubtful. 'You're your own mistress now,
remember. Your pa's gone to his last resting
place and—'

'I'm sorry. I can't. Not Sunday morning. We
all go to church and…' She shrugged.

'When then?' She was weakening, he
thought hopefully.

'I don't know. Maybe never. Unless … Tuesday afternoon might be possible.'

'Tuesday afternoon then. At two?' Giving
her no time to change her mind, he rushed
on. 'I'll buy you an ice cream and we'll watch
the squirrels and I'll tell you my life story and

56

you can...' He stopped as she gave a little cry of distress.

'Oh no! It's Leo! He's back early. Oh dear...'

Her desperation was plain to see and Ned turned. A man was approaching at a fast walk, a frown settled already on his face. So had she lied to him, Ned wondered unhappily. She had called him Leo. His stomach churned. Was this her husband?

Neither spoke until he reached them.

Before he could speak she said, 'This is the bailiff, Leo. The man who has my furniture in store – or rather, his father does. He came to – to ask if I needed any of my things.'

Ned understood immediately. He said, 'People always store something they later need. We always check up within the first few months.'

Leo's frown vanished. He turned to her. 'And is there anything, Millie?'

So that was her name, thought Ned: Millie. Must be short for Millicent. Yes. It suited her.

Now she gave Leo a quick glance. 'A few odds and ends. I said I might collect them Tuesday afternoon.'

The man seemed to be reassured and made to go up the steps. Then he said, 'Have you still got those tickets for the supper room, Millie? Mr...?'

'Ned Warren, at your service, sir.'

'Mr Warren might like to make use of them, Millie.' With a polite nod he went inside, leaving Millie twisting her fingers in embarrassment.

She said, 'He's my brother-in-law.'

Ned almost jumped with relief. A brother-in-law was no kind of threat. 'So I'll see you Tuesday afternoon, will I, *Millie*? Where will that be exactly?'

'In the park.' She began to stammer explanations, but he shook his head.

'Save it all for Tuesday,' he told her gently. 'We can talk then.'

She said, 'Oh! The tickets!' and hurried back into the house, to reappear shortly with an envelope. 'Three tickets. Tapper's Supper Room. Any evening. I can't use them but I expect you can. Now I must go!' She was already closing the door.

He said, 'I'll be looking forward to it. Two o'clock by the bandstand!' He winked, but she didn't respond and seconds later he was staring at a firmly closed door.

Later that night Millie had just undressed when there was a knock on her door. Fastening her dressing gown, she opened the door and found Leo with a finger to his lips. Nervously she stepped back and he followed her into the room.

'If Esme finds out...' she began.

'Esme's already in bed and snoring!' he smiled. 'I simply want to tell you that I consider myself your guardian while you're under—'

'My *guardian*? No, Leo! I don't need a guardian at my age! I mean, I appreciate the thought but...'

'Millie, you must let me look after you. Fate has played into our hands so fortuitously and you must see...'

His nearness was undermining her and Millie took a few steps backwards, determined that this line of thought must be stopped before it went too far.

'I don't see any thing like that, Leo. I'm eternally grateful to you and Esme for giving me a home until I decide what to do with my life, but I won't have you or anyone else treating me like a dependent. This situation...'

He stepped nearer. 'Millie, please don't pretend. We both know that my marriage to Esme was a mistake and we are both paying for it. In fact I suppose we are all three paying for it. All I want is to look after you in the best way I can. You don't have to search for a new life. Stay with us. Please, Millie.'

Millie's heart was racing. How fatally easy it would be to avail herself of his offer, but she knew she could not live indefinitely with the two of them. Both Esme and Leo had been aware of her earlier love for him, but for years now she had referred to her past feelings as an infatuation and that was how it must stay. Pride would not allow her to do otherwise.

'I'm sorry, Leo,' she told him. 'You are kindness itself, but I am determined to have a life of my own. I want a husband and a family before it is too late.'

She saw the shock in his eyes. 'Millie!' he stammered. 'You must be careful not to rush into marriage for the sake of it. Believe me, marriage to the wrong person is a terrible burden and I wouldn't want you to make the same mistake.'

'You and Esme seem happy enough—' Millie began, but he interrupted her.

'You're so wrong, Millie. We are not at all happy. We are not united in marriage. It's all a farce. A sham. We are polite most of the time, and civilized; but between ourselves we no longer pretend.'

'Leo! Please don't tell me these things!' Millie's voice was anguished. 'At least let me believe that you are happy, since there is no undoing your bonds.'

'I'm sorry, Millie, but I simply needed to confide in someone and I know you care for me.' He regarded her despairingly and Millie longed to put her arms around him. Only common sense held her back. In spite of her entreaties he went on in a low voice. 'If you only knew ... We are no longer husband and wife. For months now. She will not come near me...'

Millie covered her ears with her hands. 'Don't, Leo! *Don't* tell me. I cannot bear to learn these hateful truths!' She was aware of tears dangerously close. 'What can I do to help you? I can never be your wife. Esme will never leave you, and even if she did, a marriage between us would be impossible. Would you begrudge me the chance of happiness with someone else?'

His expression was agonized. Suddenly it changed. 'Not that fellow who came to the door? Surely you are not involved with him!'

'Certainly not!' she cried. 'I told you: he is a bailiff and my belongings are lodged with his father.'

'I saw the way he looked at you.'

'There is no law against a man admiring a woman. He's cheerful, and if he looks at me that way, it simply flatters me. That's not such a bad thing for me. I feel as if I am at a crossroads and nothing is impossible.' Seeing that this digression had stopped him in his tracks, she went further. 'The truth is, Leo, that he has asked me to go for a walk in the park on Tuesday and I...'

His eyes widened. 'So you are not going to retrieve things from the store? You lied to me, Millie'

'Yes. I didn't want to hurt you unnecessarily, so I lied. Now I see that was foolish. I'm a grown woman and I must make my own decisions.'

She saw that he was struggling with the shock of her revelations. He said, 'As long as a walk in the park is not the beginning of something more intense. You will be careful, Millie, I hope. You hardly know the man.' He swallowed hard. 'I finally have you under my roof, Millie, and I don't want to lose you.'

She sighed deeply. 'I'm not yours to lose, Leo. You made that impossible when you abandoned me for Esme, and now there is nothing either of us can do about it. You must never talk to me like this again. It is so unfair to Esme. She is...'

'I've told you she doesn't love me.'

Millie still found that impossible to believe. How could anyone *not* love Leo? 'But she is still my sister and I don't want to be the cause of her heartache. She must never find us together like this. Please go back to your own room, Leo.' He made no move and she moved to the door and held it open. 'The kindest thing you can do is to let me go and wish me well. I have to make a life for myself somehow.'

He stepped closer, but she avoided his outstretched hands. If she allowed him to touch her she would be lost. He hesitated, then turned away. When he had gone, she threw herself on the bed and wept – not only for herself but for Leo and her sister. The past, it seemed, held them all in thrall.

It was just after ten o'clock on the following Friday night and Tapper's Supper Room was at its noisiest. All the tables were full and the barmaids rushed to and fro serving drinks and fending off unwelcome attentions from the mostly male clients. Towards the back, where the lighting was less bright, older men congregated, many hoping not to be recognized.

In the middle were a few mixed groups of working-class men and women, spending their hard-earned wages on food, ale and entertainment. Nearest to the stage the young men gathered, shouting and booing. Many of these were medical students; others were uniformed men from the armed forces, making the most of a few days' leave. They had just seen off the unfortunate comic, whose jokes had failed to impress. Now they were looking forward to the Grecian tableau and that would be followed by the appearance of Lennard Hornby.

Outside in the foyer every coat-hanger held a coat, and hats were piled up on the wide window ledge. The small muscular man guarded the silk-tasselled rope, insisting on seeing a ticket and ordering out anyone who failed to produce one. A much larger man with a battered nose lounged against the counter, talking to the woman in charge of the coats. If there was any trouble, he would step in and frogmarch the offender to the door and throw him on to the pavement outside. It had been a busy evening, but few clients appeared as late as this. Supper was no longer being served, although the smell of beef pie and onions still lingered in the air.

In the wings beside the stage Poppy waited with the other women for the steps of the 'temple' to be dragged into position on the stage. The women, some slim and willowy, others plumply voluptuous, wore skin-coloured body stockings that clung to their bodies to reveal every curve. Their hair had been coaxed into a variety of classic Grecian styles. Lengths of cream-coloured silk were draped around them and floated temptingly over plump shoulders and legs.

Poppy muttered, 'Get a move on!' to the

nearest scene shifter. 'It's cold!'

'Should have worn your woollies!' he replied. 'No one asked you to bare all!'

'They certainly wouldn't ask you, you great lump!'

Poppy was eager to get on stage to see whether Henry had shown up as promised. She had hinted to several of her fellow artistes that her gentleman friend would be in the audience at the back, though she had not mentioned his name. Nobody would recognize him as an MP, she knew, because women took very little interest in politics. Poppy herself had no idea which political party he represented. Having no vote, the women wouldn't know any of the MPs' names, with the possible exception of the Prime Minister. Poppy simply wanted her friends to see her 'gentleman friend', to know that he existed and to envy her. Only she could know him by his full name: Henry Walter Granger, the Member of Parliament for a small borough of London on the south side of the river. Not that she cared for his position. What thrilled her was his adoration and the money he lavished on her.

At a signal from the stage manager the small orchestra began to play an elegant piece of music suited to the Grecian scene. At last everything was in place.

'OK, girls. On you go!'

Obediently they scampered on stage and took up their various positions. The curtains had yet to be pulled back and they had less than a minute to arrange their draperies to maximum effect without actually revealing anything. At the slightest hint of indecency, the Supper Room licence would be revoked.

With a whoosh the curtains parted and the audience went wild with excitement. Men stood and cheered, women laughed, handkerchieves were waved and names were called. A young subaltern climbed on to his table shouting, 'Maisie, luv! Give us a smile!'

Intrigued, Poppy didn't even move her eyes. The rule was that they had to remain stock-still. She had fixed her gaze on the back of the room and she could see Henry in the agreed place – the third table from the left. He was standing up, applauding heartily, and he had eyes for no one but her.

Henry W. Granger was a solidly built man in his early fifties. Too much food and drink had already resulted in a distinct paunch and his face was heavily veined. As he applauded, he thought of the amorous night to come with his adored Poppy and the weekend to come with his wife and children in their home in Somerset. The former inspired him, but the latter, had he dwelled upon it, would have depressed him. In a small village in Somerset he owned a large seven-bedroomed house with stables, a lake and a wooded area perfect for shooting. This weekend he would be entertaining four friends and they would bag a few pheasants.

His two unlovely sons – one seventeen, the

other eleven – were still at home for the summer holidays and would not return to their expensive private school until the tenth of October but would not take part in the shoot, preferring to spend their time with their own friends in the village. His wife Dorcas would hover in the background, leaving all the arrangements to the cook and housekeeper. He thought of her small, bird-like frame with distaste, but she had brought money and land to the marriage and she turned a blind eye to whatever went on in London, where she believed he had a small studio convenient to Westminster. This was the 'den' to which he retired after a late sitting in the House or after a late dinner at his club. He never entertained women in the studio, although he did occasionally rent a hotel room for casual flings – women who came and went but rarely lasted more than a few weeks or months. He even forgot their names on occasion He was a weak man where women were concerned, and fickle – except with Poppy, with whom he spent most of his nights. She was different. He thought of her as his other wife. His affair with her was well established and he had installed her in her own flat seven years ago and never regretted it. A kind-hearted girl, she was always pleased to see him. Never moody, never demanding, always grateful. She loved him despite the paunch and the thinning hair and he dared not imagine life without her. Poppy was the one bright star in his clouded sky.

As he watched her on stage he thought her worth all the risks he took to possess her and his loud shouts of 'Bravo!' were from the heart.

Some men shouted the names of their favourites, but Henry dared not do that. He was under the impression that nobody knew him by name. but to link himself to one of the women would be very unwise. However, he caught Poppy's gaze, smiled broadly and winked. Dear loyal little girl, he thought fondly.

All too soon the time allotted to the tableau came to an end; with a soft roll of drums the curtain slowly closed and the Grecian Temple was gone. Loud groans followed its disappearance and some of the men shouted 'Encore', but they all knew it was out of the question. He imagined the scene behind the curtains as the girls abandoned their poses and rushed giggling into the wings to change.

Henry downed the last few mouthfuls of his ale and dabbed at his moustache with a handkerchief. The beef pie had settled comfortably in his stomach and he sighed with contentment as he rose to leave. Avoiding his fellow diners, he collected his coat and, smiling broadly, headed for the exit.

Sunday morning arrived with a blustery wind and fitful clouds, so Millie dressed warmly for church. Twenty minutes before they were due to leave the house, Esme tapped on Millie's bedroom door and entered without waiting to be told. Her face was flushed and her eyes sparkled and Millie looked at her in amazement. In her autumn suit of golden-brown tweed, Esme looked not only beautiful but positively radiant.

'I want you to be the first to know,' she told Millie. 'I went to the doctor yesterday and he confirmed my suspicions: I'm going to have a baby!'

Millie uttered a soft cry, stepped back and sat on the bed. Esme was having a child. A wave of jealousy swept through her and she closed her eyes for fear that her sister would recognize the emotion. The thought of Esme with Leo's child hurt immeasurably. She searched for something to say – something that she *could* say without sounding insincere.

'That's – that's wonderful news,' she stammered, almost drowning in misery. 'A baby at last!'

Esme smiled. 'I've waited a long time,' she agreed. 'But now my prayers have been answered. Doctor Mellor says I'm in good health and shouldn't expect any complications. I'm to eat well, and rest often, and keep my spirits up. You are happy for me, aren't you, Millie?'

She actually sounded sincere and Millie struggled to think kindly of her sister. 'Of course I am. And Leo will be delighted. He always wanted a family.'

The words slipped out, reminding them both that at one time Millie had been close to Leo and probably understood the workings of his mind as well as Esme did.

Esme crossed to the window, stared out briefly then turned. 'I'm going to need your support, Millie, in the months ahead. I do hope you realize that. The doctor says it's not an event a woman should go through without another woman and since Mama is dead I hope...'

Millie caught her breath. 'I can't promise anything, Esme. I did tell you I shall be looking for employment and a place of my own.'

Esme frowned. 'But you can delay that, can't you? And when the child is born I shall need even more help. If you aren't with me I shall have to find a nanny and I don't fancy that idea.'

Millie could feel the trap closing and said desperately, 'What does Leo say about it? He knows I am planning to...'

'Leo doesn't know yet! The baby's not due until the beginning of March and...'

Suddenly Millie felt her stomach churn and she no longer heard what her sister was saying. Hadn't Leo told her that they were no longer man and wife in the true sense of the words? She felt sure he had not lied, but if that were true, then he could not possibly be the father of Esme's child.

She said, 'You haven't told him? He should be the first to know surely.'

Esme shrugged. 'Men are such worriers. I recall how Papa fussed when you were expected. Mama became quite irritated. I shall tell him all in good time – and you are not to say a word. I mean it, Millie. It is our secret until I think the time is right.'

Millie was tempted to challenge Esme and ask if Leo was the father, but if she did, Esme would know that Leo had discussed their marriage, and that would be disastrous. Her thoughts swam. Her natural loyalty lay with Leo, but she dared not tell him what she knew ... although he would find out eventually, when his wife broke the news. What would he do then? And whose child was it? It now seemed certain that Esme's Friday outings were connected with a lover. Millie put a hand to her head.

Esme said, 'What is it? You look pale.'

'It's nothing. A headache. I was debating whether or not to come with you to church or not.'

'Oh but you must! Leo likes to be seen with both of us. And I might need you.'

Millie frowned. 'How can you need me? You'll have Leo.' She doubted that she would be able to follow the service in her present state and longed to be alone with her thoughts. She had a sudden vision of the birth of the infant, with Esme triumphant and Leo and herself distraught by the knowledge that she had given birth to another man's child.

'*Millie!* You're not listening to me! I said I might come over faint. You should be with me.'

'I can't. My head...' To prove the point

70

Millie unpinned her hat. 'I shall rest. When I feel better I shall make a start on the vegetables and put the meat in the oven. Don't worry about me.'

Esme gave an exaggerated sigh. 'Well, I can't make you go to church. I'll tell Leo you are unwell.' She crossed to the door. 'But you'll have to pull yourself together, Millie. I need to be able to depend on you. I'm the one that's in a delicate state, not you.' She went out, closing the door a little too firmly behind her.

Millie groaned. 'Don't rely on me,' she muttered. 'I shall get away from here as quickly as I can.'

If the baby was Leo's she would have stayed as long as they needed her, but if Esme was foisting another man's child on to him, she would not be party to the deception. He must know, she told herself. If they have – have not been intimate for a long time then the baby cannot be Leo's. Whatever will he do when he is told the news? Millie did not want to be around when that particular storm broke. But how could she leave with no money, no income and nowhere to live?

Composing herself with an effort, she waited until they had left the house then hurried downstairs for *The Times* newspaper and spent the next half-hour searching the advertisements for a suitable position for which she might apply.

When she finally threw down the paper in disgust, she was forced to face the unpalatable fact that with no references she was unlikely to find anything suitable.

Left alone with her thoughts she almost forgot that she was supposed to be preparing vegetables and dealing with the joint of beef. Rushing downstairs, she larded the beef and slid it into the oven. She washed and sliced the cabbage, peeled and sliced the carrots and prepared the potatoes. Esme would make the gravy – she insisted that hers was superior to most and Millie wasn't going to argue. She rinsed the rice, added sugar, milk and butter to the dish and slid it into the oven on a lower shelf. Rice pudding was one of Leo's favourites. As an afterthought she retrieved the dish and ground some nutmeg on to the surface before returning it to the heat. She had just finished laying the table in the dining room when she heard them return.

Esme followed her into the kitchen, laughing gaily. 'I've had so many compliments!' she told Millie. 'Everyone says how well I look. And I do feel well. In the very best of spirits.' She gave Millie a conspiratorial smile. 'Mrs Anneky sent her best wishes to you and the Misses Blaine asked to be remembered. It was a very nice service. The sermon was about respect for God's teachings. A shame you had to miss it.' She pulled off her gloves and bent to peer into the oven. 'Rice pudding? I wanted tapioca.'

'Did you? I forgot.'

'Honestly, Millie, you're such a scatterbrain.'

Leo appeared in the doorway and said, 'Something smells good!' Before she could answer he asked after the headache and Millie lied, pretending it was much better.

Esme said, 'You'll be pleased to hear, Leo, that Millie is going to stay with us. You are, aren't you, Millie?' Her expression said: 'Argue if you dare'!

Leo looked at Millie hopefully. 'Is that so? I'm delighted.'

Millie said, 'I haven't said yea or nay. I'm still considering it.'

Esme gave a snort of irritation. 'Trust you, Millie! You were always the same. Afraid to commit yourself. Papa used to say...'

Leo said, 'Oh dear! Family reminiscences! I'm glad I don't have an older brother to recall all my childhood sins!'

Esme gave him a poisonous glance. 'Do you always have to take Millie's side against mine, dear heart? It's so disloyal.'

She only called him 'dear heart' when she was angry. Ignoring her sister's comment, Millie busied herself at the sink, rinsing a few dishes, willing Esme to get out of the kitchen.

Esme said, 'Well, I'll get changed and then I'll make the gravy. You've done enough, Millie. You go and relax with Leo.'

Glad of any excuse, Millie walked through to the dining room and checked the table. Leo followed her.

He said, 'Has Esme been drinking? She behaved very oddly after church. Chattering away like a magpie with people she hardly

73

knows or doesn't like.'

Millie fiddled with the cutlery, unable to face him. 'Drinking? I don't think so, but she certainly seems rather ... excitable.'

He came close to her and lowered his voice. 'Mrs Anneky said something very strange to me. She asked if Esme was in "a certain condition". I said no, and she shook her head and said, "The eyes give it away, if you know what to look for."'

Millie felt the colour rush to her face. 'What did you say?'

'What could I say? I could hardly say that it was impossible.' Greatly agitated, he glanced towards the door to make sure that Esme was not within earshot. 'Would she tell you if – if anything of the kind ... I mean – would *you* recognize the signs?'

Millie forced herself to look him in the eye. 'That would mean...'

He swallowed awkwardly, as though his throat was dry. 'Another man. I know. I don't want to even think it.'

Millie hated herself for deceiving him, but she could not bring herself to tell him what she knew. Esme must be the one to tell him. Millie put a hand on his arm. 'If you seriously suspect such a thing, you must ask her outright, Leo. You have a right to know.'

'And if she won't tell me? If she denies it?'

Millie shook her head without answering. He rubbed his eyes and she saw that his hand was shaking. She wanted to say something that would give him hope, but that would have been cruel.

He said, 'I suppose I could ask the doctor. He would be bound to tell me, wouldn't he? Or would he insist on that damned patient confidentiality? Oh damn! I don't know what to do.'

'Could you wait a few days. If she has ... If she *is* ... maybe she will tell you. Are you certain it couldn't be your child?'

He frowned. 'I've been trying to think if there was any one isolated occasion but ... I don't think so.'

Millie clutched at the only straw. 'But if there were such an occasion, and there *is* a child, and it *is* yours – then that would be wonderful!'

He smiled faintly. 'Dearest Millie, you are trying so hard to help, but I think we both know this might be the beginning of a major disaster. For some reason heaven refuses to smile on me.'

For a moment they stared helplessly at one another; then he patted Millie's arm, murmured something non-committal and left her alone with her thoughts.

Four

By the time Tuesday afternoon arrived Millie was alternating between excitement and fear. How could she have been so rash, she thought, to arrange to meet with Ned Warren, who was almost a stranger? Leo was right: she should have refused the invitation. Three minutes later, however, she was breathless with excitement at the prospect of a promenade in the park with a young man – *any* young man – who found her attractive. What on earth should she wear? she wondered. Her wardrobe was small and she would have to wear her grey serge skirt, but which jacket would look best with it? Which scarf? Which shoes? She didn't want to look as if she had made too much effort; yet if she didn't make any effort, she might look dowdy compared with the other young women who would be out with their beaux. She had the black she had worn to her father's funeral, but that was rather sombre and Esme was no longer in mourning, so presumably she, too, could wear something brighter.

Having settled the matter to her satisfaction (the grey skirt and a blue-and-grey jacket), she surveyed herself in the mirror and felt satisfied. She had trimmed the grey straw hat with a red rose made of silk and had arranged her hair so that a few curls softened her face. Snatching up her gloves, she hurried downstairs but was met at the bottom by Esme.

'Oh Millie, you're not off already? I fancy some walnuts in butter and you do them so much better than I do.'

Millie stared at her. 'I can't fry walnuts now. I'm dressed to go out.'

'But you're very early. It won't take ten minutes to reach the park. You could slip an apron over your...'

Millie felt a surge of anger. 'No!' she cried. 'I could, but I won't! It's a simple enough task. You can do it.'

Esme said, 'Well really, Millie! I can't think what's got into you. This young man must have turned your brains. You aren't usually so unreasonable.'

Millie was breathing quickly, trying to contain her anger. She did not want anything to spoil her meeting with Ned, but now she realized that was exactly what Esme was hoping for. It was the old jealous streak appearing once again.

Millie forced a smile, unwilling to appear ruffled. 'You'll manage, Esme. I have to go.' With that she pushed past her sister and headed for the front door. As she opened it, Leo came into the hall.

'When should we expect you back, Millie?' he asked. 'If you're too late we shall worry about you.'

'A couple of hours, maybe.' She turned and gave them both a bright smile. 'I'll see you later.'

Ned was waiting, as promised, by the bandstand, an ornate erection which allowed seating for a dozen musicians, who were already taking their seats and tuning their instruments.

'Ned! There you are. I hope I'm not late.'

He was wearing his Sunday-best suit of dark-brown worsted and a gleaming tiepin beneath his stand-up collar. She had never imagined he would look so smart and was glad she had taken so much trouble over her own appearance. His eyes lit up at the sight of her and all negative thoughts of Esme and Leo faded.

'My, my!' he said, rolling his eyes as he doffed his hat. 'You look a real corker, Miss Bayley!' He replaced his hat and crooked his arm and, after a second's hesitation, Millie slipped her arm through his.

'I thought we'd head for the ice-cream man,' he told her as they walked. 'Then a walk by the pond to watch the ducks and a stroll back to the bandstand to enjoy the music. How does that strike you?'

'It sounds wonderful, Mr Warren,' she admitted. Not that she had ever eaten an ice cream in the park before. Her parents would have been scandalized at the thought of eating anything in public, but they were gone; today she was throwing caution to the winds. At that moment she would have agreed to almost anything. Ned Warren's bright-blue eyes and happy face made her feel that everything in the world was fine, and she walked beside him with her head held high.

He gave her a teasing glance and said, 'So I suppose you want to hear my life story. It's not very long.'

'Do I then have to tell you mine?'

'Only if you want to.' He bent down to catch a ball that was rolling towards them over the grass and toss it back to the young lad who came running after it.

She said, 'I'll give you an edited version.'

'Aha! That has me all agog!' He tightened his grip on her arm, pulling her a little closer. 'Born Edward Warren twenty-two years ago. Two sisters younger than me but one died aged five of diphtheria, poor little soul ... The other sister is married and lives in Bermondsey. My pa – his name's Stanley – runs the removals and storage business and I help out when I'm not being a bailiff. That about sums me up.' He gave her a sly glance. 'Any questions, Miss Bayley?'

'No, except...' She blushed.

He grinned. 'Course you have a question – or you ought to have. What about: "Are you married, Mr Warren?" That might be a wise question in the circumstances, don't you think?'

She laughed self-consciously and with a sense of relief. She had been wondering if he was single and hoping he was. 'Very well then. *Are* you married, Mr Warren? I should hope the answer's no!' Not that she was planning to marry him, she reminded herself quickly, but she certainly wouldn't wish to walk in the park with someone else's husband.

At that moment they passed a young nursemaid who led a small child by the hand. She gave Millie a sharp glance, smiled coyly at Ned Warren and said, 'Good day to you, Ned.'

'Afternoon, Bessie.' To Millie he whispered, 'An old friend.'

Aware of a twinge of something approaching jealousy, Millie said, 'Not your wife, then.'

He laughed. 'I don't have a wife. Never have had a wife and might never have one! How's that for an answer?'

'Perfect,' she replied, slightly confused. 'You might never marry, then. How's that?'

'Might never find anyone rash enough to have me,' he answered. 'My sister reckons I'm a hopeless case and only a fool would consider marrying me. But now it's your turn. How many husbands have you had?'

She laughed. 'None.' Immediately she felt herself at a disadvantage. Suppose he thought that no man had ever taken a shine to her. She must say something about Leo. She took a deep breath. 'I was almost engaged once to a very nice man but – but nothing came of it. There were ... problems.' She fell silent. How could she talk about Leo without revealing her feelings for him?

He was looking at her closely. 'What sort of problems? You changed your mind?'

'*He* changed *his* mind.' The words were almost a whisper.

'Thank the Lord for that!' he exclaimed. 'More chance for the rest of us men!' He squeezed her arm in a gesture of support. 'He must have been an idiot. I hope you said "Good riddance" to him.'

'That would be difficult,' she told him. 'He married my sister instead.'

Ned stopped abruptly in his tracks and stared at her. 'Not Mr Walmsley!'

'The same.' She held her breath. What would he think of that?

His eyes widened. 'He chose your sister? Is the man weak in the head or something?' He tapped his forehead in amazement and she had to laugh at his expression.

Suddenly all the words came out in a rush. 'Esme made up her mind to have him and he – he was overwhelmed by her attention. He had bought a ring for me but he gave it to Esme. They were married two months later before he could change his mind.'

'And you were heartbroken.'

'No! At least, I mean ... Yes but...' To her dismay the pain and humiliation flooded back and she burst into tears.

Immediately his arm went round her waist and he led her gently towards a nearby seat. They sat together while he gave her a large handkerchief and allowed her the luxury of uninterrupted tears. He didn't say anything, but his arm was round her – unbelievably comforting. His quiet presence was warm

81

and reassuring and gradually her sobs lessened.

'I'm sorry,' she whispered when at last she regained control. She glanced round in agitation to see how many people had witnessed the breakdown. 'I'm so sorry. I've embarrassed you, Mr Warren.'

'Me? Embarrassed?' He laughed at the idea. 'I don't know the meaning of the word. I'm just glad you were able to get rid of all that hurt. Leo Walmsley's an idiot and I bet he knows it.'

Millie said nothing. She felt she had already said too much and was regretting her weakness. Why had she revealed so much that was painful to her? What on earth would he think of her?

'Right!' he said briskly. 'You sit here and don't move an inch and I'll fetch the ice creams. A good ice cream is a great pick-me-up. What shall it be? Strawberry, vanilla or chocolate?'

'Strawberry, please, Mr Warren.'

'Strawberry it is, Miss Bayley. I shall have vanilla.' He gave her a mock salute and darted away. She watched him go with mixed feelings. Perhaps Leo was right and she should have turned down the invitation, but a strange feeling of calm was beginning to steal over her. The tears had washed away some of the grief and anger she had been living with for so many years; and Ned Warren had called Leo an idiot, which made her feel marginally better. She knew he was no such thing, but she saw now that he *had* been weak. Not that she entirely blamed him. Esme had been very persuasive and not many young men could have resisted her. Her eyes narrowed slightly. Ned Warren had been very perceptive. He had guessed that Leo now regretted his choice.

'There is more to Mr Warren than meets the eye!' she muttered, amused.

With a deep sigh she wiped her eyes for the last time and put the handkerchief into her pocket. She had probably already ruined Ned Warren's afternoon, but at least she could pull herself together and make sure that they enjoyed what was left of it. She looked up to see him approaching at a run, an ice-cream cornet in each hand. He was laughing and looked much younger than his twenty-two years.

'One strawberry ice for madame!' He handed it to her with a flourish. 'I bought the same for myself.'

'I thought you preferred vanilla.'

'It's a sign of togetherness!' He grinned. 'Start licking it before it melts.'

Friday came and as usual Esme left the house with a happy heart. Excitement bubbled within her as she thought of the news she was going to share with the man she loved. She knew that the coming child would be a shock, but she also knew the depth of Wally's love for her. She knew, for he had told her many times, that he had been saving himself for the right woman. He was no spring chicken, but he had waited. He had never married, and had no children, so there was nothing to prevent him from marrying Esme as soon as her divorce could be arranged. A few more months and she could be free of Leo and starting a new life with Wally.

Esme climbed into the hackney cab and gave the driver the address. She settled in her seat and smiled as she recalled the expression on her sister's face. So suspicious. She shrugged. Poor, foolish Millie. It seemed she was doomed to become an old maid. It would never be possible for her to marr Leo even when the divorce came through, and she would never look at another man. This stupid business with the young bailiff was simply a ploy to make Leo jealous, and maybe it was working; but there was no way Millie would marry a man so far beneath her. It would be social disaster and Millie knew it.

Whatever would she say when she knew Esme was going to marry a man with money to burn? Wally was rich, and generous with it. True, she had never been to his home, but he bought her expensive presents (which she had to hide from her husband) and took her to expensive restaurants. They also spent romantic hours in an expensive hotel room. There was no doubt about it: Wally knew how to enjoy himself and was certainly no skinflint.

Alighting at their favoured hotel in Chelsea, Esme made her way up to room 309 on the third floor and tapped three times on the door. Their secret knock! She smiled and tweaked a curl down on to her forehead. The door opened and Wally swept her into his arms. He had already been drinking, she noticed, and his eyes were a little dull. She wished he would drink less, but on this occasion would say nothing. Nothing must spoil the moment.

'My little darling!' he murmured into her hair. 'You're three minutes late and the waiting has been an agony!'

They both laughed and then she was taking off her coat and he was pouring the champagne and they were immediately in the mood for love-making. His face was flushed with excitement and she had scarcely had time to sip her drink before he was carrying her to the large bed with the brass bedhead and familiar red silk coverlet. Esme gave herself up to his passion. Her news could wait. He quite obviously could not.

When he was satisfied and she had tidied herself, he poured more champagne and they sat together on the bed.

He said, 'I do believe my little sparrow is growing fatter.' He patted her arm. 'It's the fault of all those chocolates I buy you.'

She pouted. 'You used to say I was too thin.'

'Oh I'm not complaining, little darling. I love you just the way you are.' He kissed her and she was aware of a flutter of anxiety. She must break the news gently. He had said he loved children, but they had not planned the child she was carrying.

'Wally, my dear, have you ever thought we might one day marry and have a child?'

'I've thought about it. One day perhaps, when the time is right.' He ran his hand up and down her arm. 'You're such a pretty little thing, Esme. I'm the luckiest man in the world!'

'Haven't you ever wondered why I have no children?'

'Not really. I try not to think about your marriage and I *never* think about your husband. I like to pretend you're all mine!' He drained his glass and refilled it.

Esme looked at him and a small frown puckered her forehead. If he drank too much he might not fully understand what she was saying and she needed him to keep his wits about him.

'Would you like me to belong only to you? That is, if I could grant you a wish, is that what it would be? That I leave my husband and become your wife ... and the mother of your children?'

It was his turn to frown. 'Is this a riddle, Esme? I'm no good at riddles. Here, let me fill your glass. You're not drinking enough. I'll send down for another bottle.'

'No, Wally! Not just yet.' She put out a restraining hand. 'I have something to tell you, Wally darling. Something wonderful. Something that has made me very, *very* happy.' Esme felt a faint perspiration break out on her forehead. 'We're going to have a child,

Wally. You and me! Isn't that great news?'

He drew back sharply, staring at her, and his face paled.

'Wally, *darling*!' she cried. 'Don't look at me that way! Don't you understand? This is our chance. Leo can't stop me from leaving him now. He'll *want* to let me go when he knows about us and the child. He'll have to divorce me and...' She faltered and stopped, dismayed.

Wally had risen from the bed and was staring down at her with something like panic in his eyes. 'Stop!' he cried. 'I can't take this in. You're saying you're *with child*?'

'Yes, Wally. I thought you'd be...'

'It's not mine! It's your husband's. You should be telling him, not me!'

'But Wally...?' Her voice shook. What was the matter with him? Why wasn't he pleased? 'You have no ties, Wally. We can be together with our child.'

He was recovering himself with an obvious effort and now sat down on a chair by the window, at least three yards away from her. He eyed her, she thought resentfully, as though she were a dangerous dog that might bite him if he came any nearer.

He said, 'Look here, Esme ... I mean – I'm sorry, but this is a most dreadful shock. How can you say the child is mine? You're a married woman.'

'But Leo and I ... Don't you see, Walter. We haven't been ... Since I met you four months ago he and I have never been lovers...' She swallowed hard. 'I was saving myself for you! Please understand, Wally. It can't be his child and he will know that.'

Wally's mouth opened and closed. 'You didn't tell me ... How was I to know that the two of you weren't ...You denied him his rights and he didn't question it?'

She shrugged. 'Our marriage isn't exactly harmonious. He made no protest when I claimed a headache. And even before that ... he was never able to give us a child. I told you that. That was part of the problem between us. He knew I blamed him.'

'But I assumed the fault lay with you! Who's to say...'

'But *you* have given me a child, Wally. How could it have been my fault? Do please be sensible.'

He crossed to the window, putting a greater distance between them, and Esme's hopes began to fade.

Staring out, he muttered, 'You should have told me, Esme! This isn't right. Springing it on me this way!' He turned and now he was positively glaring at her. 'How do you expect a man to behave when, out of the blue, he hears news like this?'

Esme could think of nothing to say. She was devastated by his reaction to the news and for a moment they sat in an unhappy silence.

Then Wally said, 'You'll have to pretend it's his. Somehow ... you'll have to convince him. He mustn't know about me. You know that very well. Nobody must. I told you that right

88

from the start.'

A horrible suspicion entered Esme's mind. 'You're not saying that you *are* married?' Instinctively she put a hand to her heart. Had she fallen for the oldest lie in the book? 'Are you? Did you lie to me, Wally?'

He hesitated. 'I refuse to be interrogated, Esme. All I'm saying is that I can't marry you. It's out of the question.'

She slid from the bed and crossed to the window. Anger was rising within her, but she knew she mustn't antagonize him. 'Can't or won't, Wally? You said you liked children. You can afford a wife and child. Why is it so impossible?'

He looked at her with unfamiliar irritation. 'I don't have to explain myself to you, Esme. Just accept it. You have to convince your husband the child is his. Even if he doesn't believe you, you must stay married. He'll get over it. He won't be the first husband to be cuckolded and he won't be the last. Stay married.'

Esme felt a deep coldness within her. Shock made her tremble and her legs felt weak. Somehow she persisted. 'But you love me, Wally. We love each other. And we have made a child together.'

'It wasn't by design,' he snapped. 'I thought you were barren. All those years married and no child. You misled me.'

Esme was struggling to find a way out of the situation. She desperately needed Wally to marry her. She had set her heart on becoming his wife and she wanted to be rid of Leo. 'And suppose I won't pretend it's his? Suppose he doesn't believe me and demands to know the name of the father? I shall have to tell him. It will all come out anyway, so why not be decent about it, Wally? Do the right thing by me without any ... Oh!'

He had grabbed her arm and was shaking her violently. 'Don't you dare to threaten me, young woman! You'll find out your mistake if you try to manipulate me!' He was red in the face and his eyes bulged with anger.

Esme was suddenly frightened. She had never seen this side of him and now all she wanted was to get out of the room and go home. There she could think things out. There must be a way.

Snatching her arm from his grasp, she stumbled to her clothes and began to pull them on. All fingers and thumbs, it seemed that every garment intended to frustrate her efforts. Wally watched her, breathing heavily.

He said, 'Wait a moment. You can get rid of the child. I can find someone. A doctor. I'll pay for it. That's the answer, Esme.'

'Is it? Well, it might not be the answer for me. I'm going to think things over.'

He changed his tone. 'Please, Esme. I just want us to go on as before without complications. I simply...'

'I see. Our child is a complication. Nothing more than that. Well...' She pulled on her jacket and fumbled with the buttons. 'I've wanted a child for years and I'm not about to

90

give this one up.' She faced him. 'I might have to see a solicitor. I don't know yet.'

'If you get rid of the child I'll give you a hundred pounds! And we'll never see each other again!'

'A hundred pounds! You think that you can bribe me to—'

'Three hundred! Five, and that's my last offer. But only if you get rid of it.'

'You disgust me, Wally! I never thought I'd say that but...' Tears ran down Esme's face and her voice cracked as the disappointment and rage swept over her. Wally stepped forward, but she pushed him away with what remained of her strength and fled from the room.

Millie was mending pillowslips when Esme returned to the house. She took one look at her sister's tear-stained face and abandoned her sewing.

'Esme! Whatever is the matter? You look terrible!'

Esme slumped into chair and began to cry, in loud racking sobs. 'I feel terrible,' she cried, 'but I can't explain, Millie. It's just too awful! Too unfair!'

For a moment Millie hovered beside her, but her attempt at consolation – an arm round her sister's shoulder – was angrily rejected.

'Leave me alone, can't you? You can't do anything. Nobody can.' She took the towel that Millie handed her and wiped furiously at her ravaged face.

'I'll make a pot of tea.' Millie was wondering what had brought her sister to this desperate state and concluded it might be Leo. Perhaps her sister had told him about the child. Yet that did not make sense. Logically, if that were the case, it would be Leo who would be upset and angry, not Esme. One thing was certain. She, Millie, must say nothing about her conversation with Leo. That could only make matters worse.

'I've given you two sugars,' she told Esme as she placed the mug of tea in front of her. 'It's good for shock.'

Esme stared at her grimly over the top of the blue-and-white-striped mug. 'I've been thinking,' she said shakily. '*You* must tell Leo about the baby. He'll take the news better from you.'

'Me? I will not!' Millie felt hot at the very thought of breaking such news. 'A wife should tell her husband. What are you thinking of?'

Esme, closing her eyes, gulped at the warm, sweet tea. 'I can't. I daren't. He'll be so angry.'

Millie opened her eyes wider and tried to look innocent of any knowledge. 'But why? He always wanted...'

'This baby isn't Leo's! There! Now you know.' Esme took another mouthful of tea, which went down the wrong way and made her splutter. When she had recovered, she said, 'I have a lover. It's his child. It can't be

92

Leo's baby because ... he doesn't make love to me any more. Now you know that, too, and I hope you're satisfied.'

Millie felt as though she were stepping on glass, so carefully did she have to choose her words. 'Your love affairs are nothing to do with me and I don't want to hear any more. I certainly don't see why I should break such terrible news to Leo. It's between the two of you.'

Esme rolled her eyes. 'I knew I couldn't depend on you!' she said bitterly. 'I expect you're loving every minute of this. Just like you to gloat.'

For a moment Millie felt guilty. If it hadn't been for Leo and his unhappiness she might well have been gloating. As it was, she could foresee so much grief for the man she loved and no way out of the morass.

Esme emptied the mug and set it down on the table with a bang. Then she picked it up again and hurled it across the room. Her face crumpled and with a loud groan she covered her face with her hands. After a moment she looked up. 'The doctor said I was to stay calm and relaxed! How am I supposed to do that?'

Without answering, Millie fetched a dustpan and brush and swept up the remains of the shattered mug. Then, overcome by curiosity, she asked, 'Does your lover know?'

Esme nodded. 'He doesn't want it. He wants me to go to a doctor he knows to – to have that dreadful surgery.'

For the first time, Millie was truly shocked.

Getting rid of an unborn child was not only dangerous and against all Christian teaching, it was against the law. She sat down suddenly and stared in horror at her sister. 'I hope you're not thinking ... Oh Esme, you mustn't even *think* of such a thing.'

'He offered me five hundred pounds if I would go through with it. How can I? I did want a family once upon a time. Now it seems years ago that I was happy and everything was normal. Oh God! What a fool I've been.'

She began to cry again and Millie glanced anxiously at the clock. It was nearly time for Leo to return from the bank.

She said, 'Why don't you go upstairs to bed and I'll bring you some hot milk and honey and tell Leo you're ... I'll say you've had a bit of a dizzy turn and you need to rest.'

'And you'll tell him what's happened? *Please*, Millie! If I have to tell him I'll be so frightened and he'll be so angry – he might hit me or something. And all that emotion won't be good for the baby. Or me ... I might even have a miscarriage.'

Millie closed her eyes. Why was it that Esme could manipulate people so easily? She had such a way with words, not to mention a devious mind.

She said, 'I won't promise anything, Esme – nothing at all. But if I see an opportunity to break it gently, I might. But don't count on it.'

She helped her sister up the stairs, un-

94

dressed her, settled her into bed and made her way downstairs again with a heavy heart. Somehow she would tell Leo. Coming from her it would be easier for him to bear. But what on earth was Esme going to do? None of the options at her disposal offered much hope of a happy ending. Millie had no idea what would happen next.

When Leo arrived home, however, he strode into the house with such a cheerful expression that Millie was distracted from her mission and all her carefully planned phrases were driven from her mind.

'Leo! You look like a cat with cream!' she told him. 'What has happened?'

To her surprise, he seized her round the waist and swung her round, lifting her feet off the ground and making her feel dizzy.

'Wonderful news!' he cried, setting her down. 'Where's Esme? I want you both to hear it. I never expected ... not this early. I had hopes, of course, but this has come as a bolt from the blue. Poor Mr Ferguson. I shouldn't be too pleased but...'

Millie laughed. 'You're not making any sense, Leo! I've no idea what you're talking about. Who's Mr Ferguson? Should I know him?'

'Gus Ferguson is the manager.' He went to the bottom of the stairs and called, 'Esme! I've some wonderful news! Come down quickly.'

Millie was beginning to share his excitement and she suddenly realized that there was no way she was going to spoil his day. Esme must either tell him about the child herself or she must wait.

She said quickly, 'She won't hear you, Leo. She's resting. She had a bad turn earlier – a dizzy spell. Nothing too serious, but I put her to bed. Will you tell me the good news or do I have to guess?'

He tossed his hat on to the hatstand and ignored it when it missed and fell to the floor. Unbuttoning his coat, he said, 'We have to celebrate, Millie! We'll all go out somewhere and...'

'Tell me!' she insisted.

Leo took her hand, then, glancing upstairs, gave her a hearty kiss. 'There!' he said. 'You have now been kissed ... *by the new bank manager*!'

She stared at him. He looked years younger and his eyes shone. 'You are the new manager? Heavens! That's marvellous news!' Instinctively she threw her arms round him and hugged him. For a moment they clung together, sharing the moment.

A cry from upstairs pulled them apart. 'Millie! *Millie!*'

Thinking rapidly, Millie said, 'Wait here, Leo. I'll see how she is. I won't tell her your news.'

She hurried upstairs and into their bedroom. Esme was sitting up in bed. 'What did he say?' she asked. 'Is he very angry?'

'I haven't told him,' Millie confessed, 'and I

96

won't. Not today. He's got some good news, Esme, and he's so excited. Your news must wait. Another day or two won't matter – in fact, it will give you time to think it all over. That way you won't do or say anything you regret.' As Esme began to protest, Millie held up a finger to silence her. 'If you want me to break the bad news, you will have to wait. If you can't wait, go ahead. Go downstairs and tell him yourself!'

It was a gamble, Millie knew, and she waited with her heart thumping.

Esme sank back on the pillows, her mouth a thin hard line. 'You're so worried about *his* happiness. You don't care a jot about mine.'

Millie counted to ten. 'If you must know, Esme, I don't see that you are entitled to any happiness. You've brought your troubles on yourself by your selfish behaviour. Once Leo hears your news, *neither* of you will be happy for quite a long time. I think Leo is entitled to enjoy whatever it is he has to tell us. So I suggest you make an effort and come down and we'll hear the details together.'

Esme gave in with a bad grace and five minutes later the two sisters went downstairs together.

Leo hugged his wife and told her about his promotion, and she managed to smile and say the right things. They sat down and listened to the background.

'I did think Mr Ferguson had been taking rather more sick leave than usual,' Leo told them. 'Poor chap. He seemed to be losing a little weight but always denied that there was anything to worry about. He had another six years to go to his retirement and I had secretly hoped I would be considered for his position when that time came.'

'And he confided in nobody?' Millie tried to imagine what the poor man had been going through.

Leo shook his head. 'He was a very private person – not very forthcoming, if you know what I mean. If anyone enquired after his health, he became irritable, so we gave up asking. It seems he has a tumour in his stomach and has to undergo surgery within the next few weeks. There's no way he can come back to work, apparently.' He leaned forward and patted Esme's arm. 'So you are now the wife of the manager!'

She smiled again and Millie wondered if Leo could see how false the smile was. Esme's mouth had moved, but her eyes remained expressionless.

Esme said, 'I thought the bank's policy was to advertise vacancies.'

'It is normally, but this was all very sudden, so the board met and decided to make this an exception. Head Office gave their approval, so here we are!' He beamed at them.

Millie said, 'Congratulations, Leo! I'm sure you deserve it.' She gave Esme a meaningful look to prompt a suitable response.

'Yes, Leo! Well done!'

He kissed her. 'It will make such a differ-ence. We could rent a larger house – or maybe have a holiday. Or travel. We could go to France for a week. To Paris!' He looked at Millie. 'We might all go. The three of us. How about that?'

Taken aback, Millie glanced at Esme, but her sister merely nodded. Of course, she reminded herself, none of these exciting plans would come to fruition. Once Leo knew about the child, everything would change. Their bright new future would be hopelessly tarnished.

Unaware, Leo was determined to celebrate. 'We'll go to the zoo,' he suggested.

'Oh no!' Esme wrinkled her nose. 'All those smelly monkeys and bears and things!'

Leo smiled. 'Better still, we'll go the opera at Covent Garden!'

Esme shook her head. 'The operas are all so dreary and sung in Italian. Last time we went I was utterly bored.'

Millie hid her disappointment: to go any-where would be a welcome distraction. Caring for her father had made it impossible to go far and the thought of an outing was exciting. She tried to think what might inter-est her sister.

'What about the river?' she suggested. 'Do you remember, Esme, when we hired a boat with Papa and went to Hampton Court. Mama made up a picnic and ... I think I was about seven so you...'

Esme gave her a withering look. 'That was in summer, Millie. It's now October. Do be sensible.'

'I know!' Leo refused to be deprived of his outing. 'We'll have a day at the seaside. We'll get some sea air. It will do you good, Esme – blow away the cobwebs, as my mother used to say.' Seeing that Esme was about to protest again, he went on quickly: 'And if it rains, we'll go inside somewhere – an art gallery or a museum. Or we'll wander round the shops. We'll go to Margate. What d'you say?'

Millie said, 'Wonderful!' but Esme frowned. 'Margate is so common,' she said. 'It attracts all the wrong people. I'd prefer Ramsgate, if we must go.'

Leo accepted the change before she could find another objection. 'Ramsgate it is, then. The three of us shall catch an early train tomorrow.' He turned to Millie. 'You'll enjoy Ramsgate. There are some fine buildings – the Pier House, with its dome. They say it's made of copper – and the Clock House and obelisk.'

Esme refused to show any real enthusiasm. 'Millie won't be interested in architecture,' she told her husband. 'She may enjoy the sands and the entertainers. Possibly the man with the performing dogs.'

'I shall enjoy it all,' said Millie firmly. She now decided that she would delay the revelation about the baby until Monday. Let Leo have what little pleasure he had left, she thought with a sigh. Before long his world would be shattered and the future would look unbearably bleak.

★   ★   ★

100

Later that evening Millie waited until Leo had settled himself with *The Times* and then made her way upstairs. Esme had complained of a headache and retired early to bed. Nervously she tapped on the door of their bedroom and on entering found Esme reading a magazine with a box of chocolates on the bed beside her.

'Help yourself, Millie,' Esme told her with a wave of her hand. 'The ones with walnuts on the top are coffee cream. Those in gold foil are soft caramel.'

'I'm too full,' Millie told her. 'I ate too much at supper.'

'Nonsense. You eat like a sparrow. Take one ... Oh trust you to choose the coconut! You know they're my favourites.'

'Sorry. I forgot.' The small lie pleased Millie.

'How's Leo? Still triumphant?'

'Very cheerful. He's reading the paper. Listen, Esme...' She perched herself unceremoniously on the end of the bed. 'I've had an idea. I don't know if it will help, but ... suppose you went ahead and had the baby. You could have it adopted. Plenty of women cannot bear children and are desperate for a child. A child from a respectable home would be in demand, I would think.' She watched Esme's expression and saw that she was listening intently.

'But then Leo would have to know.'

'He's going to know anyway – unless you go to that awful quack doctor. You could confess

101

and tell Leo you don't want the child – it was all a dreadful mistake.'

'But I do want it. I want the baby and I want...' She clapped a hand to her mouth. 'I want to be with his father. I want to leave Leo. Your idea wouldn't help at all.'

Millie wanted to shake her. Stubborn as always. She had a sudden vision of Esme at fifteen, insisting on wearing her new shoes for a long walk. By the time they arrived home, Esme had a broken blister on each heel and the insides of the new shoes were stained with blood. When her mother protested, Esme had insisted that she hadn't felt a thing!

'Listen, Esme, you might not have to tell Leo,' Millie said carefully. 'I was reading an article in the *Woman's Companion*.' She laid it on the bed in front of Esme. 'There's a story about a woman who bound herself firmly around the lower body so that the growing child was not noticeable. She was a single woman living at home and her mother didn't suspect a thing. She went away to stay with her grandmother, had the baby, and it was taken away on the third day by the new parents who adopted it.'

Esme considered the idea briefly. 'But Grandmother is no longer alive.'

'Aunt Flora is.'

Esme pushed the chocolates aside and sat up a little straighter. She tapped her fingers over the article Millie had shown her. 'I want to leave Leo and I want to be with Wally,' she insisted. 'It still might be possible. Now he's had a day to think it over, he might be changing his mind.'

'Are you meeting him again?' Millie thought it highly unlikely that the man would put in an appearance.

'I see him every Friday. We meet at the same place. He might have come to his senses. He might realize he should start a family before he's too old. He's just a sad old bachelor.' She looked at Millie thoughtfully. 'If he doesn't, I could think about your idea. It just might be possible. I wonder ... Do you truly think it possible?'

'It does mean deceiving Leo.'

'I've been deceiving him for months!' Esme gave a long sigh and rubbed her eyes. For the first time Millie felt an unwilling sympathy for her sister. It was true that Esme had brought this disaster upon herself by her infidelity, but she was likely to pay a high price for the pleasures of her romance with the nameless man while he, no doubt, would escape scot-free. Was that fair? Millie felt a rush of solidarity with her sister and with it came compassion. All that Esme had ever been or hoped to be was now swept away, and she faced a future as uncertain as Millie's.

Five

The following day's weather was unpromising, with a brisk wind and heavy clouds; but the air was warm and, ignoring his wife's objections, Leo insisted that they go ahead with their plans. For Millie it was wonderful to be away from the house and out in the world. The noisy bustle of the station, the cross-section of humanity in the carriage and the train ride itself were to be savoured, and she enjoyed every moment. It pleased her to see that Leo was relishing the experience and they exchanged more than one delighted glance. Only Esme grumbled, but Millie gave her the benefit of the doubt. Millie had never been with child and she imagined that Esme's emotions were confused as well as her conscience.

By eleven o'clock they had arrived in Ramsgate and were strolling along the beach beside a grey sea. Intermittent sunshine escaped the clouds and there was a slight breeze off the sea, but they were dressed for autumn weather. Leo, determined to enjoy himself, decided to have a donkey ride, but Esme refused.

'It's so childish, Leo!' she grumbled. 'And

you *are* a bank manager. You do have a certain position to maintain! Whatever would people think?'

'They won't see me!' He looked at Millie. 'Will you join me?'

Millie saw at once that if she also refused he would give up and Esme would have succeeded. She said, 'I do believe I will!'

His eyes lit up. 'You're a real trouper, Millie!'

Esme tutted. 'You shouldn't encourage him, Millie. You only do it to annoy me. I know you.'

Millie didn't bother to argue.

As they rode along over the damp sand, she glanced sideways at Leo, who, to her eyes, looked entirely attractive, his good-looking face creased with uncharacteristic laughter. He looked suddenly young and carefree and, knowing what lay ahead, Millie's heart ached for him.

A thought struck her. Suppose when he knew about the child he wanted Esme to keep it. Suppose he offered to overlook her indiscretion and claim the child as his own. That way he would save his marriage and avoid a scandal; but was that a way out that would eventually lead to more heartbreak? If Esme spent the rest of her life pining for the absent lover, she would hardly make Leo happy.

Riding across the sands and leaving Esme behind them reminded Millie of the time when she and Leo had been so much in love and had spent so much time together. With an effort she pushed the memories to the back of her mind and hoped the same thought would not occur to Leo. If it did, it would certainly spoil the moment for him.

The ride came to an end; he helped her down from the animal and together they rejoined Esme, who was waiting in the lee of the cliff. She was surrounded by men with telescopes who were sweeping the horizon for interesting ships, and ladies in shawls who were engrossed in their magazines and novels. Further over, men in striped costumes ran in and out of the bathing machines; children ran shrieking after a ball while another, older child struggled unsuccessfully to fly a kite.

As soon as they rejoined Esme she complained that she was chilly, so they left the beach and Leo took them in search of a coffee shop, where they had a hot drink and shared a plate of mixed biscuits. Away from the sea breeze they strolled in and out of the shops and Leo bought Esme an expensive fan by way of a celebratory present. When they returned to the promenade, they met a great many bath chairs being pushed by grim-faced relatives or trim young nurses and, frequently needing to dodge these, conversation became difficult, so that Millie was left to her own thoughts. Lagging slightly behind, she watched Esme and Leo and found it hard to imagine a time when they might no longer be a married couple. Instead she tried to imagine them with a baby in a pram – maybe pushed by a young nursemaid. Nobody seeing them for the first time would suspect the serious problems which confronted them.

The train ride home later that evening was a vaguely subdued affair. The carriage was almost empty and the rhythm of the carriages over the track was soothing. No one spoke. Esme seemed half-asleep, her head resting on Leo's shoulder. He seemed relaxed and cheerful, but Millie, sitting opposite them, had the sudden feeling that the three of them would never again spend time together. It sent a shudder through her body and left her depressed and strangely fearful.

Later that night, Millie was awoken by a persistent tapping on her door. Not again, she thought. She had made it quite clear that she did not want Leo to come to her room. For a moment or two she pretended not to have heard, but eventually was forced to get out of bed. She opened the door a crack – and found Esme standing there.

'I have to talk to you,' Esme hissed, and reluctantly Millie opened the door.

Millie returned to her bed and now it was Esme's turn to sit on the end of it, huddled in her dressing gown.

'I'm not going to make a decision until I've seen Wally again,' she repeated. 'If he will make an honest woman of me – and I know he will – I'll tell Leo what has happened and then I'll leave. I'll write Leo a letter and you must help me pack.'

'And what will I do then?' Millie asked. 'I can't stay here with your husband!'

'For heaven's sake, Millie!' Esme rolled her eyes, exasperated. 'Do I have to think for everyone? You must find a situation, I suppose.' She hesitated; then her face brightened. 'Maybe Wally could take you on as *our* housekeeper. It's not as though he's poor. He could afford it.'

Silenced by this dreadful prospect, Millie studied her sister. At least Esme had abandoned the idea of getting rid of the unborn child, and that was a relief.

'You could find yourself a husband,' Esme told her. 'Don't *you* want a family? You're quite presentable, you know, but you never make the best of yourself. If you end up an old maid, you'll only have yourself to blame!'

Shocked, Millie felt herself colour. 'I don't want to be married. At least ... Well, I think you know what I mean. I can never marry Leo and there'll never be anyone else.'

'There won't be if you've made up your mind to it. Suppose you had never met Leo? You would almost certainly have married someone else, so don't talk so foolishly, Millie.'

Startled, Mille was forced to consider this point. Could she have loved anyone else? When Millie made no reply, Esme tightened her lips. 'Oh, I see! You want to blame me for your single state. That is so like you, Millie: lay the responsibility at someone else's door.

108

That's the easy way out, isn't it! Suppose Leo had chosen you instead of me. Do you think I'd have remained single? Of course not. I have more pride. I'd have gone straight out and found another man. Any woman would – except you! You have to mope around making me feel guilty.'

'At least I wouldn't have betrayed Leo with another man!' Millie glared at her sister. 'I have more pride than to lower myself to *that* level!' Her chest was heaving with anger. 'At least I'm not in the position you're in – expecting an illegitimate child! Thank God Mama and Papa are no longer alive to see you in this mess.' Esme was staring at her in shock but Millie rushed on. 'Leo's shown you nothing but love and affection and this is the thanks he gets. I hope this Wally is worth it, Esme, because, if there's any justice in the world, he's all you've got now!' She scrambled to her feet. 'Now please, Esme! Get out of my room! I'm ashamed to call you my sister!'

Ashen-faced, Esme seemed about to protest, but then she changed her mind and with a slowness intended to provoke, she slid from the bed and walked to the door.

As soon as she had gone Millie locked the door and climbed back into bed, shaking violently from the bitter exchange. Already she regretted her loss of control. She had never spoken to Esme in that way before and she felt she had gone too far, but she couldn't wish the words unsaid. As she slipped under the blankets, she knew without a doubt that she had probably made matters ten times worse for all of them.

Two days later, Ned Warren and his father were unloading the van while a young lad held the horse's head. A Mrs Ada Samuels, recently widowed, was storing her furniture while she moved in with an elderly aunt. She had explained to Ned that when the aunt died she would need to find her own lodgings and would recover the furniture. Without conversation, the two men tugged and heaved the heavy, old-fashioned pieces from the van down on to the pavement outside Haddon's Yard. First came a mahogany headboard and the iron bedstead plus a deep flock mattress, stained and frayed, that went with it. An old leather trunk followed, frayed at the corners.

'Weighs a bloomin' ton!' gasped Stanley. 'What's she got in it, for Gawd's sake? Gold bullion?'

Ned carried out a rolled-up carpet. Stanley dragged out lino and a rug.

Two ragged little boys watched them with gleeful interest until Stanley grew tired of their jibes.

' 'Op it, you two scallywags! You've had your fun!'

The taller boy said, 'You can't make us!'

'No? A clout says I can!' He darted forward and the boy retreated. His companion poked out his tongue; but, reluctantly, they finally sloped off disappointed and left the two men to their labours.

Next Stanley and Ned struggled with an oak chest that had seen better days and then a large, very solid chest of drawers – one drawer at a time and then the bulky frame. Finally a vast wardrobe.

'Watch it, Ned! It's slippin'!'

'Down a bit, Pa; it's jammed against the table!'

'Jesus O'Riley!'

Eventually the work was done and Stanley mopped his brow with a red neckerchief. 'That's the lot!' he gasped. 'Either I'm getting old or the stuff's getting heavier. We'll have a cuppa and then we'll get the stuff upstairs. If I'd realized there was so much, I'd have charged a bit more.'

They retired to the end of the workshop, where a small wood stove heated the kettle. While Stanley lit up his clay pipe, Ned made the tea.

The workshop was the usual muddle of timber, tools and what Ned called 'assorted junk'. His father would never throw out anything that might come in useful later. Old locks, oily rags, brackets, bits of guttering, rusty hinges – all tumbled together on the workshop counters and all gathering dust and rust and growing old disgracefully. The workshop smelled of wood and oil and smoke and to Ned it was his second home. He couldn't recall a time when his father had not pottered about, making and mending and somehow scraping a living. The space in the loft earned its keep, but Ned had always known there was not enough work for two, and the bailiff's job suited him well enough. Now he watched his father from the corner of his eye.

'I'm thinking of getting wed,' Ned remarked casually. 'About time, I guess.'

Stanley dropped the pipe and the stem snapped off. 'Dammit! Now look what you've done!' He kicked the pieces into a corner and frowned at his son. 'Getting wed? What – proper wed? In a church?'

Ned nodded. 'Why not?'

'I didn't know you was courting. Bit sudden, isn't it?'

Ned shrugged. 'What's the point in waiting?' He blew on his tea.

His father looked at him doubtfully. 'It's that nursemaid, I suppose.'

'No, it isn't. It's Miss Bayley.'

His jaw dropped. *'Miss Bayley?* The one that stored her bits of furniture? Come off it, Ned. A woman like Miss Bayley's not going to take up with a chap like you!'

Ned grinned. 'She doesn't know it, but she is!'

Stanley shook his head. 'Don't you go getting fancy ideas, Ned. You'll only come a cropper. Anyway, you shouldn't wed too young. Give yourself a chance to save a bit first. Wait a year or two, Ned. That's my advice, for what it's worth.'

'You wed Ma when you were nineteen!'

'There was a reason for that!' His eyes

112

narrowed. 'Her father kicked up such a hulla-baloo … You haven't got her in the … have you?'

'No, I haven't! She's refined. I like that.'

'Maybe you do like it. The question is: does she like you? I can't see a lady like Miss Bay-ley—'

'She's not exactly a lady, Pa!' Ned con-sidered, his head on one side. 'I'd say nicely brought up but fallen on hard times. Hap-pens all the time.'

'She's lady-*like*, any road, I'll grant you that. Nice manners. Speaks well enough. Have you asked her?'

'I'm getting round to it.' He winked. 'Com-ing to the wedding, are you?'

'Oh, I'll come to it if you can get her to the altar.' His father chuckled. 'I'll be there. Haven't been to a wedding for years. Couple of pints of ale and a nice piece of ham!' He laughed. 'Well, well! This should be inter-esting. Half a crown says there isn't one – no wedding, that is.'

'Done! Start saving up, Pa! You know me when I make up my mind.'

'I know you, but I don't know her – and nor do you! She might have other ideas. Why isn't she already wed, eh? Have you asked yourself that?'

'Some fellow jilted her years ago. More fool him. He's done me a favour.'

'And she didn't find anyone else?'

'She was nursing her ailing father.'

Stanley eyed his son warily. 'I hope you

know what you're doing, Ned.'

He tossed the tea leaves into the sawdust that covered the workshop floor. Some of them splashed on to the dog, who blinked reproachfully before settling his head on his paws once more. 'Right. Let's get that furniture under cover. We'll never get those big pieces up the stairs, so we'd best find some oilcloths and old sacks.' He stood up and stretched, easing his back. 'Bit of a nuisance. Still, it's a few extra bob.'

'I'll be wanting my cut, Pa. Got a wife-to-be now. Need to save my pennies!'

'Wife-to-be ! Hah!' He slapped his thigh, enjoying the joke. 'You'll be lucky, Ned – but I'll give you your cut, right enough.'

He gave his son an affectionate punch on the shoulder and moved outside, still chuckling, and the subject of his marriage was not mentioned again.

That same evening, in Allbrin Street, there was a prolonged ring at the Walmsleys' front door. Esme was resting in her room and Millie was in the garden, so Leo answered it. The young bailiff stood on the doorstep.

'Evening, Mr Walmsley,' he said. 'I'd like a word with Miss Bayley, if I may.'

Warren was the last person Leo wanted to see. Annoyed, he hesitated. Should he pretend that Millie was out? Reluctantly he decided that he dared not take such a risk. He might be found out and Millie would be furious. She was so damnably independent lately and he was unsure how to deal with it. Since she had come to Allbrin Street she had been very defensive and he blamed Esme for some of that. His wife tended to treat Millie as a servant rather than a family member and he had taken her to task on several occasions. Esme, however, was also becoming difficult and emotional lately and he assumed that Millie's presence had caused this change. Women were so difficult to read, he thought unhappily. He had wanted Millie safely under his roof and was trying to be fair to both of them, but the situation was proving much harder than he had expected.

'I said I'd like to speak with Miss Bayley, if she's in.' The young man had raised his voice slightly as though he thought Leo might be deaf.

'I heard you the first time,' Leo snapped. 'I'm afraid she's busy. Perhaps you could call back some other time.' Preferably never, he thought, aware of an uncharacteristic chill in his voice. This young man was becoming too interested in Millie. 'Unless you want to leave a message.'

'I'll wait.' He gave Leo a challenging look.

'She might be some time.'

'She's worth waiting for!' He grinned. 'Please tell her I'm out here on the steps. I think she'll find time to have a word with me.'

Leo bit back an angry retort. This chap worried him. He was a sight too confident. Surely Millie could never be interested in a man like this. He gave in with a few muttered words and went in search of Millie. She was staggering back from the garden with a basket of dry washing that she would soon start to iron. He said, 'That fellow's on the doorstep again. You really shouldn't encourage him, Millie.'

'That fellow? You don't mean Ned Warren, do you?'

Her eager expression went straight to his heart. 'The bailiff fellow. I don't like him.'

Without another word Millie dropped the basket and walked quickly past him and along the passage. Feeling a complete fool, Leo followed quietly until he stor where he could hear them, but out of sight in case the wretched man should glance past Millie into the gloom of the hallway.

'I was bringing in the washing,' Millie told her visitor. 'The wind has dried it beautifully. I love a windy Monday!'

Leo closed his eyes. She sounded like a servant. He must speak to Esme again. She was much too keen these days on resting in the afternoons and leaving the lion's share to Millie.

'I thought we might go out one evening,' Warren told her. 'I've still got those tickets you gave me. I thought maybe you and me and my pa could go. You'd be safe with us if things got rowdy, although I must say Tapper's has got a good reputation compared with many supper rooms. What d'you say?'

Leo crossed his fingers. 'Say no, Millie,' he willed silently; 'it's not at all suitable.' He

116

certainly didn't want Millie spending an evening with this fellow and his father. Anything might happen. He waited for Millie to refuse the invitation.

She said, 'Tapper's Supper Room? Oh!' and then there was a short silence.

Warren said, 'You've already met my pa. We'd look after you, I promise. Do say yes, Millie. It would be a great evening.' There was another silence. 'They do a great beef pie with onions and you could have a glass of wine, if you don't care for ale.'

Leo leaned closer. She wasn't going to agree, surely.

Millie said, 'The thing is – I know someone who's in the show. She's in the Grecian Temple scene. I'd love to see that but ... I don't think they would approve – Leo and Esme, I mean.'

She had lowered her voice, but Leo caught most of it and smiled with relief.

Warren said something, also in a low voice and Leo frowned. He stepped forward a couple of feet, still hidden from them, and heard Millie laugh. At that moment there were sounds on the landing above him and Leo retreated hurriedly. Trust Esme! As he slipped back into the kitchen, she came downstairs, hovered in the hallway and then joined him in the kitchen.

She asked, 'Who on earth is Millie talking to?'

'That bailiff fellow. You really should have a word with her, Esme. He's most unsuitable.'

117

'It's hardly our business, Leo. She must make her own mistakes. We did.'

He paused at the back door. 'What do you mean?'

She gave him a long, cool stare. 'We both know, Leo: marry in haste, repent at leisure.' She poured a glass of water and drank it quickly.

'It's only a mistake, Esme, if we allow it to be so.' His heart was racing suddenly. 'Or if you want it to be so.'

Esme gave him a strange look but said nothing. Instead, glancing at the dried washing, she said, 'Oh dear! I can't deal with that. Standing makes my back ache.'

'Aren't you leaving too much for Millie?'

'I don't think so. She's quite fit.'

'Aren't you?'

At that moment Millie rejoined them and they both stared at her expectantly.

She stared back, volunteering nothing.

Leo said, 'What did he want?'

Millie began to sort the washing, shaking out the clothes and folding them into a neat pile on the kitchen table. Leo was in an awkward situation: he could hardly admit that he had been listening to the conversation.

Millie glanced up. 'He asked to take me out on Saturday, that's all. I said yes. I shall look forward to that.'

Leo caught his wife's gaze and said, 'Where is he taking you?'

Before Millie could answer, Esme said, 'I don't think it's any of our business, Leo.

Millie isn't a ward of court! She's old enough to go where she pleases without our approval.'

Leo groaned inwardly. First the two women were at daggers drawn and now they were uniting against him. He said, 'Lord's sake!', went out into the garden and shut the back door firmly behind him.

On Friday, promptly at two o'clock, Esme arrived at the hotel, smiled at the receptionist and proceeded to the lift. The lift boy, usually very talkative, gave her an odd look and remained silent, but she was so busy with her own worries that she paid him no attention. Leaving the lift, she hurried along the carpeted passage, trying to contort her face into a happy smile. She rapped on the door of number 309 and waited, her heart beating particularly loudly. She had bought herself a new jacket of quilted blue velvet with covered buttons and had redecorated her hat with blue silk forget-me-nots, although she doubted if Wally would recognize their significance.

When no one answered, she rapped more loudly and then tried the handle, thinking he had perhaps left it open for her. After a few moments the truth dawned that the room was empty – either that, or he was deliberately excluding her; but if that were the case, he would hardly have bothered to rent the room.

Shocked, she leaned against the wall, willing herself not to faint. Nothing had led her to suggest that he would disappear from her life – that she might never see him again. She drew a deep breath, and then another, and straightened up. Telling herself not to panic, she made her way down the stairs to give herself time to think. At the desk she again managed a smile.

'I think there may be a letter for me,' she said. 'My friend in room 309 seems to...'

He shuffled a few papers on the counter in front of him. 'Mr Granger has cancelled the Friday arrangement,' he told her. 'He didn't tell you?'

Granger! So that was his name. She thought quickly. 'He's probably been trying to reach me, but I – I've been away in the country.'

'There is a letter.' He turned, selected one from the bank of pigeon-holes and handed it to her with what she suspected was a mocking bow. Esme walked away with an attempt at dignity, but as soon as she was out of sight she scurried to the Ladies' Powder Room and locked herself in one of the cubicles.

Opening the envelope with trembling fingers, she had to blink away tears of anger before she could read it.

My dear Esme,
We can have no future together. I did warn you right at the beginning that I am not the marrying kind. I'm sure you now realize this but I am willing to offer five hundred pounds if you will agree to see my doctor friend who will look after you well. A quiet chat with him will calm

120

all your fears on the subject. If you are willing, I shall be in the lounge of the hotel in one week from now at our usual time. I will take you to the doctor myself and he will send you home in a taxi. Out of the money you will pay the doctor and keep the rest. If you are not here I shall leave and we will never meet again. You only have this one chance, Esme. I am truly sorry we have to end our friendship this way but for reasons I need not explain, there is no other way out.

Yours sincerely –
Wally

Esme continued to sit there, shaken to the core and numb with despair, losing all track of time. Someone knocked on the door and she hastily pulled the chain.

'You all right in there?'

She drew a quick breath and stuffed the letter into her purse. 'I'm quite well, thank you.' She let herself out, to be confronted by a motherly-looking woman in a dark-green uniform.

'I thought you was never coming out!' she told Esme as she began to polish the taps.

'I – I was daydreaming!' Esme laughed shakily.

'That's all right then, dearie,' she said, 'only sometimes people are took ill and it's my responsibility, you see. People don't realize that. They see me as a cleaner, pure and

121

simple.' She breathed heavily on the mirror and gave it a polish. 'Oh dear me no! There's more to it than that. Once I had a woman faint clean away. I heard her go down, crash! I had to get down on my hands and knees to look under the door to see if she was dead or not. I had to give her a good sniff of sal volatile. That brought her round, but it gave me a scare, that did!'

'I see that it would.' Esme washed her hands and when she had finished, the woman handed her a small towel.

'Thank you.' Still badly shaken, Esme longed to sit down on the small cane chair, but if she did, the attendant would probably assume she was ill after all and might call the management. Instead she said, 'I must get along. Here ... please take this.' She held out a shilling, which the woman took gratefully, trying unsuccessfully to hide her surprise.

On the way home, resting on a park bench, Esme drew on unexpected reserves of courage. She would meet Wally next Friday, but what would she say to him? If she decided to visit the doctor, she would persuade Millie to accompany her. She would certainly need a woman friend. But if she decided to keep the child, she would need more than five hundred pounds from Wally. Somehow she would have to persuade him to make her an allowance. That would keep them in touch and when the child was older, he might take an interest. He might even change his mind and marry her.

She lay back in the seat, exhausted by shock and a growing sense of anger. 'Wally Granger – you are not going to treat me like this!' she muttered. 'I'm going to make you acknowledge our child if it's the last thing I do!'

Tapper's Supper Room was all Millie had hoped for and more. She sat between Ned Warren and his father and could hardly eat for excitement. As promised, the steaming plates of beef pie and onions could hardly have been better and the exciting venue made it taste even better. The chandeliers glinted and sparkled overhead and the room was full of gaiety and relaxed good humour. The air was full of cigar smoke, perfume and patchouli oil and there was a constant murmur of voices and clattering cutlery as the diners chatted while they devoured the food. Smiling faces appeared wherever she looked and Ned Warren watched her with amusement as he tucked in to his pie.

'Eat up, Miss Bayley,' he said between mouthfuls. 'If you leave anything, Pa will have it off your plate!'

With a reproachful look at his grinning son, his father explained; 'I can't abide waste,' he told her earnestly. 'I was brought up very strict like that. If it was on your plate, it was yours to be eaten.' He grinned. 'I love spuds, so watch them!'

Stanley Warren had surprised Millie by his smart appearance. Gone was the battered corduroy cap and instead he wore a bowler.

His suit, too, was obviously meant for Sundays, high days and holidays and he had shaved himself carefully to remove his normal stubble. He was taller and thinner than his broad-shouldered son and his clothes looked well on him. Ned Warren was also a revelation in a tweed suit and brown Derby with a white shirt and collar that appeared to be strangling him. Both men had been a little shy with her at first, no doubt wondering how she would react, but Tapper's friendly atmosphere worked its magic on all three. It was impossible not to feel comfortable and share in the fun.

They had already seen a comedian and a juggler and a plump woman with five little poodles which were trained to jump through hoops, roll balls and even count! Millie was longing for the Grecian Temple tableau. She had already made up her mind that tomorrow she would deliver a note to the stage door, congratulating Poppy on her performance.

At last, as the jam pudding and custard was arriving at their table, the tableau was announced and all eyes turned towards the stage. Something approaching silence fell as knives, forks and spoons were lowered and the chatter that had accompanied the earlier acts faded. Millie watched transfixed as the red curtain was slowly raised and the tableau was revealed in all its glory. A spontaneous burst of applause rang out and a barrage of lustful male eyes darted from one 'statue' to another, comparing their various merits and arousing unmentionable excitement. The atmosphere was electric, but Millie found herself smiling and was quite unshocked by either the feigned nudity on stage or the effect it had on most of the audience.

She soon spotted Poppy, upright against a graceful white column, one hand on her right hip, the other resting seductively against the column. She looked wonderful in her creamy silk drapes and wispy veiling, which were just enough to create an impression of modesty. Millie applauded ecstatically and pointed Poppy out to her companions. Men began to shout the names of their favourites and somewhere at the back of the room a man called for Poppy to give him a smile. Millie turned curiously. Was this by any chance the man who rented Poppy's flat for her? She saw a burly, middle-aged man on his feet and blowing kisses. He was very red in the face and looked as though he had been drinking heavily.

Millie turned to look at Poppy who, without moving her limbs, swivelled her eyes in his direction. So this was Henry! Poppy's MP. Millie found it difficult to see what Poppy saw in the man, but she reminded herself that beauty was in the eye of the beholder.

Ned Warren said, 'D'you know him?'

'No. I've heard him mentioned, that's all.' She turned back to the stage, reluctant to reveal any details of Poppy's gentleman friend. As she did so, there was a crash from somewhere at the back of the room and several cries of alarm. Millie turned back to

125

see Poppy's friend sprawled face down on the carpet. A waiter narrowly missed tripping over the prostrate form; someone called for a doctor and another shouted to a waiter to fetch the manager.

'Heart attack!' said Ned. 'Pound to a penny!'

'Oh dear!' Millie glanced up at the stage and saw that Poppy was staring down, a look of deep concern on her face. For a moment her arm moved and she covered her mouth with her hand, but immediately, at a hissed command from the wings, she resumed her original position.

Because of the commotion the curtain was lowered, amid groans from the men, and the next turn was announced. The unfortunate singer, a buxom young woman, was hurried on stage but sang largely ignored by the indifferent audience. Most people were watching the drama off stage as a doctor appeared and knelt beside the fallen man. After a whispered consultation with the manager, a stretcher was brought in and the insensible man rolled on to it. Two waiters then staggered off with him and the atmosphere lightened a little. Conversation resumed, but in hushed tones, and the singer went off to muted applause. After the unhappy interruption the show did not regain its lost momentum and the management announced that in view of the 'accident' the show would close early. Within half an hour the evening came to an end and Millie was taken home by her two

126

escorts.

'I don't know how to thank you,' she told them. 'I've had a wonderful time.'

As they stood at the bottom of the steps, Ned Warren made her promise that she would spend another evening with him, and she agreed willingly. They all shook hands and parted company. Millie was sure she had seen someone watching them from behind the curtain, but she decided not to mention it. She wondered how ill Poppy's gentleman friend was and what difference it would make to her friend if he died.

When she let herself in, Leo was waiting for her. Esme had gone up to bed.

'You needn't have waited up, Leo,' Millie protested. 'I was quite safe.'

'It's nearly half past ten!'

'Is it really?' Smiling, she pulled off her gloves.

'Have you been drinking?' he demanded.

'Two glasses of wine, and a very nice beef pie. Not to mention the jam pudding.'

'So you went to a restaurant.'

'Not exactly. We went to Tapper's Supper Room. Don't you remember? – you suggested I gave the free tickets to Ned Warren. I went with him and his father. They looked after me very well.' Putting a hand to her mouth, she covered a yawn. 'But I'm ready for bed now.'

He hesitated. 'We could have a hot drink,' he suggested. 'We never get any time to talk. There's so much...' He looked at her with such appeal in his eyes that, for just a moment, Millie was tempted. But that way lay disaster, she reminded herself. She must keep a distance between herself and her sister's husband.

'I'm sorry, Leo. I'm too sleepy. Another time, perhaps'; and with a quick smile she made her way upstairs to her little attic rooms and was soon in bed. Her last waking thought was of Poppy Gayford.

Six

As soon as the curtains closed Poppy made a dash for the wings, elbowed the other girls out of the way, and ran for the dressing room. This was a large, cold room with a row of mirrors edged with lights in which the artistes watched their reflections as they applied their make-up. Paint flaked from the walls, and a cupboard and a row of hooks were definitely the worse for wear. Higher up, on one wall, a broad shelf supported dozens of hatboxes.

Pulling her clothes on but forgetting to dismantle her elaborate Grecian hairstyle, Poppy snatched up her coat and shouted a hasty goodnight to the rest of the cast, who were now filling the dressing room. Minutes later she was in the foyer, asking for news of the man who had collapsed.

The front-of-house manager shook his head. 'Can't say, darling.' He called them all 'darling'. 'He was still breathing when they carted him off. You'd best ask at the hospital. They'll have taken him to the nearest one. And don't speak to any newspaper hacks. It's hardly good publicity for...'

But Poppy had heard enough. She darted outside to the pavement, hailed the first hansom cab and told the driver to take her to the nearest hospital. Usually she enjoyed the thrill of the ride – the soothing clip-clop of the horse's hooves and the occasional flick of the driver's whip as they clattered through the gaslit streets in the darkness. Now she thought only of Henry and his possible fate.

At the hospital she was met by a steely-eyed receptionist.

Poppy gave her a nervous smile. She hated hospitals. The smell of the disinfectant was enough to alarm her. 'The gentleman who's just been admitted,' she said, '– a possible heart attack.'

The woman glanced at a paper on the desk in front of her. 'You don't mean the MP?'

'Yes. Henry Granger.'

The woman stared at her and Poppy realized that she had forgotten her hat and that it was raining. No doubt her Grecian plaits and curls were looking a trifle dishevelled.

'Only next-of-kin are allowed to see the patient. Are you next-of-kin?'

Poppy made a split second decision. She said firmly, 'I'm his wife. I heard the news and came straight here.' Poppy hardly expected to get away with such a blatant lie, but to her surprise, after the smallest hesitation, the receptionist nodded. 'Go up to ward three,' she told her. 'Ask the sister there whether the patient is well enough to have a visitor.' She smiled at Poppy. 'Your husband is in good hands, Mrs Granger. You must try not to worry.'

Thanking her, Poppy hurried up the stairs and along a corridor. Her footsteps rang on the polished wooden floor and she whispered a prayer for Henry's survival. Without him to pay her rent she would soon find herself in desperate straits. Her meagre wages would pay for her food but accommodation would be reduced to more dingy surroundings and life would be a constant struggle.

The nursing sister was obviously a little suspicious. Perhaps, thought Poppy, they considered she was too young to be married to a much older man. Too late she remembered that Henry had sons who were no longer children.

'Mrs Granger?'

Poppy returned the stare as confidently as she could. 'Yes. I'd like to see my husband, please. This has been a great shock.'

The woman's eyes narrowed. 'Not such a shock, surely. He came in here earlier in the year with a minor attack. The doctor did warn you then that there might be worse to come.'

Drat! Poppy rallied quickly. 'But he has been so much better recently. I thought the danger had passed. May I see him? Is he conscious?' Had she been sufficiently convincing? She waited nervously.

After a short hesitation the nursing sister said, 'Just for a few minutes, then. I'm sure he'll be pleased to see you. The doctor is due at any moment, but I'll show you the way.'

She led Poppy into a small private room, where Henry lay in bed, his face ashen.

131

Poppy said, 'May we have a little privacy. I promise not to tire him.'

Taking the hint, the sister left them alone, closing the door quietly behind her.

'Henry? How are you, my love?' Poppy leaned over to kiss him. 'You gave me such a fright. Tell me you're not as bad as you look. You're so dreadfully pale.'

'Not ... not to worry ... pretty little...' His eyes closed and Poppy patted his hand sharply.

'Don't go to sleep, Henry! Stay awake, please! Talk to me. How do you feel?' She leaned closer. 'When will I see you again?'

'Don't ... don't come here ... again,' he murmured. 'My wife ... she mustn't ... mustn't see you.'

'I know that, Henry. Just tell me you'll write or something. Promise me. Send a letter to the flat or to the theatre. I must know what is happening.'

His eyes closed again and she gave a little cry of fright. Was he going to die on her, right here in the hospital?

Without opening his eyes he murmured, 'I'll write ... to you, little darling . . . never ... fear. Now go, Poppy, please.'

With tears in her eyes, Poppy gave him a last kiss and hurried from the ward. As she passed the nurses' room, she saw the nursing sister talking urgently with a young man holding a notebook. A doctor, possibly. Averting her eyes, Poppy almost ran down the corridor, fearing that at any moment an arm

132

would reach out for her and she would be accused of deception or fraud or whatever the name was for her crime. By the time she burst out into the street her heart was thumping so loudly that she half-expected a heart attack herself.

Had they discovered the lie? She would never dare return. Presumably Henry's wife would be notified and would travel up from their country house. Maybe she would stay in town for a few days. Henry's studio was available to her. What would happen when the real wife announced herself as Mrs Granger?

Frantic with worry, Poppy asked directions and set off to walk home alone through the dark streets. There was no point in wasting good money on a cab, now there was no urgency, and she was going to need every penny. But Henry *would* write to her. He had promised. She would be patient. It occurred to her that the news of Henry's attack would find its way into the newspapers. With a jolt, she realized that the young man with the notebook might have been a reporter.

Millie found herself alone with Leo at breakfast next morning and for a while he continued to read the newspaper while she ate bacon and eggs with a slice of toast.

Suddenly he lowered the paper. 'Did you see anything of this?' he asked. 'It says that Granger, the MP, had a heart attack last night while he was having a meal at Tapper's Supper Room!' He looked at her accusingly. 'You didn't mention it.'

'I didn't think it was important. I suppose I'd forgotten about it. I did see him collapse, but I didn't know he was an MP.' Lies, Millie reflected sadly. Why was it so difficult to remain honest?

He turned back to the relevant column and read aloud:

> ...A young woman appeared at the hospital claiming to be the MP's wife but staff were alerted by a young reporter from the *Daily Echo*, who claimed that Mr Granger's wife was in Somerset with their two sons and was intending to travel to London today to visit her husband. The identity of the mystery woman is not known...

Millie shrugged and tried to look innocent. Presumably it was Poppy who had rushed to the hospital, pretending to be Henry's wife. Did the unfortunate wife know already that there was another woman involved? Surely a woman could tell if her husband was betraying her with someone else. There would be small giveaway signs and indiscretions.

At that moment Esme joined them, refusing the usual Sunday-morning ritual of eggs and bacon and preferring a slice of plain toast.

Leo said, 'You look pale, Esme.'

'I feel pale. I feel very low, if you must know – what Grandmama used to call "out of sorts".' She smiled faintly.

Leo read out the extract about the MP.

'I've never heard of him,' Esme told him irritably. 'You know I take no interest in politics.'

'Middle-aged, overweight, gingery hair and a too-ruddy complexion,' Leo told her helpfully. 'Well known in the House for speaking his mind. Always smokes a meerschaum pipe in the shape of a skull.'

'A skull?' Esme stared at him.

'Yes. A bit eccentric, I suppose. He married Lady Dorcas Denton years ago and almost immediately her parents were killed in a road accident in Switzerland; the daughter inherited the estate in Somerset because there was no male heir. They say he's a bit of a womanizer.'

Esme swallowed a mouthful of toast with difficulty. Millie ignored her. They had barely spoken since the row the previous week, partly because Millie had managed on many occasions to be in another room or out of the house altogether but partly because Esme had spent a great many hours resting on the bed.

Now Leo glanced from one sister to the other. 'Have you two had a falling-out?'

Before Millie could answer Esme said, 'If we have, it's nothing to do with you. Falling out is what sisters do. It doesn't mean anything. You wouldn't understand, being an only child.' She smiled at Millie and they exchanged sheepish looks; Millie felt hopeful that maybe their differences had faded into the background – for the moment at least. Her sister could be charming, but she could also be very sharp-tempered and Millie, as the younger child, had learned to treat her cautiously.

Millie finished her breakfast and rose to leave the table. She intended to visit Poppy as soon as they had finished the midday meal. Today Esme would have to wash up.

Poppy opened the door to her just after three o'clock and Millie at once saw the effect her lover's illness had had on her. Her smile was less radiant and her face bore fewer traces of make-up. Her eyes were reddened and she clutched a handkerchief. She did, however, seem genuinely pleased to see Millie and at once drew her inside and up the stairs.

The flat, previously so elegant, now showed small signs of neglect. Petals had fallen from the roses in the bowl on the window sill and the ashes had not been cleared from the grate.

'Sit down, my dear Millie, and make youself comfortable,' Poppy told her. 'You are just what I need to cheer me up. Poor Henry has been taken ill with – but of course, you know that. You were there! I saw you.' She sank into the armchair opposite Millie and sat forward, hugging her knees. Millie saw how hard she was trying to maintain her usual bright manner, but the strain showed in her eyes.

'I came to say how sorry I am about Henry,' Millie said, 'but also, of course, to congratulate you on the Grecian Temple scene. It was wonderful and so were you.'

'Was I? Oh that's so kind of you.' Poppy brightened visibly. 'He was so happy, at that moment, blowing kisses and calling out my name! Poor dear darling! I could hardly believe my eyes when he fell to the floor. I was so shocked I *moved*, and that's a cardinal sin; but in the circumstances Mr Jennings forgave me.'

Millie said, 'You're almost famous, Poppy – except that nobody knows your name. At the hospital – it was in the paper this morning.'

'In the paper? Good heavens!' She stared at Millie, obviously startled by the information. 'I haven't been out this morning. I slept so badly I didn't feel up to preparing myself for the outside world.'

'You are described as a "mystery woman"! It *was* you, I take it?'

'It was me all right.' She poured them each a glass of sherry and settled down again. 'Oh! What will Henry say?' She stared at Millie, then began to laugh. '"Mystery woman"? That's too funny for words! Poor Henry. He would see the funny side of that.'

'I thought you ought to know, Poppy, in case any reporters come sniffing round the stage door. Someone might put two and two together...'

'And make four. I'll have to be careful. But I don't think the young man at the hospital noticed me slipping past.' Her expression darkened. 'I've been wondering what to do if

137

Henry dies. I shall want to go to his funeral, but then they'll ask me who I am. I can't go upsetting his poor wife, can I?' She sighed heavily. 'And I shan't be able to stay here. It's expensive, so near Leicester Square.'

'What were you doing before you came here?'

'Sharing a room with two of the other girls...' She drew a long breath. 'Still, I'll survive. Beggars can't be choosers.'

She jumped up and took a photograph from the mantelpiece. 'Look: me and Henry. We were at the seaside. We went to Brighton because Henry thought there'd be less chance of bumping into anyone he knows. He didn't really want the photograph taken – afraid of being recognized – but I insisted. It's the only one I have of him.'

Millie stared at the two lovers – Poppy looking carefree and windblown and smiling happily, Henry looking anxious and not a little furtive. Poppy was leaning against Henry and he had his arm round her waist. Once again Millie was stricken with envy. Her time with Leo had been so brief and they had never had a photograph taken together. She had nothing but memories to prove that they had ever been in love and although she and Leo both knew it, there was nothing but pain now. It was worse since she had been forced to move in to The Laurels, and once again Millie determined to seek her independence.

Millie returned the photograph. 'I do wish I could say something helpful, Poppy, but I

138

can't think of anything – except that Henry will almost certainly survive. He looks a big strong man.'

Poppy shook her head. 'He was once, I daresay, but his heart isn't strong. He had a minor attack earlier in the year. Poor Henry. I wish I could be the one to look after him instead of Dorcas – that's his wife. He says she doesn't love him any more, but I'd be a devoted nurse.' She sighed. 'If he has to convalesce, they might send him to Bognor. That's where he went last time he was ill. There's a convalescent home close to the Downs. I'd hardly ever see him, but it would be better than him being sent to his home in Somerset. I'd *never* see him if that happened.'

Millie smiled. 'If they advertised for a nurse, you could apply! – pretend to have nursing skills!'

Poppy brightened. 'I'd do it,' she said stoutly, 'except that then I'd lose my job at Tapper's and if Henry died I'd have no one to nurse and I'd be back to square one.'

When it was time to leave, Millie gave Poppy a hug and promised to call and see her again. 'And you know where I live,' she added. 'If anything urgent happens and you need me, come round. Two heads are better than one. I may not be able to solve the problem, but I *can* offer moral support. That's what friends are for!'

That evening, while Leo checked the household accounts, Esme took Millie aside and showed her Wally's letter. Millie read it in silence and then looked at her sister in horror. 'I thought he loved you, this man? This is so – so *cruel*.'

'It is, I know, but ... the truth is he did tell me once that he would never marry; but men say things like that. I didn't pay any attention. The thing is, Millie, that I have to meet him on Friday to...'

'Not to have the operation? You don't mean that, Esme?'

'Of course not, but I'm certain I can make him change his mind. The only thing is, if I can't – if he won't budge – he might try to make me go. I do need that money, Millie, in case Leo deserts me. What will I do if he turns me out. Many men would. Many men *do*!'

And who could blame them? thought Millie; but she remained silent.

Esme leaned closer. 'I want you to come with me, Millie. I'd feel a lot safer and stronger if I knew I had an ally.'

Millie was already shaking her head. 'No, Esme. It means joining the deception against Leo and I won't be part of it. I'm sorry.' Even as she uttered the words she felt a twinge of guilt. Would she have refused Poppy? Did she have one answer for her friends and another for her sister? Esme was her own flesh and blood. 'I don't think I'd be any help,' she added, but knew how unconvincing she sounded.

Esme ignored her words. 'I think it would be reasonable to take a woman friend with me, especially a family member. He might be more reasonable if you were there. You could sit on the other side of the lounge, out of earshot.'

Millie avoided her sister's eyes. This really was an impossible situation.

Esme said, 'The truth is I'm half-afraid of what he might do. If he becomes angry ... he might force me to accompany him to the doctor. He wouldn't attempt that if you were there as well.'

'I've already said I won't do it!'

Esme continued as though Millie hadn't spoken: 'I really do need to persuade him to give me the money, Millie, even though I'm going to keep the child; but I could sign something to say that the five hundred is all I shall ask from him. You could witness my signature. Oh Millie!' Suddenly her voice shook. '*Please*, forgive me for everything I've ever done to hurt you – and help me.'

Millie was forced to admit that Esme sounded genuinely frightened. Suppose she refused her sister's request for help and then Esme died from the illegal surgery? She would never be able to forgive herself. Millie sat for a while with her head in her hands, desperate to discover a way out, but finally concluded reluctantly that she must agree.

'I'll come with you, Esme,' she said at last, but the words had an ominous ring to them and as Esme clung to her, weeping tears of relief, Millie immediately suspected that she had made the wrong decision.

The promise to accompany Esme galvanized Millie into decisive action. She was going to find herself a job and leave Esme and Leo to sort out their own problems. On Wednesday morning, neatly turned out in a plain navy-blue skirt and jacket, she presented herself at a private employment agency and waited in some trepidation for her turn. She was finally called to a desk, where a stern-looking woman announced herself as Mrs Britton. Millie sat down in front of the imposing desk and tried to hide her nervousness. Mrs Britton wore black, her hair was black and Millie suspected, from her bad-tempered expression, that her heart was also black. Without preamble Mrs Britton took down a few details: Millie's name, address and age.

'You have references, of course.' Mrs Britton held out her hand for them.

Millie hesitated. 'I'm afraid not. I – I have never been employed,' she explained. 'I have nursed both my parents and now they are dead I need to earn a living. I think I am fairly adaptable...' She trailed into silence as the woman pursed her lips unhappily.

'Does that mean you have no references at all, Miss Bayley?'

'Yes. I mean, no – I don't have any references.'

Mrs Britton assumed an expression of exaggerated disbelief and wrote at length in

142

her notebook. 'Are you also saying that you have no training?' Dipping the pen carefully into the inkwell, she waited for Millie's answer.

'I suppose I am saying that, but I do have experience: I nursed...'

Mrs Britton leaned forward and sighed loudly. 'Our clients, Miss Bayley, are not looking for unskilled workers. They would go elsewhere for that kind of employee. Do you see my dilemma?'

Millie stared at her with growing embarrassment. She was clearly beginning to see her *own* dilemma. For a moment they faced each other in silence.

Mrs Britton sighed again. 'Exactly what kind of employment are you expecting to find, Miss Bayley?'

Millie clasped her hands in her lap to keep them from trembling. 'I think I could be a companion to someone.'

'Nursing an elderly lady, perhaps – is that what you have in mind?' As she spoke, Mrs Britton allowed her fingers to riffle through a box filled with index cards. She pulled one out and studied it. *'Elderly man requires housekeeper. Some nursing qualifications required.'* She raised her eyebrows and replaced the card. Choosing another she read: *'Companion between twenty and thirty years old for elderly widow. Some previous references essential.'* She looked at Millie. 'You take my point, Miss Bayley? Our clients expect superior qualifications from...'

Millie swallowed hard. 'I could be a nanny, perhaps.'

'Where did you do your training?'

'I haven't been trained but I could learn as I go along. I like children.'

The eyebrows went up again. 'You have children of your own?'

'No, but I'm certain...' Again she fell silent. How certain was she that she could cope with lively children? Babies, even?

The fingers extracted another card and Mrs Britton handed it to Millie. '*Wanted, nanny for three young children (one almost blind) and an infant. Live in. One day off every three weeks. Holidays taken in Cornwall without parental supervision, share large nursery...*'

Millie looked up slowly and met Mrs Britton's triumphant gaze.

Mrs Britton said, 'You can't always expect a room of your own, you see, and the nanny takes the children to Cornwall in the summer for six weeks – alone. It's a big responsibility.'

Millie shook her head. Surely she was capable of *something*.

Mrs Britton fussed with her lace collar then began once more to glance through the file for a suitable card. 'Here is one for a cook,' she suggested. 'I don't know how well you cook. *Plain cook required for large family (five children, parents plus invalid grandmother), stews and vegetable dishes preferred but cake and pudding on Sundays. Hours from 6 a.m. to 9 p.m., full board and lodgings and spending money to be negotiated. One day off in ten. No followers. Widow preferred.'* She shrugged. 'So that's no good.'

Millie made a last attempt. 'I am quite well read. What about a governess?'

'You would have to do more than *read*, Miss Bayley. You would have to teach the three Rs – reading, writing and arithmetic. Can you do mental arithmetic?'

'Yes.'

'Fifteen, twenty-five, six and nine make...?'

'Oh! I see. It's a test. Would you please repeat the numbers? I didn't...'

Mrs Britton closed the lid of the box. Obviously she despaired of finding any position in her file that Millie might possibly fill. Humiliated, Millie tried to protest, but her throat was dry. She was also angry.

'What about road-sweeper?' she suggested. 'Or bird-scarer. Maybe a Thameside scavenger – or chimney sweep! There must be something low enough that I could do!'

Mrs Britton drew herself up, her mouth a thin line of disapproval. 'There's no call for that kind of talk, Miss Bayley. You simply prove to me that you are not at all the sort of person we like to deal with...'

'And this is not the sort of agency I could ever recommend to any reasonable woman in search of a reasonable position!' Millie felt tears pressing against her eyelids. 'Good day to you!'

Trembling, Millie somehow found her way down the stairs to the street, where she rushed blindly along the pavement, willing herself not to cry – past the bootmaker's, the pawn shop, a ladies' hatter and a wig-maker's shop. Just as she turned the corner the first tears trickled down her cheeks, but almost immediately someone grabbed her arm and swung her round.

'Miss Bayley! I thought it was you! Why, what's the matter?'

A blurred version of Ned Warren swam into view and Millie felt weak with relief. Here was someone who appreciated her qualities.

'There's nothing the matter – at least, nothing important.' Hastily she brushed away the tears and forced a smile. 'What are you doing here?'

'Just about to throw someone out into the street. Mr Burrows the wig man can't pay his rent.' Seeing Millie's expression he said, 'Well, not exactly, but I've already served a summons, which he ignored, so they sent me round to play the heavy.'

'Oh dear! Poor man!' Millie at once forgot her own troubles. 'Doesn't anyone want wigs any more?'

Ned threw out his hands. 'He had an assistant – his nephew; but his eyesight's gone and he's given up. Mr Burrows is late with the orders and some folks cancelled and went elsewhere. It's tough, but it happens.' He stared at Millie. 'Who's upset you? I'll sort them out for you in a twinkling.'

Briefly Millie explained, citing the advertisement for the family cook as an example. 'It was really me being silly. I should have known better. She was quite right, but she needn't have been so dreadfully dismissive.'

'Mean old cow!' he said indignantly. 'You know what you should do? – you should find a nice young man who'd marry you and look after you. I mean there must be someone who'd have you.' He grinned. 'I know someone not a million miles away who'd jump at the chance.'

'Ned Warren!' Cheered by his impudence she smiled back.

'Let's see now: "Wanted, attractive young woman with kind heart willing to rescue a poor man from a life of loneliness. Cooking, laundry work, housework, bringing up babies. No days off, no followers..." ' He laughed. 'I mean, who could resist a job like that?'

'No followers?' she mocked, amused.

'Certainly not! My wife would have eyes only for me, Miss Bayley. She wouldn't *want* any followers because I'd be so good to her. Because I'd – I'd *love* her, Miss Bayley.' His smile had faded and he now regarded her earnestly. 'So if you were to apply...'

Before she could reply a man came clattering down the stairs at the side of the shop and stopped abruptly at the sight of Ned Warren. He was a small twig of a man in a brown curly-brimmed bowler. At once Millie stepped backwards and Ned the bailiff became businesslike.

'Today's the day, Mr Burrows,' he said sternly. 'Sorry about that, but you were warned.' He adopted a more formal tone. 'Alfred

147

Burrows, I am instructed to remove goods from your property to the value of the outstanding rent to the agreed sum as notified in the summons.'

The wig-maker glanced up and down the street as though hoping for divine intervention. Discovering none, he said, 'You could take the grandfather clock. I can hear the church clock from here – and there's a nice copper warming pan: I could use a hot brick in the bed ... and maybe the pewter teapot. Used to be my mother's, but she's not alive now to miss it, God bless her!'

The bailiff folded his arms. 'I c' .d take all that,' he agreed, 'and you wouldn't see it again.' He lowered his voice. '*Or* you could pawn it all and give me the money. Then if things look up, you could get it all back out of hock. Up to you. I could give you twenty minutes or so.' He leaned against the wall and began to whistle.

Alfred Burrows rushed back upstairs and the bailiff became Ned Warren again, but his romantic mood had been broken. 'I'll have to give him a hand,' he told Millie apologetically. 'He'll never carry all that stuff without dropping something. I'm a fool to myself sometimes. But I'll pop round to your house again and—' There was crash from somewhere upstairs. 'What did I say! You'll have to excuse me, Miss Bayley.'

He disappeared up the dark stairs and Millie was left to her own thoughts. After a few moments she resumed her walk home.

On the way she bought a bunch of violets for her window sill from the flower-seller on the corner, and by the time she reached Allbrin Street she was feeling much more cheerful.

Seven

Esme felt marginally happier, knowing that Millie was with her, as they set out for the Embassy Hotel on Friday. Although she would never admit it, she liked having Millie in the house because it meant that she and Leo were not thrown on to their own resources so often and there was less opportunity for argument and bad feeling. She was also glad to have shared the terrible secret with someone and Millie *had* agreed to accompany her today, which was a huge relief. She had only ever known Wally when he was on his best behaviour, and her last meeting and the letter had been sources of great disillusion. Now, as they went up the steps to the hotel, she wondered how she had ever thought herself in love with him.

Together they stood in the foyer while Esme looked for him. 'He's not here,' she said. 'Maybe he's in the lounge.'

'We could order coffee,' Millie suggested. 'We can't simply make use of their lounge for a conversation. None of us is renting a room.'

'Don't fuss so, Millie. You don't know anything about hotels.' She led the way into the lounge, which was half-empty, and the two

150

women settled themselves at a coffee table by the window. A waitress appeared, but Esme said, 'Not just yet. We're meeting someone. He's a little late.'

The woman smiled and walked to the next table to collect some empty cups and saucers. Esme and Millie sat in silence, watching the doors.

Esme was clasping and unclasping her hands and Millie laid her own hand on them to still them. 'You look so nervous,' she said. 'I know you are, but perhaps you should try to—'

'I can't help it. I haven't slept too well and I feel sick. My nerves are in tatters and it's all his fault.' She forced back tears. 'When he comes, I'll introduce you so that he knows you're here and then you make some excuse and wander away so that we can talk privately; but do keep an eye on us, Millie.' She lowered her voice. 'I'll ask for the money and then, when he's given it to me, I'll say you are going to accompany me and he needn't come.'

'You think he'll trust you?'

Esme frowned. Really, there was no need for Millie to make things difficult. 'I think he will,' she said, 'because I'll ask for the address. You and I will leave in a cab and he'll think we're going to the doctor but instead – Oh, there he is!' She jumped up but immediately subsided again. 'It wasn't him.'

'Instead we'll do what?' asked Millie.

Esme tidied her skirt. 'We'll tell the driver

151

to take us home. Wally will never know.'

'Unless the doctor contacts him and says you didn't turn up.'

Esme regarded her sister with growing exasperation. 'Why should he?'

'I thought you said he was a friend of Wally's. What will you do if Wally *does* find out?'

'I don't know! He'll hardly come to The Laurels to ask for the money! He won't want anyone to find out, let alone Leo! Really, Millie. You are so naïve.' She regretted the words immediately, but it was too late: Millie looked annoyed. She took offence so easily, Esme reflected – always had done; always had been a prickly child. Still, fate had not dealt her a particularly good hand and looking after their parents had hardly prepared her for the wider world.

Lost in the past, Esme continued to watch the door for Wally's arrival, until Millie drew her attention to the time.

'He's forty minutes late! Do you think he's coming?'

'Of course he is. I expect he's been delayed. All that traffic in the Strand. It only takes one vehicle to break down and there's a big hold-up.' She smiled at her sister and hoped she was impressing her with her knowledge of London life. 'One day a horse broke away from its cart and was run down by an army waggon. There was a dead horse in the road for nearly half an hour and the roads were clogged with traffic in all directions. Wally knew an alternative route, but his cab couldn't go forward or back.'

The waitress appeared again and this time Millie said quickly, 'We'll have a pot of tea, please.'

Esme looked at her in surprise. Her younger sister was rarely so masterful.

'Suppose I don't want tea?' she said.

'Then I'll drink two cups.' Millie's chin jutted defiantly and Esme decided not to pursue it. 'It's thirsty work, Esme, all this worrying! Anyway, it might help you feel better. Did you eat any breakfast?'

'No. Maybe I should have forced down a piece of toast.'

The tray of tea came and to their surprise there were four biscuits on a plate. The waitress winked. 'They're not on the bill,' she whispered.

'Thank you!' Millie poured and Esme bit hungrily into a biscuit.

By the time they had finished the refreshments it was painfully obvious that Wally wasn't coming. Millie suggested that perhaps he had telephoned and left a message, so they settled the bill and moved to the reception desk.

Esme smiled at the desk clerk. 'Has there been a telephone call for me? – Miss Walmsley.'

Esme glanced at Millie, certain that her sister would have registered the fact that Esme was pretending to be single. She slipped her left hand into the pocket of her jacket so that she would not notice the missing wedding ring. To the clerk she said, 'Would you be kind enough to check again. We were supposed to meet here.'

He consulted his notes. 'I'm afraid not, miss.'

Esme said, 'We may have missed him. We've been talking. He books a room here once a week – room 309 – and I...'

Now the clerk was staring at her. 'Room 309? I thought I recognized you...' He seemed startled by this. 'But surely you know...' He stopped, visibly confused. 'I'll just check with the manager, miss. He'll know.'

Millie said, 'Don't you know his name, Esme? Reddish hair isn't much to go on.'

'No I *don't*. He was most particular. It was a sort of game between us. He said if I didn't know his name, I couldn't let it slip out by mistake. I always called him Wally.' She felt a frisson of alarm. 'Why? Does it matter? We were – Oh, here comes the manager.'

The manager, tall, dark and painfully thin, looked grave and asked them to accompany him into the office. Esme followed, feeling faint with a dreadful premonition. This could only mean bad news.

When they were all seated, he asked for her name and noted it on the pad on his desk. He said, 'Miss Walmsley, the gentleman who used to rent room 309 was the MP Mr Henry Granger. You may have heard—'

'An MP? That's ridiculous!' Esme stared at him. 'Room 309. Please check it again.' She turned to Millie. 'Wally wasn't an MP! He'd have told me.'

'Our records show that regular payments were made on successive Fridays for that very room. We recognized him, naturally. He was very well known – a popular figure in the House. The payments were definitely paid by him.'

Millie turned to Esme. In a low voice she said, 'But you said he wouldn't tell you his name. Maybe that's why: if he's an MP, he has a reputation to protect.'

Esme's confusion was making her angry. 'I tell you it couldn't have been him! Do please mind your own business, Millie.' She turned back to the manager. 'What was his name again?'

'Henry Granger.'

'Not Walter, then!' She smiled at Millie.

The manager nodded. 'Henry Walter Granger. He's been an MP for many years. He represents somewhere south of the river – I forget where. He was recently taken ill and was taken to hospital. It was in the newspapers.'

Millie was leaning forward. 'Esme, it was Henry Granger – the man in Tapper's Supper Room! Leo read it out to us and I told you I was there with Ned Warren when it happened. A heart attack. Don't you remember?'

Esme's hand flew up to hide her mouth. 'That was Wally?' Suddenly her voice was a hoarse whisper.

'Oh, Esme!'

Millie looked as shocked as she was herself. Esme, feeling dizzy, tried to focus, gripping the arms of the chair. She looked at her sister through a dark mist and willed herself not to faint. She was trying to work out whether the fact that her child had been fathered by an MP was to her advantage or not. At least he would be comparatively wealthy and...

Millie said, 'Are you all right, Esme? You're very pale.'

The manager said, 'Would you like a glass of water?'

'No – no thank you...' Esme hardly recognized her own voice, it was so thin.

'This seems to have been a bit of a shock, Miss Walmsley.' The manager steepled his hands. 'It obviously explains why your – your friend has been unable to meet you here today.'

Esme tried to gather her wits. 'Perhaps I should visit him in hospital.'

'That may not be a good idea,' he said cautiously. 'Of course, they only allowed next-of-kin and his wife was with him until...'

Esme sat up abruptly. 'His *wife*? Wally doesn't have a wife.' Hope returning, she turned to Millie. 'It can't be him. I told you so!'

The manager said, 'I'm afraid his second name *is* Walter – named after his grandfather, who was also in politics.'

Millie whispered, 'Walter ... Wally. You don't think...'

Esme groaned and put her hands over her

156

face. Seconds passed while she struggled to accept the terrible truth. There really was no doubt that her lover was a married man, which changed everything. Unless he would agree to a divorce ... She was carrying the child of a married man. Did he have any other children? The idea was unbearable. And his wife – what was she like? Was she prettier than Esme? Another dark thought entered her head: did he truly love her or had she simply been a diversion?

Millie moved to put an arm round her shoulder. 'Esme, it obviously *is* him. We can talk about it on the way home.' She glanced at the manager, who took the hint and offered to send for a cab.

As they got up to leave, he seemed to come to a decision. 'Miss Walmsley, you will have to know sooner or later. I fear I have bad news for you. Poor Mr Granger died late last night.'

That night Millie lay in bed and tried to decide what to do. The shock of the MP's death had sent Esme deathly white and they had just managed to catch her before she fell forward in a dead faint. It had been some minutes before she recovered and the manager had insisted on calling for a doctor. This young man had declared her well enough to travel and they had been sent back home in a hansom cab paid for by the hotel management. Perhaps, thought, Millie, the manager had been hoping to avoid any adverse publicity for the hotel – or perhaps he had simply been a kindly man taking pity on two women in distress.

Esme had gone straight to bed and had sobbed unrestrainedly for some time before falling into an exhausted sleep.

'You are going to have to confess, Esme,' Millie said into the darkness of her room. There was no longer any other way out of the mess. Esme must tell Leo that she was pregnant and must explain the circumstances – and ask forgiveness. It might not be forthcoming – Millie knew that. If Leo could not bring himself to accept the child, he might turn Esme out of the house. Where would she go and how would she fare? After her own experience at the employment agency a few days ago, Millie had no illusions. Esme would find it difficult to find a job. Perhaps Esme should have a talk with Aunt Flora. She was older and wiser...

Drifting into an uneasy slumber Millie suddenly came to her senses with a start. Granger was dead! Poppy, too, would be in serious trouble now *and* unable to say a last goodbye to the man she loved. Why on earth had the wretched man played fast and loose with so many women? she wondered. A wife and family in Somerset, Poppy in London and occasional meetings with Esme. Was it greed or vanity on his part or a fatal weakness for the opposite sex? By now, of course, his unfortunate wife would know that another woman had impersonated her on that fateful

Friday evening at the hospital. Poor soul.

Wide awake again, Millie sat up in bed and stared round the moonlit room. She had been comfortable enough here, but it had always been a temporary move in spite of Leo's urging. The future for Leo and Esme looked very troubled and Millie knew that her own presence would be a further complication they could do without. She would wait until Leo knew the truth, but then she would find a way to leave. Somehow she would find a way of earning her living and she would find a place to live, however humble.

Creeping downstairs, she was startled to find Leo already in the kitchen. He was sitting by the stove, his hands clasped round a mug of milk.

He looked up. 'Who's Wally?'

In total shock, Millie stared at him. He knew! But who had told him?

'Wally?' she repeated helplessly, aware that she must look very guilty. She certainly felt guilty.

'Esme's talking in her sleep. She does that sometimes when she drinks alcohol. I have to know, Millie. Please don't lie to me.'

Shaken, Millie lowered herself on to a chair, the hot milk she had wanted now forgotten. 'I can't ... that is, you should ask her yourself, Leo. She's the one who should tell you.' Even as she said this, she remembered that at some stage she had told Esme she would break the news. She had delayed too long.

Leo said, 'She won't talk to me and I know

she's in trouble. I think she has a lover.' He looked at her. 'Please, Millie, if you still have a shred of affection for me … I have to know.'

Seeing the anguish in his eyes, Millie decided she would have to tell him. 'She did have a lover but now he's dead.' Quickly, the words tumbling out before she could change her mind, Millie told him everything about Henry Granger – except for the news about the child. Leo listened in silence, his head in his hands. Then he said, 'And is she with child?'

Millie hesitated. How would he take the news? How strong was he? Suppose he went storming out and threw himself into the Thames. Or found a way to shoot himself … or to kill Esme? Before she could reply a sound made them both turn and they saw Esme in the doorway. She was wearing only a nightdress and her feet were bare. Her eyes shone with a feverish intensity and a spot of bright colour burned in each cheek. Her hair was tousled and hung carelessly around her shoulders. And she still looked beautiful, Millie thought with a familiar rush of envy.

Esme looked at Millie. 'I went up to your bedroom. I expected to find you and Leo together. Instead I find you together down here.' She turned to her husband. 'Yes, Leo, I'm with child. I suppose my sister has told you everything else. She's waited a long time to be revenged on me, but this is her moment!' Her voice was full of bitterness and Millie knew that their relationship was all but finished. Well, so be it. She was too tired to feel anything but regret.

Leo had slowly risen to his feet. 'I made her tell me, Esme. I knew – I could see you were in some kind of trouble.'

Esme sat down while Leo walked to the back door. He opened it and stared out into the darkness, and for a moment Millie thought he was going to walk out on them; but he hesitated, closed it and sat down. He looked utterly defeated and Millie longed to comfort him, but the room was full of passionate undercurrents and she felt that a careless word or gesture could sweep them all away. A heavy silence descended, until Millie could bear it no longer. She stood up. To Esme she said, 'I've done all I can for you. I think the two of you...'

Esme said, 'Don't go, Millie!'

Leo said, 'I think on this occasion there's safety in numbers. Could you bear it, Millie? It's a lot to ask.' Reluctantly Millie sat down again. 'So what were you planning to do next, Esme?' His voice was cold.

In a few blunt sentences Esme told him about the plan to get the five hundred pounds and explained how it had backfired.

He looked from Esme to Millie. 'My God!' he whispered. 'Is any of this going to appear in tomorrow's newspapers?'

Millie, shocked by the idea, said nothing.

Esme said, 'Damn the newspapers! What are we going to do, Leo? It's your decision. I could have the child adopted, but I would

161

rather keep it. The child is not to blame for any of this and I've always longed for a family. I don't expect forgiveness, Leo. If you betrayed me, I would never forgive *you*.'

Leo said, 'I wish I had betrayed you with Millie!'

Horribly startled, Millie jumped to her feet. 'Well, I'm glad you didn't, Leo. However much I feel for you, we both know that *our* chance has gone. Betraying Esme would never have made me feel better about that. It might have felt like a sweet revenge, but I have my own life to lead and I'd never want that on my conscience!' She swallowed and drew a long breath. 'So leave me out of the equation, please, and sort out your own problems.'

Esme said, 'This doesn't mean you have to leave here, Millie. I shall need you more than...'

Millie looked at her in amazement. 'Esme! You're in no position to offer help to me. Where will you be in a month's time if Leo doesn't take pity on you? Think about that!'

Shaking with rage, Millie stumbled to the door and, ignoring Leo's pleas, made her way upstairs on legs that trembled. Whatever happened, she promised herself, she would get away from the two of them – as far away as possible!

After a sleepless night Millie had formed a plan, but she needed the co-operation of Poppy Gayford. To this end she made her way

162

to the flat and knocked on the door before she could change her mind. After an interval the door was opened and a subdued Poppy invited her inside. Millie told her how sorry she was about Henry's death without mentioning Esme. They talked it over for a while and then, encouraged by the inevitable sherry, Millie told Poppy her idea.

'Suppose I find myself a job,' she suggested. 'I could move in with you, if you would have me. I would then be able to help you with the rent and...'

Poppy leaned forward eagerly. 'Stop right there!' she told Millie. 'For once Fate is on our side. There's a job going at Tapper's Supper Room and I could ask Ivan for you...'

Millie gasped in horror. 'No! That's out of the question! I could never do what you do, Poppy. I don't have the confidence or the looks or...'

Poppy was laughing. 'Not on stage, you cuckoo! Behind the scenes. Etta, our elderly dresser, has been taken ill and there's nobody to take her place. You could do it temporarily and possibly take over when she gives up. Poor old Etta is riddled with diseases – a heart problem, trouble with her rheumatics and a cough that would have finished off a lesser mortal! She's seventy if she's a day and can't last much longer.'

'Poor soul!' Millie didn't know whether to be pleased or sorry that the ancient dresser was about to give up. She would be old herself one day.

Poppy had brightened considerably. 'If your wages aren't enough, we could take in another girl. Philly – that's Phyllida to you – might be willing to join us. Mind you, we've only one bedroom, but you two could sleep on the sofas. We'd only need an extra couple of blankets and I know somewhere we can get them cheap.' Her face clouded momentarily. 'Better than being thrown out on to the street. That happened to us once when I was about five, but I've never forgotten it. This bailiff came and started dragging our furniture into the street. All the neighbours were watching from behind the curtains and some even came on to the pavement to get a better view!' She glanced down at her hands. 'It was horrible. I felt like dirt.'

Millie said quickly, 'You can't blame the bailiffs: they were only doing their jobs.'

'I didn't say I blamed anybody. It was circumstances. That's what it always is: circumstances.' She looked at Millie. 'We'll go round to Tapper's now...'

'Oh no! That is, it's just an idea. I haven't made up my mind whether—'

'...before you lose your nerve,' Poppy finished with a smile. 'Then you can go home to your precious sister and tell her you're leaving! I'd give anything to see her face!'

Millie was already becoming nervous. Everything was happening too fast, she realized, but there was no stopping Poppy. Together they hurried round to Tapper's and bearded the manager in his den.

Ivan Tottestall (known as 'Ivan the Terrible' to his staff) was a huge man with wild white hair, eyebrows to match and a squashed nose. Despite his size he spoke in a high voice, which trembled deceptively. Anyone who opposed him learned to their cost that he had a fiery temper and no patience with the meek.

Poppy faced up to him with apparent confidence, much to Millie's admiration.

'She needs work,' Poppy told him, with a glance towards Millie, 'and I need a room-mate. Poor old Etta might never come back.'

Tottestall looked doubtfully at Millie. 'You ever worked before?' he asked.

'No, but I can work as hard as anyone else. I can iron and I can sew and if you need a dresser...'

Poppy said, 'She's a dab hand with a needle!'

Tottestall eyed her up and down. 'We could do with another girl in the Grecian Temple scene...' he began.

'No!' cried Millie. 'It's dresser or nothing!'

He shrugged. 'Please yourself. It's more money if you go on stage.'

'I can't do it. I *won't* do it!' She glared at him, shaking inwardly. The extra money was tempting, but suppose someone saw her and recognized her, draped in those flimsy veils. Suppose Leo saw her. Or Ned Warren? She would die of shame!

'You're on,' said Tottestall, with a nod of his huge head. 'Five shillings a week, including matinees. Take it or leave it.' He raised furry

165

white eyebrows and, after a moments hesitation, Millie accepted. She would offer Poppy two shillings and make do on the rest.

As they stood again on the pavement, Millie rolled her eyes. The deed was done. 'Now all I have to do is tell Esme!' she muttered.

That evening she explained the situation and told Leo and Esme of her decision. 'I shall be leaving tomorrow,' she said as firmly as she could. Ignoring their shocked expressions, she waited for their reactions. They were slow in coming.

Leo sat down heavily, his face pale. Esme stared at her furiously, her face reddening with anger. 'So you're going to leave me in the lurch!' she cried. 'Thank you for nothing, Millie! I never thought you would be so ungrateful. I can hardly believe it. Just when I need you most ... It's unforgivable!'

Millie, inclined to agree, said nothing.

Esme went on: 'My husband has forgiven me and will stand by me, but my own sister is turning her back on me!'

Millie drew a breath of relief and wondered if Esme realized how lucky she was.

Leo shook his head slowly in disbelief. 'A dresser at Tapper's Supper Room!' he gasped. 'How could you lower yourself, Millie? You will never rise above it. Do you realize that? All your friends and acquaintances – what will they think of you? What would your parents have thought? You mustn't do this, Millie. There must be another way.'

Millie took a deep breath. 'You two need to be on your own,' she told them earnestly. 'You have problems to solve and I am in the way. I want a life of my own and if that means being a dresser for a few weeks or months, then so be it. If I can bear it, so can you.' She couldn't look at Leo, imagining what was going on in his mind. 'Poppy is a sweet woman,' she insisted, 'and a good friend. Some time you must meet her.'

'I think not!' said Esme coldly. 'You hardly know the woman and yet you want to solve her problems by sharing the rent. I am your own flesh and blood, but you care nothing for my problems.'

Millie stared at her in dislike. She was strongly tempted to tell her that the wonderful 'Wally' was also Poppy's paramour – but common sense won: that would be a step too far; the unhappy coincidence that had brought the three women together was best kept to herself. If neither Poppy nor Esme knew of the other woman's involvement with Henry Granger, a great deal of heartache would be avoided. The man was dead and there was no point in unnecessary revelations. Millie had decided to keep that particular secret to herself. Poppy need never know that her beloved Henry had been bestowing occasional favours on Esme or that their relationship had resulted in the conception of a child. Esme, with all *her* problems, would never discover that she had been sharing Wally – not only with his wife, but with

167

another woman. As for Henry Granger's wife ... Millie hoped she would always remain in the shadowy depths of rural Somerset.

Millie looked at Leo. 'Please try to understand,' she begged. 'When the child is due, I will try to be here for Esme – if she still wants me.'

Esme cried, 'But that's months away! You really are a most selfish woman, Millie! You ought to be ashamed of yourself!'

Leo sighed heavily. 'No! Millie's right. Why should we expect her to involve herself in our sordid problems? You, Esme, have brought this disgrace on our heads and there is no reason why Millie should suffer also. We'll deal with our own problems and let Millie go her own way. She deserves a chance to make a new life and I for one will not stand in her way.' He stood abruptly and, with an anguished glance at Millie, strode from the room.

Esme burst into loud sobs. 'There! Now see what's happened. You've got all his sympathy and I have nothing! The sooner you get out of this house the better!'

The twenty-third of November, a Monday, was Millie's first night as dresser at Tapper's Supper Room and it was also a night she would never forget. She had moved her few belongings into Poppy's flat with the promise that she would ask Ned Warren to collect the few bits of furniture that she had left in the attic at The Laurels.

After a busy day Millie and Poppy had

made their way to Tapper's and down a short flight of steps to the poorly lit, ill-ventilated room that served the female artistes as a dressing room. To Poppy it was home from home, but to Millie's untutored eyes it was a shock. The white walls were discoloured, and damp patches had ruined the ceiling. The backs of the large mirrors were peeling and there was a noticeable lack of cupboard space, so that various costumes were thrown higgledy-piggledy on any chair or table that proved convenient. The gaslight flickered and hissed and there was a sour smell of sweat and greasepaint. At the far end a solitary table waited for Millie to begin her work. The table was covered with an old blanket, which was covered by a sheet bearing many scorch-marks.

Several young women were already there in various stages of undress and Poppy introduced them as dancers who would open and close the show. They showed mild interest in the new dresser and one of them shared the news that Etta had only a few hours to live.

'She's not alone, is she?'asked Millie.

'No. She's got a daughter. She's with her.'

Poppy initiated Millie into the mysteries of the gas iron and suggested she start on one of the costumes. This was a riot of frills and flowers, but under the owner's watchful eye Millie made a reasonable success of ironing it. She had just finished when Ivan the Terrible put his head round the door and said, 'Turn up, did she?'

Poppy said, 'Of course she did!'

Millie raised a hand and smiled at him, and received a nod by way of acknowledgement.

He regarded Poppy through narrowed eyes. 'I hear you lost your gentleman friend. Going to be all right, are you?'

It was her turn to nod. 'Millie's moved in with me and we're hoping for someone else. Got to keep the wolf from the door!' She managed a smile.

He grunted. 'Just don't come asking for a loan,' he warned. 'I'm not that kind of man!'

He withdrew and Poppy put her tongue out at his departing presence. 'We all know what kind of man he is!' She seized upon a long dress and tossed it to Millie. 'This belongs to Mara Letts, the singer. Might as well get in her good books.'

Millie did her best with it, terrified she might scorch it or otherwise damage the flimsy fabric, or detach a few precious sequins. The first half-hour passed in a whirl of bodies and voices as the inadequate room tried to accommodate more than fifteen women of assorted shapes and sizes – the dancers slim and very young and the Grecian 'models' older, their figures more matured. Red hair, sleek black hair and frizzy brown hair crossed and recrossed in front of Millie in a bewildering parade as she attempted to match a name to a face. Few gave her a second glance, for they were each wrapped up in their own lives or busily gossiping about friends and loved ones. It seemed to Millie that she would be forever on the sidelines of this bustling, colourful crowd.

As time passed, however, she felt less nervous and began to discover snippets of information about the other women who came in in ones and twos to prepare for the evening performance. There was Dotty, who also danced – she had a crippled husband who cared for their two-year-old son. Dora was a born-and-bred cockney whose grandfather was a pearly king. Greta Garner, a rising comedienne, said little, considering herself too important to chat with the lesser lights, and Bella Marks sulked in a corner because her promotion to solo dancer had not materialized as promised. The rest were a blur of names and laughter, with a vocabulary that startled Millie more than she would ever admit.

Suddenly a young lad appeared in the doorway. 'Five minutes! Hurry up, ladies!'

Millie expected an exodus, but the women continued to apply rouge, tweak their hair and smooth their tights.

He appeared again shortly after his first warning to call, 'One minute! Look lively!'

Still nobody stirred. From somewhere outside the dressing room a man bellowed, 'On stage!' and with screams and groans the dancers leaped to their feet and rushed from the room.

Poppy caught Millie's eye and grinned. 'Matter of principle,' she explained. 'We do hate to be hurried!'

Seconds later the music changed as the overture gave way to the first dance number and the sound of ten pairs of tap shoes resounded through the dressing room from somewhere overhead. For Millie that evening, the lively rhythm of that particular number signalled the start of a different life with a new home and new friends. Any doubts she may have had were immediately swept away.

As Millie chatted and ironed and smiled and ironed until her back ached, Leo sat alone in the attic she had so recently vacated. He stared at the bare boards. The room was devoid of anything that might remind him of Millie. The furniture was still there, but her clothes had gone and so had the other small items that she treasured. Her few books were missing and the pictures she had hung upon the wall had been taken away to their new home in Poppy Gayford's flat. He tried unsuccessfully to visualize Millie in her new home and cursed himself for the hundredth time for allowing her to leave them.

Why had he been so weak? he asked himself bitterly. He should have sent Esme away – she could have thrown herself on Aunt Flora's mercy. The old lady would have taken her in. Instead he had condoned Esme's adultery and had landed himself with an unborn child who was only partly Esme's and nothing at all to do with him. The child's father was dead, but the baby might take after him and Esme would doubtless dote upon it. He should have been firmer. He should have rejected her appeal for help. The worst of it was that he could not even congratulate himself on an act of compassion. Foremost in his mind had been the recent promotion. If he had thrown his wife out into the street, it would have cast a deep discredit over him. The truth would have leaked out and questions would have been asked at Head Office.

Leo groaned aloud. Suppose he *had* thrown Esme to the wolves and persuaded Millie to stay on. She could never be more than a housekeeper to him and that would have been most unfair. She might have grown to hate him for spoiling her chances of a better life. Did she *really* like this awful Warren fellow? The thought of the two of them together hurt him and he tried to change the direction of his thoughts.

Footsteps on the stairs alerted him to the fact that Esme was coming in search of him and he straightened his back. No need to let her see how low his spirits were. He must somehow regain the upper hand and become master again in his own house. They had to go through with the charade, but it would not be easy.

'Leo! Here you are.'

He stood up. 'I was just checking that Millie hasn't left anything. Do we have her address?'

'No! We don't need it.'

Her eyes were red-rimmed and he knew she had been crying but could feel no sympathy.

She had shamed him and he was never going to forgive her.

'We might need to contact her,' he pointed out. 'We might have to forward letters.'

'Maybe ... and that young man might come round trying to find her!'

That hurt, as Esme had known it would. Leo sighed. Was this how it was going to be – dealing out punishments for a lack of love? Could he bear this much hostility for the rest of his life? Could Esme live with her own disappointments?

With an effort he stood up and followed his wife downstairs. She had made a carroway-seed cake – his favourite – and he recognized it as a small peace offering, but at that moment he felt that if he took one mouthful, he would choke.

The following morning Leo sat at his desk in his office and stared into space. His arms rested on the polished desk in front of him, but the thrill of being in the manager's office *as manager* no longer excited him. His unexpected promotion had come too late – at a time when his personal life was in a state of chaos. How could he enjoy his new status when Millie had left the house and Esme was expecting another man's child. His future was bleak and no amount of money or prestige was going to alter that.

Glancing at the papers on his desk, he tried to organize his thoughts. There was a letter from a client who needed to extend his borrowing, but that request would be denied. Good money after bad, thought Leo. Amazing that his predecessor had granted him a loan in the first place: a barber's shop was not exactly a business that could earn high returns. He sighed. Surely it was time for his cup of tea. It was nearly five past eleven.

As though reading his thoughts, Dora Levine tapped on the door and entered, bearing a small tray. She was new to the bank and still learning, which meant that she made the tea. Young, nicely rounded but rather plain: Leo had scarcely registered her existence, but now, to his surprise, she gave him a shy smile.

'Good news, Mr Walmsley!' she said as she set down the tray. 'Your wife telephoned to say she may be a little late with the midday meal as she is going to the dressmaker.' Her smile broadened. 'It seems you are to be congratulated. A new addition to the family!'

Leo tried to hide his shock. He had told Esme to say nothing for at least another month and now she had confided in a member of his staff. He forced what he hoped was a smile.

'Good news, yes!'

'We're all pleased for you, Mr Walmsley.'

'Er ... yes. Thank you. It is early days. Things can go wrong.' He stirred his tea.

'Oh don't say that, Mr Walmsley.' With another bright smile she withdrew and Leo's smile disappeared. Just like Esme to take him by surprise, he thought angrily, giving him no time to prepare. Oh God! Where was all this going to end? He could anticipate no happy ending. Moodily he sipped his tea and nibbled a tea biscuit.

Almost at once Miss Levine returned. 'There's a Mr Warren to see you,' she told him. She looked flustered and the flushed cheeks gave her a bit of colour. She looked almost pretty, he thought absent-mindedly. 'I know the rules, Mr Walmsley, and he doesn't have an appointment; I've told him you can't see him, but he won't listen – Oh! Here he is!' Her voice rose as she stepped aside, her expression indignant. The man Leo least wanted to see pushed past her into the office.

Warren entered, his hat in his hands, a cheerful smile on his face. 'I won't take up much of your time...' he began.

Leo rose to his feet and waved Miss Levine away. 'I don't think you are a client of ours...' he said coldly. 'I'm a very busy...'

'A client? Good Lord no!' Ned smiled. 'I don't believe in banks. All my money goes under the mattress! No – I was wondering if you have Miss Bayley's new address. I understand from your wife that your sister-in-law has left The Laurels ... rather suddenly.'

Leo closed his eyes briefly. More trouble. Why couldn't they leave him in peace? 'She has moved, if that's what you mean,' he said, '– and before you ask, I don't have an address and wouldn't give it to you if I had it.'

'Is that so now?' The man's composure didn't falter. 'I wonder why that is? Don't you

176

like me, Mr Walmsley?'

'How can I have an opinion? – I don't even know you.' Nor do I want to, he thought bitterly. 'However, I *do* know that you are not at all a suitable companion for my sister-in-law and I won't make the mistake of passing on information about her to you.'

'Not suitable *how*, exactly?' He gave Leo an almost challenging look.

The wretched man appeared totally at ease and Leo felt an urge to throw him bodily from the room. He said, 'Miss Bayley comes from a well-to-do family that sadly fell upon hard times. She was brought up as a delicate child and is not prepared for the hurly-burly of the life *you* lead. Your sort of people...'

Ned Warren's smile vanished and his eyes grew cold. 'I doubt if jilting her has helped, Mr Walmsley.'

Leo gasped. Millie had confided in this wretched man!

'Rather harsh treatment for such a delicate flower, wouldn't you say? Being tossed aside by the man you love must have felt very much like a taste of hurly-burly, wouldn't you say?'

Badly shaken, Leo began to stammer a defence, but Warren held up a hand. 'I can promise you Millicent Bayley will never be treated so cruelly by me or by "my sort of people". I hardly think you are in any position to judge me. I have regular work; I have never been in trouble with the law; I'm not married and never have been ... and Miss Bayley trusts me.'

'She may trust you – she is hardly a good judge of people – but are your intentions...?'

'Are they honourable? Oh yes, Mr Walmsley, they are most honourable. I hope to persuade Millie to become my wife, Mr Walmsley.'

For a few seconds there was silence and Leo fancied he could hear his heart beating erratically. Millie and this hateful wretch? It was unbearable. Anger and fear swept through him. Somehow he gathered his wits and stabbed a shaking finger towards the door.

'Get out! I have no time for this nonsense,' he said hoarsely. 'I have work to do.' He had hoped to rid himself of the man but was immediately disappointed.

'You have work to do?' Warren nodded. 'So do I, Mr Walmsley, and plenty of it; but I have my priorities and Miss Bayley is one of them. So you can't help me. I'm surprised she didn't leave a forwarding address. I hope you didn't part on bad terms.'

'Certainly not.'

'Yet you don't know where she is? Isn't that rather ... shall we say *odd*?'

Leo felt his face burn. 'You may use whichever word you wish, Mr Warren. If Miss Bayley chose not to leave an address, that is her business – she was in rather a hurry. Something to do with a friend in trouble. I'm sure she will be in touch shortly. Mrs Walmsley is her sister, after all.'

'So you're not bothered. Well, well! Me

now, I am. I'm very bothered. She's young and very innocent and I shan't rest until I'm sure she is all right. I'm *concerned* for her, Mr Walmsley, and would like to find her.' He regarded his hat for a moment, turning it this way and that. 'But then she knows where I live and will no doubt come to me before long.'

'That's possible, I suppose.' Leo's tone was icy and he made no attempt to hide his dislike. 'Now if you'll excuse me...' He waved a hand at the various papers on his desk.

Ned tutted sympathetically. 'All this paper to push around! I don't envy you. Well, I'll be about *my* business. When I see her, shall I say you'd like to know where she's living? I'm quite happy to pass on a message.'

Leo drew in his breath in a short hiss. 'That won't be necessary. I am perfectly capable—' He stopped abruptly. This might be his last chance to hammer home a few facts about his relationship with Millie. He said, 'You may wish to know that since Miss Bayley's father's recent death I have looked upon myself as her protector. I should see it as a duty to ensure that, if she ever marries, it is to someone I consider suitable.'

'Meaning someone who would love her and take care of her?'

'Exactly.'

'I'd wish no less for her. That's what I would offer her, were I to believe that she loves me.'

Warren turned quickly on his heel and left

the room and Leo sat down, breathing heavily. Had Millie given Esme any idea of where this Poppy woman lived? He would ask her as soon as he arrived home for his dinner – when she arrived back from the dressmaker's. He glanced at the clock. Another hour to go. Suddenly it became important to him that he find out Millie's whereabouts before the obnoxious Ned Warren did.

Eight

When Millie opened the door the following Friday evening, she didn't know who to expect. Poppy had gone out to visit one of the other girls from Tapper's, who had been off sick for a week with what seemed to be a form of pneumonia. The doctor, young and inexperienced, had been uncertain, but Betsy was running a high temperature and was having trouble breathing. Poppy had made some soup and had taken it round to try to tempt her friend to take some nourishment.

A man stood on the threshold. He was probably about mid-thirties, Millie guessed, perhaps a little older. He had smooth dark hair with grey eyes and was well dressed in a fashionable coat with a slim fur collar. His face lit up when he saw her and he said, 'At last! I knew it would happen if I were patient enough.'

Millie waited, puzzled by the comment. She supposed this man was a friend of Poppy's. Or maybe Poppy had a brother. She smiled tentatively, secretly admiring the cut of his coat and the confidence that radiated from him.

He said, 'I've been longing to meet you.

181

May I come in?'

'Are you sure you've come to the right flat?' she asked. 'No one is expected at this address and the – the owner is in mourning.'

'I'm aware of that and this most certainly *is* the address!' He frowned. 'Aren't you the owner?'

Millie shook her head, wondering what to do. He seemed very much at ease and appeared to find her confusion amusing; she wondered fleetingly if he could have been drinking, so early in the day.

He said, 'Aren't you going to ask me in?'

Millie shook her head, but in fact she was undecided. Inviting a stranger into the flat might be a recipe for disaster – but, on the other hand, Poppy might be annoyed if she had turned away one of her friends. She did like the look of him; and the way he was looking at her *was* rather flattering. His gaze swept over her in a lingering way, as though he appreciated what he saw.

'Who are you?' she asked, blocking the doorway so that he could not push his way in. 'I don't even know your name.'

With a dramatic gesture he brought up his right hand in a mock salute. 'Your most honoured servant, Edmund Bernard Granger.' He thrust his hand into an an inside pocket of his coat and withdrew a large envelope, which he held up for her inspection. 'I've been sent to give this to the owner. You could describe me as a messenger bearing good news.'

Granger? But that was the name of Poppy's

admirer. On the envelope Millie saw the name 'Miss P. Gayford' written in a large, masculine script and was finally convinced that the man had a legitimate reason for being there.

Her said, 'Might I ask *your* name, since you say you are not Poppy Gayford.'

'I'm a friend. My name's Millicent Bayley.' Reluctantly she opened the door and allowed him to enter.

He stepped into the room with a look of great interest. 'He certainly did her proud,' he told her with a smile, 'and I'm sure she deserved his largesse. And you are Poppy's friend ... and very personable, if I may say so without offence.'

Seeing that Millie still eyed him with suspicion, he laughed again. 'This is too cruel of me, isn't it? – to tease you like this. Sweet Millicent, I'm Edmund – Henry's brother.'

Millie felt a rush of relief. This man was a family member. She assumed that Poppy *would* be pleased to see him.

Hastily she invited him to take off his coat and sit down, which he did. 'But I'm just sharing the flat,' she explained, '–at least for the time being. I'm a dresser at Tapper's Supper Bar.'

His expression was comical, but then he shook his head, amused by the mistake he had made.

'Lucky old Henry!' he said. 'Two beauties for the price of one!'

'There was nothing like that!' Millie informed him, instantly on her guard, although she was pleased to be considered a beauty. 'I have never even met your late brother, though I did see him the night he collapsed. I was in Tapper's Supper Room having supper with friends.'

He eyed her with interest. 'So, Miss Millicent Bayley. Do you forgive me for teasing you?'

'Of course. I was naturally rather uneasy, but no doubt you will forgive me.' She tried not to stare into the handsome face. 'Now I do understand, you are welcome to stay. Poppy will be delighted to see you.' And I will be delighted if you stay, she thought, with a frisson of excitement.

He settled himself in an armchair and languidly crossed one leg over the other, leaning back, apparently completely at ease. 'I wouldn't count on that,' he told her. 'Henry and I were like most brothers: constantly falling out. I disapproved of Henry's relationship with Poppy and he knew it.'

'So why...?'

'Why bring round the envelope? Because it was left for her secretly at Henry's bank and someone had to bring it round. The bank notified me when I went in to close my brother's account – and I thought: why not? I'd always been curious about his little piece of fluff. And a little jealous, if I'm honest. See the wonderful Poppy for yourself, Edmund, I thought.'

Millie was somewhat affronted by his

attitude to Henry's death. He seemed re-markably cheerful in the circumstances and he was less than chivalrous about Poppy. She was beginning to revise her opinion of him and almost regretted inviting him in. But she suspected that the envelope contained money that Henry had left for Poppy in the event of such an emergency as his unexpected death – money that Poppy desperately needed. She wondered anxiously how long it would be before Poppy returned.

Edmund was staring at her and she hastily lowered her gaze. The situation was difficult and Millie had little idea how to cope with it. She glanced up at him and saw the twinkle in his eye.

'Poor little Millicent. I've embarrassed you by barging in like this. Please accept my apologies,, but I couldn't resist coming un-announced. I wanted to see Poppy's face but I've seen yours instead. And yours is just as pretty, I'm sure. What would you say to supper at Tapper's with me? We could watch Poppy in her famous Grecian scene.'

Millie was startled. 'Oh no!' she cried. 'That would be most – be most unsuitable And anyway, I work in the evenings. I told you: I'm a dresser. I look after the costumes and help the girls to get dressed.'

He leaned forward suddenly. 'So why are you not married, Millicent Bayley? Crossed in love?' He laughed, but then, seeing her face, put a hand to his mouth. 'You *were*! Oh what a careless fool I am! Please forgive me.'

'It doesn't matter,' Millie told him hastily. 'It was a long time ago.'

He reached for her hand and took it firmly in his own. 'The man must have been blind or stupid to let you go!'

With some reluctance, Millie withdrew her hand. 'Really, I have forgotten all about it.' The lie pleased her, but he looked unconvinced.

'We shall have to make it up to you somehow,' he insisted, 'for the honour and reputation of all decent and trustworthy men. I shall take you out somewhere when you are not hidden away at Tapper's, dressing your girls, and convince you that all men are not rotters and bounders.'

Ignoring Millie's protests, he consulted a very expensive gold watch and tutted. 'I have to go, but give Miss Gayford the envelope and with it my kindest regards. My brother confessed to the relationship after I had seen them together at the theatre. He was none too pleased and I was furious, but time, the great healer ... Isn't that what they say?' He stood up. 'Tell her not to believe everything Henry told her about me. There is good in the worst of us.'

He saw himself out and left Millie feeling slightly dazed from the encounter. It all seemed most irregular, she thought, but she hoped she had behaved correctly in the circumstances. She went at once to the mirror over the fireplace and stared at her reflection to try to see what Edmund had seen. Her hair looked a little tousled – she tidied it hastily – but apart from that she was reasonably presentable. A pity she hadn't been wearing her best blouse ... She smiled at herself. Perhaps he had liked her smile – Ned Warren had said it was one of her best features. She tried to remember the conversation, but the few snippets she could recall were hardly sparkling. Had he found her dull? If so, he had hidden it well. Was he married?

Hastily she turned from the mirror, feeling her face grow hot with embarrassment. 'Stop it, you idiot!' she whispered. Edmund Granger was the brother of a politician – correction: the brother of a *dead* politician. He obviously came from a wealthy family and no doubt had a wife or someone to whom he was betrothed. With a shake of her head she tried to put all thoughts of him out of her mind. She felt the envelope he had given her for Poppy and was certain it contained money. Delighted for Poppy's sake, she waited impatiently for her friend to return.

When Poppy came home, she was in a pensive mood. Betsy was no better. Millie told her, rather tentatively, who had called in her absence and her friend was immediately distracted by the news.

'His brother?' she echoed, her eyes wide with surprise. 'Oh Lord! Not Edmund! He and Henry were at daggers drawn! That horrible creature has been threatening to tell Henry's wife about me for simply years. And I half-expected him to do it!' She threw herself into a chair and rolled her eyes heavenwards. 'Why didn't you push him down the stairs?' she demanded. 'That would be an act of friendship. Instead you have invited a viper into our nest!' She laughed at Millie's expression. 'Oh don't worry. He's not exactly evil, but he must have known he wouldn't be welcome here. I'm glad I was out. That spoilt his little game!'

Millie interrupted hastily. 'He brought you this envelope. It was left for you at Henry's bank. It feels like money.' She held out the envelope and Poppy snatched it from her, her irritation forgotten.

'Money? Oh my God, Henry!' She kissed the envelope. 'You see, Millie: the darling man didn't forget me!' She tore at the envelope and shook out the contents. Paper money fluttered to the floor and with it came a letter.

Feeling superfluous, Millie excused herself, went into the kitchen and closed the door. After a moment or two she heard a shriek of excitement followed by heartfelt sobs and rushed back to find Poppy on her hands and knees, scrabbling for the money. She lifted a tear-stained face to Millie.

'He left me a hundred pounds,' she gasped, 'and a small annuity for life. He *provided* for me. And he never said a word. Can you believe it? What a darling man. Oh Henry!' Tears flowed down her cheeks. 'My darling Henry! I do miss you. What will I do without you?' She dabbed at her eyes with a fragile lace handkerchief that was already useless and Millie handed her her own, which was more substantial.

She waited until Poppy's sobs lessened, then gave her a comforting hug. She picked up a stray five-pound note and handed it back. 'So have you forgiven his brother? He seemed nice enough although a bit ... scatter-brained.'

Poppy flopped on to the sofa, clutching her money. 'Henry hated him. He was so much younger and a real nuisance. Henry often referred to him as "the afterthought"!' Her smile was watery, but Millie took it as a good sign. She went on: 'When he saw us – he surprised us together at the Drury Lane theatre – he threatened to tell Dorcas, Henry's wife, as well as his mother. That would have been disastrous. Poor Henry was terrified of his mother. It seems the old woman is a proper battleaxe. I was terrified. I thought she'd come to the flat and confront me!'

'But she didn't?'

'No. I'm sure he didn't betray us, but the threat was always there; and it made it so easy for Edmund to borrow money from Henry. He didn't need to actually blackmail him. You know what army men are like.'

'Army men?'

'Yes. He's some kind of officer at Sandhurst – teaches military history or some such. They are all like Edmund, according to Henry: drinking, gambling, *women*!' She raised her eyebrows. 'Their pay never lasts from one week to the next, especially for men like Edmund. Single, selfish ... The possibility was there that he would betray us and Henry knew it. Edmund had him over a barrel!' She frowned. 'If he comes again, you must refuse to let him in, Millie. Tell him I won't have him in the place. Tell him I have a long memory. He can tell his mother whatever he likes now – and the wife. It won't matter, will it?'

'I daresay not.' Millie hid her doubts. 'He seemed very nice,' she ventured.

Poppy rolled her eyes. 'Well, he isn't, so don't be seduced by his good looks and charming manner.'

'So you found him charming?' Millie felt relieved. She *had* been impressed by Edmund and hated to think her judgement was at fault.

'We never actually met,' Poppy explained, 'because when Henry saw him at the theatre he whisked me away. Edmund caught a glimpse of me, but that was all – enough to know that Henry was with another woman. According to Henry, Edmund can sweep a woman off her feet with a flutter of his eyelashes. So be warned.'

Millie muttered, 'I will,' and fiddled with the cuff of her blouse. 'I wonder what his wife's like,' she asked innocently.

'He doesn't have a wife. Men like that marry late. Henry said his mother keeps hinting that he should settle down, but his friendships never last. Either the women get tired of his boyish charm or he gets tired of them.'

Millie pondered this information. 'Maybe he's never met the right woman,' she suggested, but Poppy was re-counting her windfall and seemed not to hear.

So Edmund was single. Millie wondered how Poppy would react when she actually met Edmund. And how *he* would react to her. With a sigh she realized that Poppy would probably sweep him off his feet. She might even change her mind about him, fall in love and marry him. If Millie had been honest with herself, she would have admitted that the thought depressed her.

'Suppose he refuses to go away when I tell him,' she said. 'I think he's determined to see you.'

Poppy slid the money back into the envelope, then glanced up. 'Hopefully I shall be here when he next calls and you will see how it's done. I shall send him off with a flea in his ear. Henry would turn in his grave if I made Edmund welcome in this flat.'

She slid from the sofa and checked the time. 'Good heavens! No time to prepare a meal. I think we'll pick up a couple of mutton pies on the way to Tapper's.' She grinned at Millie. 'Cheer up! I'm not blaming you for letting him in. You weren't to know he was the enemy. We'll be late if we don't hurry. It won't matter for me, but they'll all be screaming for the dresser, and that's you!'

Sunday morning at The Laurels found Esme pale and nauseous. She appeared at breakfast looking dull and miserable and pulled a face at the sight of her husband eating egg and bacon.

'Aren't you well?' Leo asked.

Esme sat down carefully and wondered whether she could face a cup of tea. 'I feel sick,' she muttered. 'I've *been* sick. It's called morning sickness.'

'Poor old you.' He regarded her with sympathy, for which she felt ridiculously grateful. At least he could appreciate what she was going through. He said, 'Let me pour you some tea. What else do you fancy?'

'Nothing!' she declared irritably. 'I'll try and sip some tea.'

He passed her a cup and she clutched it in both hands, trying to find comfort in the warmth.

He looked concerned. 'Aren't you coming to church, then?'

'Do I look well enough?' She took a tentative sip.

'There's no need to snap my head off.'

Esme put down the cup and, with a soft moan, covered her face with her hands. Then she stood up and stumbled hastily from the room, clutching her mouth.

After she had vomited she washed out her mouth with cold water, then made her way back to the dining room.

Leo was wiping his mouth with the serviette. 'Better now?'

'Hardly. You'll have to go to church without me.' She sat down, her face ashen. 'I shall go back to bed and tomorrow you must take me to the doctor's. There must be something he can give me. And, Leo ... I want Millie back. I need her. I know I sent her away, but she'll come back. She can't like it where she is. She's had more than a week to ponder her mistake...'

Leo frowned. 'I'm not going after her, Esme. I told you: she deserves a life of her own, whatever it is.'

'But she didn't mean that! She was angry – that's all it was – and wanted to upset me. We could pay her more. Please, Leo.'

He hesitated. 'We don't know where she lives.'

'You know where she works – at that Tapper's place. The supper room. You could ask for her there.'

He shook his head. 'If you want her, *you* ask for her.'

'Leo! You *beast*! I'm not well enough to go traipsing round London. How could you expect me to? You really are the most selfish wretch!' Her misery overtook her and she began to cry. 'She's my sister!' she managed, between sobs. 'We've always fallen out. It doesn't mean anything. She'll come back if she knows I need her.' She gave him a sly glance through her tears. 'Don't you miss her, Leo? Don't you want her back?'

Again he wavered. 'Only if she is going to be happy here,' he said at last. 'Only if you are going to treat her like a sister and not like a servant. You can be very unkind, Esme.'

Minutes later it was agreed that he would go to the supper room and find Millie. Esme brightened at once: Millie would come back and they would be friends again. With a hopeful smile she reached for a slice of cold toast and began to butter it.

Later that evening Millie dressed warmly, put up her umbrella against the rain and set off for Mr Warren's workshop. It was nearly six and the light was fading. She hurried through the dark streets, dodging the puddles and, warned by the sound of approaching hoof-beats, keeping well back whenever a van or waggon passed, sending a spray of muddy water over the pavements. When she reached the workshop at Haddon's Yard, she was glad to see the glare of gaslights within and rapped loudly on the door. It opened and Ned Warren's father peered out cautiously into the gloom.

'It's only me – Millie Bayley,' she reassured him.

His face broke into a broad smile as he opened the door and invited her in. He swept sawdust from a nearby stool and said, 'Sit down, my dear Miss Bayley; we were beginning to wonder what had happened to you.'

He wore a large canvas apron and his hair was full of sawdust. Millie looked round the workshop. Wood was stacked everywhere, in planks of various shades, many leaning against the walls, others slung overhead in makeshift racks. There were tools hung on the walls – saws, hammers, others that she could not name, and a few bigger ones set out on a large workbench. The overriding smell was familiar: it was sawdust, but there were hints of something else that she took to be cedar oil and what might have been wood-stain and fish glue.

Millie said, 'Oh dear! I'm disturbing your work. I just wanted a few words with...'

'With my son?' His expression changed and he sat down gingerly on the end of a trestle. 'I expect you've been busy, but Ned did wonder if you was all right. It's been a while since we had word from you.'

She nodded guiltily. Taken up with her new life and thoughts about Edmund Granger, she had neglected them. She began to explain how her life had changed, when her companion held up a hand to silence her. 'You'll be wanting to know that Ned's been to the hospital with a sprained wrist and pains in his inside from the kicking.'

'The kicking? The hospital! What's happened?'

'The usual: one of his clients turned nasty.' He shook his head in disgust. 'Ned was sent to turf him out. Big fellow – all brawn and no brains, as my old ma used to say – and very drunk and in a foul mood. Ned tried to reason with him, but he wasn't having any – not no way!'

'Did he owe a lot of rent?'

'Not really, but he was ruining the place and the other tenants, they was all complaining, and who could blame them? Quarrelling with everyone, he was, and living like a pig! Filling the place with rubbish so the rats came! He even sold some of the furniture to buy gin ... and one night he nearly set fire to the whole building by falling asleep with his pipe still burning!' He rolled his eyes heavenwards. 'Set the bed alight, the dimwit! The landlord couldn't get him to go and the police wasn't interested, so they called Ned's firm in and he got landed with it.'

'Poor Ned! How dreadful for him.' She wished immediately that she had been in contact with him at the time and her guilt increased. 'Is he still in the hospital? Could I visit him?'

'He's at home now. I'm going back any minute, so you can come with me.'

Five minutes later Millie scurried along beside him, trying to keep up. Overhead the street lights hissed and flickered and sent shadows across the wet streets, but at least the rain had stopped.

Inside the basement flat they found Ned sitting in an armchair, writing a letter. The room was shabby, but neat and clean, and a small fire burned in the grate. The table bore a tablecloth on which knives and forks had been laid for their supper. The brass coal scuttle had been polished and a kitten was curled up in front of the fire.

'Brought you a visitor,' Stanley told him, and Millie was touched by the pleasure on Ned's face when he saw her. He was sitting at the table with a piece of paper and a stub of pencil. There was a huge bruise over his right eye and his lip had been split but was healing. He might have been killed, she thought, shocked by the idea of such violence towards him.

'I was writing you a letter!' he exclaimed. 'I was going to leave it for you at Tapper's in the hope you'd find it. I badgered your sister until she told me where you worked.'

Millie sat down and expressed her condolences for his injury. 'The man must have been a brute!' she said.

Ned shrugged. 'You meet all sorts in my job – but at least he's cooling his heels in the town jail for a few days. They arrested him for assault.' He held up his bandaged left wrist. 'Could have been worse. A couple of the other tenants came to help me when they heard the din. One old duck hit him with a frying pan!' He laughed.

Stanley offered Millie tea, but she declined. 'I have to get back to Poppy's and do some long overdue washing.' She told them about her new life, making it sound as exciting as possible but omitting the details about Edmund Granger. Some instinct warned her that Ned would disapprove. She also thought he might detect a little too much enthusiasm in her voice.

'Pretty kitten,' she said to change the direction of the conversation.

Ned nodded. 'A kid brought it to the door with two others from the litter – wanted good homes for them. We fancied this one. Tiddles. That's her name. She keeps the mice at bay!'

For a moment Millie wondered how it would be to be part of this family – getting up in the mornings to light the fire, feeding the kitten, going out to the market for fresh vegetables. She wondered about Ned's mother and his life as a young boy. For a moment she was consumed with a strange desire to belong to such a family, but then she remembered Poppy and her new exciting friends. And Edmund.

When it was time to go, Ned limped with her to the door and pulled on a coat. 'I'm not letting you wander through the streets alone,' he said in answer to her protests. He pushed the unfinished letter into her hand and grinned. 'Read it later and imagine a row of kisses at the end!'

As they walked, he tucked her arm through his and Millie wondered if Edmund would ever be close enough to do the same. They made their way to Poppy's flat in a mainly companionable silence and Millie felt wonderfully relaxed. Their closeness seemed entirely natural and comfortable. We're friends, Millie told herself earnestly. He's like a brother. Nothing more. Ned and I can always be friends even if anything comes of my relationship with Edmund. She wanted to believe that, but in her heart she doubted it was true.

'We're here!' she announced, withdrawing her arm with regret. 'It's flat 2A if you should ever want to call on me.'

'I reckon I will, but when shall we meet next?'

Millie hesitated. She wanted to be free all the following week in case Edmund came round or wanted to take her out. 'I'm rather busy for the next few days but...'

'Tuesday,' he said firmly. 'Like before.'

'Oh but...' Looking into his eager face she faltered to a stop. 'Right then. Tuesday.' She nodded brightly.

'The park? I'll buy you another ice cream. I'm like that. Money's no object!'

They both laughed and then settled on the same bandstand at the same time on the same day and he lingered as they said their goodbyes.

'Should we risk a kiss?' he asked, suddenly shy.

She looked at him nervously: 'What do you think?' and then asked, 'But your poor lip?' She was afraid that a kiss would mean too much. Would she be misleading him? Would he read too much into it?

'I won't even notice it!' He leaned forward, tilted her head slightly and kissed her once, very gently.

In spite of her reservations, Millie wanted it to happen again. It was so long since Leo had kissed her – since *any* man had kissed her – she had almost forgotten how thrilling it could be.

He said, 'See you Tuesday. Don't be late, Miss Bayley!' and within moments had been swallowed up by the darkness.

Once inside the flat, Millie read the letter, which was short and to the point.

Dear Miss Bayley,
    I have been in hospital thanks to a nasty peece of work but will soon come to Tappers to ask for your wairabouts. As your brother-in-law was not helpful.
    Hoping to see you soon,
    Your devoted friend Ned Warren

That night, wrapped in her blankets on Poppy's sofa, she thought about him and the kiss he had given her and tried not to think about the brute who had hurt him. She certainly did like Ned a lot ... and admired him for the way he lived his life. It seemed so enviably straightforward compared to her own confused world, which seemed full of betrayals and deceits. Sadly, though, he did not excite her in the way Edmund did and although she could not seriously believe that an army officer would want to marry her, she craved the excitement of the unknown and the glitter of a different existence. If she was honest, even Leo had not stirred her emotions in the same way that Edmund did. Leo had been respectable and even rather...

'No!' she muttered. 'Not *boring*!' Poor Leo. He had never been boring, but he *had* been predictable ... but then he had been an assistant bank manager and was expected to behave as a reliable member of the community. A solid citizen. A church-goer. A sober dresser. Utterly trustworthy ... He would have made a perfect husband.

'Until Esme threw her cap into the ring!'

She drew in a sharp breath, struggling with the familiar resentment. No, she would not go down that road again, she promised herself. Maybe Esme had done her a good turn by releasing her from a marriage with Leo. Maybe. If she married Edmund, she would thank Esme for stealing the man she loved.

To banish the last of the uncomfortable thoughts she focused her mind on Edmund and imagined him standing beside her at the altar in his smart army uniform. Outside the church his fellow officers would make an archway with their swords for the happy pair to walk under ... She finally fell asleep with a smile on her face.

The following evening – Monday – Leo went in search of Millie. Esme had suggested he enquire for her at Tapper's Supper Room and he arrived just after eight. His vague misgivings about the venue appeared at first to be unfounded. As he looked round the well-lit vestibule, he saw nothing to alarm him. People were leaving their coats and heading into a large room, where tables were set out and where the cheerful sound of cutlery and china mingled with the sounds of laughter and conversation. Someone was singing a well-known ballad and when it ended, there was generous applause. He found it hard to disapprove and moved towards a short man who was collecting tickets.

'I'm looking for a Miss Bayley,' he said. 'Can you help me?'

'Artiste, is she? They finish around eleven.' He reached past Leo, smiling. 'Evening, sir, madam. Hope you enjoy your meal.'

The couple thanked him, handed over their tickets and moved in to the supper room. They were young and obviously wealthy. He was a cadet from Sandhurst and he kept his arm round the woman, who was very dark, with an eastern look about her. Leo thought wistfully that he would never enter such a place with someone he loved, young and carefree. His chance for that had passed. His own life seemed sterile by comparison; yet once upon a time to be a bank manager had been the height of his aspirations.

'She's not an artiste, no,' he said. 'She's a dresser.'

He imagined that he went down in the man's opinion. 'Go round to the stage door.' He jerked his head, smiling again at a large man who was taking off an expensive coat trimmed with astrakhan. 'Evening, Lord Humphrey. Lady wife not coming tonight?'

'I'm meeting my niece,' came the reply, accompanied by a large wink.

'We've saved your favourite table, Lord Humphrey. A nice quiet corner, eh?'

There was a burst of raucous laughter from inside the hall and Leo hesitated, suddenly tempted, wondering if he dared venture into the supper room itself. He could have a meal and see the show ... but that would take time and Esme would be furious when he returned. The doctor had given her some pills to limit the nausea, but they were proving slow to take effect and she had spent the day in bed. He hoped he had shown suitable sympathy, but the child was not his and he was finding it difficult to pretend that he cared anything for her suffering. She had brought it all upon herself.

At church he had been besieged by friends congratulating him on the coming child and he and Esme had received three letters in the same vein. Esme was playing the part of delighted wife and mother-to-be very convincingly, but he had found it almost impossible and had said nothing to the staff at the bank. Esme, however, had obviously mentioned it to someone when she telephoned, because the word had spread.

Three young women came in, gaudily dressed, their eyes everywhere, their laughter shrill. His desire to dine faded. As a solitary male he might well be accosted and he knew that he would be unable to deal with the embarrassment. These three might be women of the night, he thought with a shudder and, turning abruptly, he hurried outside again and made his way round to the stage door.

He found an elderly man in a small room and enquired for Millie. Tapping on the dressing-room door he was confronted by five scantily dressed women in tap shoes who burst out in a flurry of scarlet frills and ribbons and, ignoring him completely, fluttered their way towards the stage. They had left the door ajar and he called. 'Millie! Miss Bayley! Are you there?'

A busty woman dressed as a man-about-town came to the door. 'Who wants her?'

'I'm a friend. A – a family friend. Leo Walmsley.'

She withdrew and Millie took her place. 'Leo! What on earth...?' She frowned. 'I can't talk. I'm busy.' She glanced over her shoulder to where several of the other women were giggling.

Leo stared, shaken by his longing for her, which was as fierce as ever. For a moment words failed him.

'Leo! I'm in the middle of an urgent repair!'

Urgent repair? His mind was blank.

She said, 'I'm repairing a costume. A tear. She's waiting for it!'

With an effort he said, 'It's Esme. She's very sick. She wants you to...'

Millie's expression changed. 'She may want all she likes. I'm not coming back! She threw me out and I'm staying out. I don't need her...'

'No! *She* needs *you*! It's morning sickness. I took her to the doctor but...'

'I'm sorry. I don't have time for this. I'm paid to work, not chat. Tell her I'll call in one day soon but not to stay. I'm quite happy where I am. Now *please* go, Leo.'

Leo went home in a daze, stunned by her

attitude. He had forgotten just how much he loved her.

'Well?' Esme demanded from her sickbed, propping herself up on one elbow.

He told her what had happened. Ignoring his wife's immediate sulk, he told her a little about Tapper's. 'It doesn't seem at all bad,' he said. 'Quite respectable and – and cheerful. There was a certain gaiety about the place. I was almost tempted to stay for a while. We could go one evening, if you like, when you feel better.'

'If I ever do!' She frowned. 'How did Millie look?'

' Just as...' He stopped himself just in time. 'Just as beautiful,' was what he had intended to say. 'Just as always,' he amended. 'She was busy repairing someone's costume. I suppose that's what dressers do. That and ironing.'

'And helping the artistes to dress. Did she ask how I was? Did she seem to care?'

'I told her you were sick. She was very busy.' He had left out much of Millie's answer. To mollify Esme he said, 'She looked upset that you weren't well. Perhaps if we have supper there one evening we could both go round to see her afterwards. If *you* ask her to come back, she might say yes.'

Esme considered this idea. 'I have to admit I'm curious.' She fell back on to her pillows. 'Perhaps we will. Perhaps we'll seek her out in her lair! Confront her. The novelty might have worn off if we give her another week.'

Leo turned away to hide his delight. He

would see Millie again and if Lady Luck smiled upon them, she might relent and come home. Buoyed up with fresh hope, he went into the kitchen to boil up some milk for their cocoa.

Nine

As Millie stood on the doorstep of The Laurels, it seemed years since she had lived there. The time spent with Poppy and the hours at Tapper's were so fresh in her mind. There was no way she would ever go back, she told herself. Whatever life might throw at her in the future, she would face it alone. She would never again admit to needing anybody and certainly not Leo or Esme.

The door opened and the two sisters faced each other.

Millie said, 'I'm not setting foot inside this door unless you say I am welcome. You sent me away...'

'Oh Millie! You're very welcome! Please do come in.'

Millie looked at her and found it hard not be sympathetic. Esme's face lacked colour and she looked thinner than Millie remembered. She had made no effort with her hair and was still wearing a nightdress although it was nearly eleven o'clock in the morning. She clutched her dressing gown to her neck and shivered.

Wordlessly Millie stepped inside. Esme certainly needed help of some kind, she thought, resisting the idea that she might be that someone. Ensconced in the kitchen they sat down on either side of the table and eyed each other warily. Millie saw unwashed dishes in the sink and the breakfast remains were on the table.

She said, 'Are you eating properly?'

Esme shook her head. 'But I drink milk and sometimes tea.'

'Why aren't you dressed?'

'I can't find the energy. Oh Millie, do please forgive me and...'

'Don't ask me to come back!' Millie said sharply. 'I have a new home and a job and I intend to keep them. You've got Mrs Wetton.'

Esme scowled. 'She's no good. I mean, she does the heavy work, but she doesn't cook or shop and I am not well enough to do it.'

'Then Leo must find a housekeeper ... or maybe a nurse to come in for a few hours each day. Or a part-time companion – someone to help you wash and dress and maybe prepare a midday meal – for Leo if not for you.'

'I don't want a stranger around the place. Oh Millie...'

'I'm not coming back, Esme. You and Leo have things to deal with and I can't be part of it. I'm much happier where I am.'

Esme rolled her eyes. 'I never thought you'd be so mean,' she said. 'Leo thinks you'll come back. He's hoping you will.' She waited, watching Millie's face carefully. 'He misses you, too.'

'I don't want to talk about Leo. I have another young man, if you must know.'

Esme scowled. 'Not that bailiff fellow, I hope. Leo thinks him quite unsuitable. He doesn't like him at all.'

'Then it's mutual!' Millie hesitated, longing to tell Esme about Edmund. She said, 'Actually it's not Ned Warren. It's someone I met at Poppy's. He's an officer at Sandhurst. Very dashing.' She smiled.

Esme's mouth fell open with shock. 'You and an officer from Sandhurst? I don't believe it. You're making it up. That's just like you, Millie. You always did tell lies.'

'So did you!' She glared at her sister, remembering their many squabbles as children. 'You lied about my doll – the one you hid when you'd broken the arm!'

'So! You lied about my hat. You cut off the ribbons and you never did admit it, but it couldn't have been anyone else!' Furiously, Millie searched her mind for more of Esme's transgressions.

'You lied–' She stopped abruptly, aware of the stupidity of the exchange. 'Anyway,' she said, 'it's not a lie about Edmund, but I'm not going to tell you any more about him.'

'That's because he doesn't exist. You're so transparent, Millie. You always were. Officer indeed! You're trying to impress me. I can see right through you and I always could.'

Millie was fighting to keep control of her temper. Esme had always had the ability to upset her. She forced a smile. 'Then I will tell

209

you,' she declared recklessly. 'His name's Edmund Granger and he's Henry's younger brother. So he's your child's uncle –but he doesn't know it!'

A flurry of emotions showed in Esme's face as she took in what Millie had told her. Shock, disbelief, belief, and finally incredulity – and then envy.

She stammered, 'You're going out with Wally's – I mean Henry's *brother*?'

Too late for Millie to wish the words unsaid. They were out now no matter how much she might regret them. She wondered at once if she could swear her sister to silence but knew it was unlikely. Esme might tell Leo and whatever would he think of her? He would no doubt imagine that her relationship resembled Poppy's, which was not the case and never would be. Since there was no going back, she went on: 'So you see, Esme, there is no reason why I should come running back to you and Leo. I'm sorry you're unwell and I'll help you when I can but...'

Esme leaned over and clutched her hand. 'You mustn't tell Leo – about the baby's uncle. Please, Millie. I want him to forget about the Grangers. Mentioning this Edmund would ruin everything. At the moment we are managing to live together. Not wonderfully happy – not happy at all, but it's bearable. We're polite and ... going through the motions.' Her mouth quivered. 'I hope as time goes by...' She drew back. 'Well, I hope Leo will forget the baby's not his.' She watched Millie's face anxiously.

'I'll spend some time with you now – for Leo's sake,' Millie said slowly. 'But you have to be nicer to him, Esme. You have to appreciate him and the sacrifice he's making for you. Most men would have—'

'I know!' Esme cried peevishly. 'You don't have to keep reminding me. It's bad enough losing Henry and being sick all the time. You've no idea how miserable I am and you don't even care!'

Millie felt a pang of conscience. 'I *do* care,' she said. 'But we all have to live with our mistakes.' And one of mine, she reflected grimly, was to allow you to steal Leo. I should have made a fight for him, but my pride wouldn't let me. She sighed. All water under the bridge now. They both had to make the most of what they had – and she, Millie, had Edmund. At least, she *might* have him.

Esme roused from her despair and made a pot of tea.

Millie said, 'What's Leo having for his midday meal when he gets back?'

'I don't know yet. Probably egg and bacon. He can make that for himself. Cooking makes me feel sick.' She poured the tea and sipped hers tentatively. 'Couldn't you come round each morning for an hour or two?'

'No, Esme. I'm sorry, but I have things to do. Sometimes I shop and sometimes Poppy does it. Occasionally we go out together. One day I cook, the next Poppy does.' She smiled. 'Not that she's much of a cook. Her idea is to

211

pop out and bring back two mutton pies!' She laughed and added milk to her tea so that she coud drink it quickly. 'I'll wash up for you now and tidy the kitchen while you you go upstairs and dress and do your hair. Leo doesn't want to see you like this. And then I must go.'

'Oh Millie! It's nearly time for Leo to come home for his meal. He's looking forward to seeing you. He said—'

'I can't stay, Esme. Give him my best wishes. I'll see you again some time.'

Ten minutes later Millie left the house with a sigh of relief, pleased to be aw⌐ ⌐rom the gloomy atmosphere and back to her own life. Her only regret was in having shared her news about Edmund. That had been rather unwise, she reflected. Her sister had stolen the man she loved once before. She mustn't let it happen again.

Later that night Millie lay in bed struggling with her conscience. She admitted to herself that she was gloating over her sister's misfortunes and that was a spiteful thing to do. She had said a prayer asking God to help her be more charitable. Now she was wondering whether she could bear to spend one morning a week with Esme, helping her with the house and cheering her up. They could go for a walk together; or chat while they did some embroidery. Maybe they could sort out the family photographs and put them in an album.

She sighed. The tables had really turned,

she thought, and could not resist a smile. She now had a life of her own and all Esme had was heartache. But – and it was a big 'but' – Esme was expecting a child. She would have a *family*. She, Millie, had no prospects in that direction – unless Edmund was becoming seriously interested in her, and she suspected he might be. He wanted to see her again, and it was mutual. Could she ever be married to an officer from Sandhurst? She wondered what Edmund would look like in his uniform ... But what would Poppy say when she knew? Poppy couldn't stand him and made no bones about it. Millie longed to talk about him to someone and Poppy would have been the ideal choice if circumstances had been different. Now she would have to keep their friendship to herself.

For a moment she thought of Ned Warren and her conscience pricked her again. But she had made no promises. They were little more than friends. Yes, that was it: good friends. As long as he realized that and didn't hope for more. Guilt washed over her because she knew in her heart that in Ned's mind he was more than a friend. She would have to step carefully, she thought, for fear of hurting him.

Dorcas stood at the French windows which looked out across the extensive lawn, but her small brown eyes were closed and her face was set in anguished lines. She was dressed in black bombazine, which was relieved only by the pearls Henry had given her when they were married. As her fingers felt the beads, she thought wistfully of happier times when they had been young and she hopelessly in love with him. The years had tempered her passion, but in a way she still loved him, in spite of his failings – and in spite of the woman who had impersonated her at the hospital.

At last she turned. Behind her, sprawled on the ottoman, her brother-in-law rolled his eyes. Exasperated, he said, 'But you asked me to find out who she is. That's all I've done. So why the mood? You asked her name and I've told you. It's Prunella, better known as Poppy.'

'*Poppy!*'

'Awful, isn't it? She's nothing special, just one of the Grecian models. Pretty enough, but she doesn't sing, she doesn't dance.' He shrugged. 'A silly little talentless nobody. I can't see what Henry saw in her.'

Dorcas felt a little comforted by this description. 'You've spoken to her?'

'Not yet, but I've spoken about her with the young woman who shares the flat.'

She hesitated. 'Did Henry pay the rent?'

'I don't know. Maybe not, if she has a flat-mate. This other girl says she shares the flat.' He shrugged. 'I'm not a private detective, Dorcas. I can't do miracles and I can't just blunder in and ask questions. I'm cultivating the friend – Millie Something. I'll get all the information I need from her if I don't get to see Poppy. No doubt Henry gave me a bad

214

write-up. Poppy probably hates the sound of me.'

Dorcas twisted her fingers together, a habit she had when she was worried. 'I've learned that Henry left her something at the bank – an envelope – and that it was collected.' She gave him a searching look. She had never really trusted him after the business with the maid and in some ways she was longing for his leave to come to an end. Back to the army and discipline – that was what he needed. Henry had always said that, left to his own devices, Edmund would go to the bad. He already gambled on the horses and lost more than he could afford.

Edmund shrugged. 'Don't look at me!'

'You didn't collect it, then – this envelope?'

He looked indignant. 'Certainly not!' he insisted. 'Henry wouldn't have trusted me with such a mission. I suppose she collected it herself.'

Dorcas took a deep breath and tried to steady her voice. 'I assume she isn't ... in an interesting condition. I want the truth, Ed.'

'She looked normal enough.'

'I thought you hadn't met her!' He *was* lying, she thought desperately.

'For heaven's sake, Dorcas! Don't be so paranoid. I saw the woman on stage wearing very little and she looked normal. I hope to get to speak with her some time, but I can hardly ask her such a question. I do think you're making too much of this, Dorcas. Henry's dead. His philandering days are –

Hell's bells!'

She had slapped his face and didn't regret it. They were a pair, she thought bitterly. Henry and Ed. How had sons with a strict, God-fearing mother like Maria turned out so badly?

'Don't speak of Henry that way!' she snapped. 'He's dead. Show a little respect. You are no better. For all I know you may be worse!'

'At least I'm not married!' He rubbed his cheek where she had slapped him. 'Come on, old girl. Why not let it drop? How can she hurt you now, this Poppy creature? He's dead and she's got nothing.'

'We don't know that.' Dorcas sank into an armchair and stared round at the beautifully furnished drawing room: chandeliers, family portraits, highly polished chairs and tables and elaborate flower arrangements. 'He worked so hard for all this. Poor Henry...' She sighed heavily. 'I'm sorry, Ed. I lost my temper. I just want to be certain there isn't a child,' she explained. 'Then I can rest easy in my mind. No surprises. Jack inherits. Lance follows you into the army. The boys' future settled. Then I can relax.'

Edmund rose languidly to his feet and smiled down at her. 'You always were a worrier. Look, even if she were to have a child, it wouldn't affect the boys. Jack would still be the oldest. Lance would still go to Sandhurst.'

She frowned unhappily. 'You may say it wouldn't change anything, but it would. The

216

boys would have a half-brother – or half-sister. The child would be part of the family in a way.' She swallowed hard at the thought that Henry might have fathered another child – a child she would never hold in her arms.

'Nonsense! It would simply be a love-child. Wrong side of the blanket. Happens all the time. You are so awfully dramatic, Dorcas.'

'On the contrary, I am looking at the worst scenario. I'm trying to prepare myself for any emergency. It *could* happen and then what would we do? This Poppy might come knocking on the door one day, asking for maintenance for the child.'

'You'll have to fight that battle if it happens, but probably it won't come to that. If it does, you simply ask her to prove that the child is Henry's, and how can she? But I'll find out what I can and tell you. I promise.'

'Thank you, Ed. I appreciate that.'

He glanced at the clock. 'Good Lord! I'm playing tennis with Bullet in ten minutes. He'll be here in a jiff. I must change.'

She groaned inwardly. Tim Bull, otherwise known as Bullet, was one of her brother-in-law's many wild friends who descended on them whenever he was on leave. She watched him hurry out of the room and listened to his footsteps on the stairs. Now she must make *her* way up to her mother-in-law's room and tell her a suitable version of Ed's news. The old lady might be bedridden, but she had all her wits about her and no illusions about her two sons.

217

Maria Granger was sitting up in bed wearing an expensive shawl of soft blue wool. Despite her age and infirmity she was very vain and rarely allowed anyone to see her when she looked less than perfect. Her back was straight against the pillows and her long grey hair was immaculate – pulled back into the chignon she had adopted when on holiday in Trouville in happier times. Now rheumatism had claimed her knees and hips and she was forced to spend her days in bed or downstairs on the chaise longue reserved especially for her. When Dorcas entered the room, the nurse was fluttering round the bed, but at a glance from her mistress she gave a dutiful nod in Dorcas's direction and scurried out of the room, leaving the two women alone.

'Well?' Maria fixed her daughter-in-law with a piercing look. 'Is there a woman?'

Dorcas told her briefly what she had learned from Edmund.

'And is there a child?'

Dorcas remained standing, her hands clasped in front of her chest. 'Not as far as we know. Ed is still making enquiries. He hasn't reached the woman yet, only a friend of hers, but he will keep us informed.'

Maria sighed heavily. 'What's taking him so long?'

'The woman won't want to see him. He says Henry probably poisoned her mind against him because he...'

'Go on!'

'Because Ed used to tap Henry for money.

218

For debts.'

'Gambling debts?' As Dorcas hesitated, she snapped, 'I've never thought Edmund was a saint. He inherited his father's weaknesses.'

'Yes. Gambling debts.'

There was a long silence. 'If there is a child, it will be a Granger. You realize that.'

Dorcas nodded silently then amended, 'Only partly.'

'It will be my grandchild. In my book that makes it a Granger.'

Dorcas swallowed hard. She had always wanted a girl, but Henry had given her two sons, both of whom had disappointed her. She loved them both but recognized their faults. Jack was a bully and Lance was mean-spirited. At best she suspected that neither of them would ever amount to anything. She asked, 'What point are you making? If there is a child ... perhaps it would be better to know nothing about it.'

'Ignorance is bliss, you mean?' Maria tossed her head. 'That is not the way I think. I could not allow Henry's child to be brought up by a woman like Prunella Gayford. A cheap showgirl. Not even a real actress, though that would be even worse. From what you tell me she merely appears on stage *in a supper room*! What sort of life could such a woman make for a child? What sort of mother would she be? It's unthinkable. We would have to take in the child. Bring it up. Educate it. Surely you see that, Dorcas.'

Dorcas reeled slightly at this prospect and

219

groped for a nearby chair, which she drew up to the bed. She sat down heavily. 'Aren't you forgetting something? The mother? She may not wish to part with the child.'

'Nonsense. She will hardly be able to bring up a child in her profession.' She frowned. 'Pull the curtains to a little, will you? The sun is surprisingly warm for November and it's shining directly into my eyes.'

Dorcas obeyed. No 'please' and there would be no 'thank you', she reflected. The old lady was too used to a nurse at her beck and call all day.

Maria went on. 'Was she at the funeral, this Prunella Gayford? Did anyone see a strange woman attending the service?'

'There were several women unaccounted for!' Dorcas could not resist it.

'Lord above!' Maria exclaimed. 'What is the matter with the Granger men? My husband was as unreliable as his father before him and my two sons were no better. Your two are hardly promising – Oh don't argue with me, Dorcas. You know they are not what we might have hoped for. Don't blame yourself. I fear it runs in the family.'

Dorcas bridled in defence of her cubs. 'Jack and Lance are not—'

Maria ignored the interruption. 'My husband was as irresponsible as they come. Left to himself Cyril would have ruined the family finances – but at least he didn't chase women. Too much drink, that was his problem – that and a taste for opium, which he

220

thought he hid from me.' She shook her head. 'At least the Granger men always chose their wives wisely. Cyril had me. Henry had you. He was lucky. I didn't expect you to accept him, you know. I thought you had more sense.'

I certainly could have made a better marriage, Dorcas thought wearily. Her parents had been against Henry from the start, but she had been besotted with his good looks.

Maria glanced at the bedside table, which was in easy reach. 'Do hand me my smelling salts,' she said. 'I feel slightly light-headed. I think my midday meal was too heavy. Cook will insist on making me egg custards and they don't agree with me. Remind her when you go down. And see if she has fed Tiger.'

Dorcas nodded, rising. The old tabby cat was the only creature that Maria really loved. 'I must be going: I have some letters to write; but I'll keep you informed. Do you want to see Ed? Is there anything else he can tell you about...'

'Certainly not. Keep him away from me. I might feel inclined to give him a talking-to and that always tires me out.'

While she had the chance, Dorcas made her exit. Her thoughts were chaotic. Bring Poppy's love-child into the family – if there *was* a child? The idea appalled her.

'Not if I have any say in the matter,' she vowed. Unless ... a little girl ... No! She must not waver.

Through the landing window she saw

Edmund and Bullet playing tennis. Should she say anything to her brother-in-law? she wondered. Maybe not. She would bide her time. There might be no need for alarm. But if there was, she would be ready for it.

Tuesday arrived. As usual the park was full of people, enjoying the sunny but windy weather. Millie sat on a seat and waited for Ned to appear. A boy ran past wheeling a metal hoop, urging it on with loud cries as though it were a horse. An elderly couple strolled past arm in arm, talking in a language Millie didn't recognize. In the distance she caught sight of three soldiers laughing uproariously at a shared joke and for a moment her heart leaped, but as they came nearer and passed she could see that Edmund was not one of them. A little girl stood with her mother, throwing peanuts to a bold red squirrel.

Ned was a few minutes late but eventually hurried towards her, a large grin on his face. His wrist was still bandaged and the bruise on his face had turned a nasty yellow, but he insisted that he was fine.

'So sorry to be late. Hate to keep a lady waiting,' he told her earnestly. 'You're looking very nice today, if I may say so, Miss Bayley! Very nice indeed.' He tucked her arm through his.

'Oh! Should we?' she protested. Suppose they met Edmund Granger.

He laughed off the doubt. 'No law against

it. Look!' He pointed. 'Lots of couples walk hand in hand.'

'Yes but ... they're *couples*.'

He stopped in his tracks. 'Aren't we a couple?' he asked humorously. 'I was beginning to hope we were!'

They walked on and Millie could see by his expression that he hadn't taken her comment seriously. He was telling her something about his employer and she tried to concentrate.

'...So I said, "Mr Betts, I think I've proved my worth to this firm over the past few years and now..."'

'Mr Betts is your employer?'

He nodded. A small mongrel dog raced up to them, waving its tail in a friendly manner, and Ned bent to make a fuss of it. 'I shall have a dog one day,' he told Millie. 'My pa doesn't like dogs – he's a cat man; but I shall have a dog when I have my own place. D'you like animals?'

She nodded. Did she? She had never thought about it.

'But not one of those fancy dogs,' he went on. 'Not a poodle, or a pug with a squashed face. Nor one of those with a pedigree as long as your arm! They're not so hardy, you see. I like a dog with a bit of character. Like this little chap.' He watched with regret as the dog's owner whistled and it went scampering back.

'So I said to Mr Betts, "I think I'm due a bit of a rise. I've got commitments." "Like what?" he says. "Like I might be getting married," I tell him.' He glanced at Millie. 'That surprised him.'

'It surprises me!' Millie stammered. 'I didn't know you were...'

'Oh I didn't say it was definite. No. I only said I *might*. No harm in letting him know that much. I mean, a man's due a bit more money when he's thinking about a wife and family. Stands to reason, that does.'

'I dare say it does.' Taken aback, she stared straight ahead, afraid to catch his eye.

The pressure on her arm increased as he drew her closer. 'What I'm telling you is: Mr Betts said yes! Another five shillings a week! That's not to be sneezed at. Because he knows I'm good at my job. And it's dangerous at times.' He held up his bandaged wrist. 'His son's also in the firm, but he's not a natural like me. I can usually talk them round. He can't. Poor old Sid. He's a blusterer. Shouts a lot but then gives way too easily and folks will take advantage of him. Mr Betts knows that.' He stopped, obviously waiting for her to say something.

Millie said, 'Five shillings more. That's wonderful news, Mr Warren. I'm pleased for you.'

He gave a little skip of excitement. 'What it really means, Miss Bayley, is that I feel I am in a better position to look for a wife. Better financially. You see what I mean?' He glanced hopefully sideways, trying to gauge her reaction.

Millie said, 'Won't your father miss you?'

'Of course he will, but he'll have compensations. A daughter-in-law and some grandchildren. He'll be very content with that.'

Millie was growing hot with nervous anticipation and couldn't think of anything to say. If she was disparaging, he would be mortified, and if she said anything encouraging, he might feel inclined to ask her more directly. She tried to recall if she had ever given him any hint that she would say yes.

Tired of waiting, he said, 'I was hoping to meet a willing woman.' He laughed to show that this was a joke.

'And have you?'

He stopped abruptly and stepped in front of her in order to study her expression. 'I thought I had ... but maybe I was wrong. I rather hoped, Miss Bayley, that you were beginning to like me ... and might even...'

Millie took a deep breath. 'I like you very much, Mr Warren, but I have to confess I haven't been thinking about getting married. After my earlier unhappy experience I think I need some time to – to...'

She read the disappointment in his eyes and longed to sweeten the pill. 'I feel as though I have never lived an independent life. Caring for my parents and then being with Esme and Leo ... Sharing a flat with Poppy and having a job, however humble, is exciting and...'

To her relief he took hold of her hands. 'I've been thoughtless,' he told her. 'My pa always said I was impulsive. The thing is, I know I could make you happy and I'm afraid you will make another mistake. Leo was not the man for you. There's so little joy in his soul, you know. I knew when I went to the bank.'

'I could have made him happy!' she insisted.

'But would he have done the same for you?'

He resumed his place beside her, then suddenly abandoned her and ran after a straw hat which had been snatched from its owner's head by a gust of wind. He returned breathlessly, to reclaim her. 'My good deed for the day,' he exclaimed. 'Not enough hatpins, I told her!'

They walked in silence for a while until he said, 'So if I were to propose to you, you wouldn't say no. Not a downright no. Is that how it is? I mean, if I were to wait a little to give you a chance to enjoy your freedom and – and maybe grow tired of the single life...' He frowned. 'Help me a little, Miss Bayley, please. I'm rather out of my depth.'

Millie was feeling distinctly flummoxed and guided them to the nearest vacant seat. 'If you were to give me time, Mr Warren, I promise I would consider the idea but ... I don't want you to take that as any kind of agreement.' Inspiration struck. 'I may not want to marry *anybody*. I don't mean to – to discourage you or...' But that was exactly what she did mean. This was proving harder than she'd expected. 'Surely women can live alone and be happy and fulfilled.'

'Can they?' He sounded genuinely surprised by the notion. 'I always pitied them. How stupid of me!' He smiled. 'I'd like to put my arm around your shoulders. I might feel a bit better then. Not quite so discouraged. What d'you think?'

She hesitated, unwilling to hurt his feelings. 'Please do, Mr Warren.'

He slid his arm around her and pulled her towards him so that she rested her head against his shoulder. It was very pleasant but brought back memories.

He looked at her thoughtfully. 'But what about the women who long to have a family?' he asked. 'If they remain spinsters, how can they be fulfilled?' Before she could answer he went on: 'Would you be fulfilled if you spent your life alone? I imagined you in this very park, sitting on this very seat with twins in a pram and another child sitting beside you...' He grinned as her eyes widened. 'And you're watching me playing ball with the other one!'

'What an exhausting picture!' Millie laughed aloud. She couldn't tell him that when she had expected to marry Leo, that would have been her dream. No, she thought, she wouldn't be happy growing old alone. But whoever she married, it would have to be the right man. Sadly, she was not at all sure that Ned Warren was that man.

She returned to the flat to find a small bouquet of carnations waiting for her. Poppy, sitting with her newly washed hair in a towel, was looking none too pleased. 'There's a note with them,' she said. 'I thought they were for me and nearly opened it. Who on earth can be sending you flowers?'

'I don't know! I've never had flowers sent to me before.' She looked at them, trying to hide her excitement. Please, she begged, let them be from Edmund! That would make her day. It would make up for the past two hours, which had left her feeling horribly guilty.

Poppy said, 'Well, open it, Millie, or we'll never know!'

Millie sensed her exasperation and her fingers fumbled with the flap of the small envelope. Inside was a card decorated with flowers and ribbons: *'Millie, I shall pick you up tomorrow in a trap at ten a.m. and we will drive down Rotten Row! Edmund.'*

'Well?' Poppy repeated.

Millie looked at her. 'It's from Edmund. He's going to...'

'Read it out, Millie!'

Millie did so. There was an awkward silence.

Poppy said, 'The beast! Henry used to take me driving in that trap. He's doing it on purpose to upset me!' Her eyes were dark with anger and Millie's romantic moment died.

'I'm sure he's not,' she ventured.

Poppy covered her face with her hands. 'He *is*!' she muttered. 'I know it. It's Henry's pony and trap. He keeps it – used to keep it in livery a mile from here. We often drove down Rotten Row with all the big-wigs.'

Her voice shook and Millie felt truly unkind to even *think* of accepting Edmund's offer.

She felt sure she ought to turn him down, but a small stubborn voice within her told her not to be so rash. 'This is *your* life, Millie,' she told herself.

'I'm sorry, Poppy.'

Poppy uncovered her face. 'You're not going, are you? I've told you: he's just doing this to upset me. Because of all the things Henry's told me about him. He's using you to try and make me jealous.'

Millie threw down the offending letter. 'Stop it, Poppy. I think it's very selfish of you to want me to miss the excitement. You've done it all. Now it's my turn. I know you don't like him, but he hasn't done me any harm and—'

'Yet!' Poppy shook her head. 'Don't you see how sly he's being? He wants to get to me, for whatever reason.'

'You mean he doesn't find me attractive – is that it? You're saying I don't really interest him.' Millie almost choked on the words. 'If he wanted to send you flowers, he would have done so!' She snatched up the flowers. 'I'm going to put these in water before they droop.'

Poppy said, 'I shall be here tomorrow at ten and he doesn't set foot in this flat! Do not invite him in. Poor Henry would turn in his grave!'

Millie pretended not to hear, but as she reached for the tap to fill the vase, she was trembling.

Ten

The next day Millie was up extra early. She boarded the bus to Bond Street and went shopping. She felt she needed to update her meagre wardrobe for the outing with Edmund and bought herself a small fur-trimmed hat and a muff to match. Somehow she misjudged the time and when she ran for the bus the clock was striking a quarter to ten; she knew with a sinking heart that she would never get home in time to prevent a clash between Edmund and Poppy.

Arriving home, she found him pacing up and down, looking none too pleased; but he smiled when he saw her and admired her outfit.

'Queen Prunella refused me entry,' he laughed. 'How on earth did Henry put up with such a harridan?'

Millie began to stammer an apology, but he made light of the matter, took her arm and steered her to the smart pony and trap that waited at the kerb side. The trap was highly polished, painted a dark glossy green with a thin yellow stripe by way of decoration. The brown-and-white pony's harness matched the trap and Millie, perched beside Edmund on

230

the seat, felt extremely elegant. Edmund was an expert driver and he steered them in and out of the heavy traffic with ease until they finally drove through the gates into the park.

Glancing at Millie, Edmund leaned closer. 'I've never seen eyes that sparkle like yours,' he told her.

Millie began to protest but quickly bit back the words and thanked him instead. Perhaps he was right. Perhaps her eyes did sparkle, though Leo had never mentioned it. She wanted to say that being with Edmund was enough to make any woman's eyes sparkle, but that, too, would be a mistake. Learn to accept compliments, Millie, she urged herself.

Once inside the park the pony slowed to a sedate trot as they kept pace with the other carriages. These extravagant vehicles were filled with fashionably dressed people, many of whom Edmund knew by name. The women were warmly dressed in sumptuous furs and many wore scarves tied over their hats. The men wore beaver coats or fur collars and fine leather gloves and Millie had never seen so many top hats. The beautifully groomed horses jingled their harnesses and tossed their heads and seemed to know they were being paraded and admired. The whole thoroughfare jostled and heaved with pedestrians who had taken the walk in order to see and admire the parade.

Edmund glanced at her. 'The common people never tire of watching their superiors!'

he told her. 'Come rain or come shine, they turn out to watch and doff their hats. Half the time the poor fools don't even know who they are acknowledging!'

Millie said, 'Does Queen Victoria ever appear?'

'Hardly ever. Not for years. Not since Prince Albert died. She hides herself away in the Isle of Wight, mourning her beloved. It's morbid to mourn for so long – and politically unwise. The people need to see her or they become restless.' He raised his hat to a couple who overtook them and the man shouted, 'Granger, old son! Time we got together again!'

Edmund called, 'Indeed it is!' then muttered, 'Silly old duffer! The man's a pretentious ass!'

'But they'd recognize the Queen if she did appear?' Millie persisted.

'Oh yes. She's unmistakable, isn't she? A tough old bird!' He laughed at the shocked expression on Millie's face. 'Sorry, Miss Bayley. You must forgive a rough soldier.'

Two children waved at Millie, who quickly returned the wave. Little do they know, she thought, amused. They assume I am somebody important because I ride in a smart little trap with a handsome escort!

They left the park and made their way to a restaurant called Di Marco's, where Edmund assured her they served the best kidneys in marsala that he had ever tasted. Inside, the room glittered with lights and glassware and

Millie felt conspicuous by her less than extravagant clothes. Edmund, however, appeared unperturbed and, after he had ordered for them and Millie had drunk a glass of champagne, she began to feel more at ease.

'Tell me about your life at Sandhurst,' she suggested. 'Do you teach the men to drill?'

'Good Lord no! That's the sergeant-major's job. He bellows at them for hours – they're a lazy lot on the whole. I and my fellow officers teach them the history of the army and politics and all about weapons and tactics and how to behave in the field – camouflage and such and how not to get your head blown off!' He laughed. 'Awfully boring stuff, really. I'm thinking about applying for a transfer to somewhere more interesting.' He smiled and raised his eyebrows. 'Dare I say "somewhere more dangerous"! Life in England is too cushy. It might sound glamorous but...'

'I shouldn't like you to go anywhere too dangerous,' Millie ventured shyly.

'Millie! How awfully sweet you are!' He picked up her hand and kissed it. 'But enough about me. I have something to ask you ... But first another glass of champagne for the pretty lady!'

After the second glass was poured the food arrived and Edmund appeared to have forgotten whatever it was he was going to ask her. The meal was delicious and Millie was able to eat most of it. She had been brought up not to waste food but to leave just a little 'for Mr Manners'. After a third glass of champagne she realized that she was becoming a little light-headed and wondered whether to say anything to Edmund about it. She made an exit to the Ladies' Room on legs that felt rather unsafe and was alarmed to see from her reflection in the mirror that she looked a little drunk! Her face was flushed and her eyes were wider than normal. She thought she looked almost beautiful.

When she returned to the table he leaned closer and whispered, 'About poor departed Henry ... Is there a child on the way?'

In Millie's state the question did not seem that unseemly, but she was surprised that he had guessed. 'How did you know?' she asked, blinking in some confusion. 'It's supposed to be a secret!'

He sat back, staring at her. 'You mean there *is* a child? My God! This will put the cat among the pigeons and no mistake! So Queen Prunella has pulled off a hat-trick! Hah!' He roared with laughter. 'Wait until I tell Dorcas ... and Mother! There'll be...'

Millie frowned hazily. 'Queen Prunella? Oh, you mean Poppy! Oh no! It's Esme, not Poppy.' What on earth would Poppy think if Dorcas turned up on her doorstep accusing her of an unwanted pregnancy? Suddenly she had all his attention. His mouth opened and he stared at her.

'Esme?' he said at last. 'Who in God's name is Esme? Henry *has* been busy!'

Dimly Millie realized that she might have said too much, but it was too late.

Edmund chose a dessert for them both and ordered another bottle of champagne. Before the meal was over he had persuaded Millie to reveal all she knew about Esme and Henry.

'But don't worry your head about it,' he reassured her. 'It was only a matter of time before the truth was out. These things can't be kept quiet.' He leaned forward and kissed the side of her face. 'Poor little Millie! You look so awfully worried.'

'I think ... I've had too much to drink,' she whispered. Her head was beginning to ache and her joy in the occasion was fading minute by minute. She felt disorientated and nervous, as though she was losing control of her mind. Somehow she stammered, 'Would you be kind enough to – to take me home, Edmund?'

His face seemed to loom into hers. It was out of focus, but she could see that he was laughing.

'Poor Miss Bayley!' he whispered. 'Hasn't anyone ever told you? – you should never trust a military man!'

The ride home was a blur, but he was chivalrous enough to carry her up the stairs and knock on the door for her. He gave her a goodbye kiss and promised to write to her when he returned to Sandhurst. Then he left.

When Poppy opened the door, Millie was alone, propped up against the door jamb. She fell into Poppy's arms, only half-conscious. The last words Millie heard were: 'That blackguard! He hasn't heard the last of this!'

235

Muttering to herself about the stupidity of some young women, Poppy half-carried Millie into the bedroom and hoisted her on to her own bed. There was no way she could risk leaving her on the sofa: it was too small and she was likely to fall. She fetched cold water and a cloth and bathed the unconscious Millie's face and neck. Millie roused enough to say that she was going to be sick and Poppy rushed for the pail that was kept under her washstand.

'Just in time!' she said, wrinkling her nose. When the vomiting ended, Millie looked a little better but still very pale and shivery. Poppy made her drink some water and finally Millie came to and was able to sit up.

'I dread to ask what happened!' said Poppy. 'I'll make a guess. You've been with that wretch Edmund, he plied you with alcohol and made you feel like a princess.'

Millie nodded miserably and Poppy saw that there were tears in her eyes. Hardening her heart she pressed on with her inquisition. 'And he asked you about me and you told him everything!'

'No. He...' Millie flopped back against the brass rails of the bed head. She put a feeble hand to head and groaned softly.

Poppy said, 'Serves you right for being so gullible!' But her heart wasn't in it. She could remember when she, too, had been naïve enough to be manipulated in the same way. Poor, foolish Millie!

Millie pressed fingers against her eyes. 'He

236

asked about you – whether you were expecting Henry's child and...'

Poppy's eyes widened. 'Expecting Henry's child? He asked you that? The nerve of the man!'

'But I said *you* weren't but my sister is and...' She suddenly lunged forward for the pail, which fortunately still rested on the carpet beside the bed.

Slowly registering what Millie had said, Poppy frowned. 'You said *your sister* is having Henry's child. *Esme?* What are you talking about? She doesn't even know him!'

Millie wiped her mouth on the damp cloth and leaned back again. A fine perspiration stood out on her face. 'I'm afraid she does,' she muttered. 'I didn't want you to know. She told me about this man, but she called him Wally and...'

'She's married to Leo but she was seeing someone called Wally? What on earth are you rambling about, Millie? Are you in your right mind? What on earth have you been drinking?'

Millie blinked tiredly and her eyes closed. 'Champagne!'

Poppy jumped up and shook her. 'Don't you dare go to sleep on me, Millie Bayley! You tell me this properly. Start at the beginning.'

'I just want to sleep.'

'You may want to but you're not going to. You tell me a garbled story about a man called Wally and your sister and then drag Henry into it!' What was it that Millie didn't want her to know? Her heartbeat quickened as anxiety crept in. How could Esme be having Henry's child? That would mean that Henry had another woman and – and ... Her thoughts were spinning. She took several deep breaths and tried to quell her growing unease. There had been those days, of course, when she didn't make herself available to Henry – those certain times of the month – but surely he hadn't gone with other women on those occasions. Would he? The thought sickened her, but she had to know the truth. 'Tell me, Millie, and I promise I won't interrupt you. Start at the beginning.'

She sat on the end of the bed and prepared herself for the worst – or thought she had. She had expected some kind of muddle, but as Millie's stumbling story came out she was forced to face the unwelcome truth that her beloved Henry had availed himself of other women and Esme Walmsley had been one of them. Perhaps the others had all been married, so less of a threat to his own security.

She listened in silence to the rest of Millie's account and at last she thought she understood. Henry had used his second name so that they would never know who he was. Sly old Henry, she thought with grudging admiration – an emotion laced with bitterness. And now Esme, a married woman, was paying for her infidelity.

'Serves her right!' she told Millie. 'I have no sympathy for her.'

'But she didn't know he was married!'

238

'She knew *she* was, though! Wasn't one man enough for her?' She glared at Millie.

'Don't blame me, Poppy. I'm not responsible for her.'

Poppy nodded. 'Sorry, Millie, but it's been a nasty shock.'

Guiltily she leaned forward and squeezed Millie's hand as her friend's tears started to flow once more. Poppy reminded herself that Millie, too, had suffered a setback. She had pinned her hopes on the rascally Edmund and had been rudely awakened as to his true character. He hadn't even waited to see how she was when he had dumped her outside the door but had scuttled away without so much as a goodbye. Poor Millie would never see *him* again ... Men, she thought resentfully. Were they all tarred with the same cruel brush?

Poppy sighed. At least she still had the money Henry had left her and the small income for the future, and she certainly didn't envy Esme the child. Children had never appealed to her. A career on the stage was all she craved and she believed herself to be on her way up. With Henry's money she might take singing lessons ... or learn to tap-dance. Perhaps if she learned one song, Tapper's might give her a chance – a solo spot. It would be a start. The thought cheered her and as the initial shock of Millie's news began to fade, she finally smiled and straightened her back.

'So what will happen now?' she asked

briskly. 'Rest assured, Edmund, the spy, will report back to the family. Esme's secret will be out – thanks to you.'

Millie dabbed at her reddened eyes and shrugged. 'I don't know. The way I feel now I don't care! They will have to sort it out between them.'

'Hmm! I doubt that very much. That sister of yours seems unable to do anything for herself. She always has to drag you into it.'

'No. I mean it, Poppy. This time it has gone too far and I shall keep out of it.'

Poppy settled her friend in the bed and left her to sleep. Later she made her way to Millie's sofa for the rest of the night, but sleep eluded her and she lay for hours considering the growing confusion and the unhappy prospects of those around her. She was cautiously optimistic about her own future and that gave her a feeling of superiority. Henry might have betrayed her in small ways, but he had thought about her future and had left her secure. The same could hardly be said for Esme Walmsley or any of Henry's other women. Whatever Leo said to his wife now, he might sing a very different tune when the child arrived. And what would Dorcas say when Edmund passed on his news about the illegitimate child? Henry's mother would be furious when she knew what had happened. Poppy's only worry was that Edmund would one day reveal the money Henry had left her. Would he tell? And if so, would the Granger's lawyers be able to put a stop to it?

She tossed uncomfortably on the sofa and longed for the comfort of her own bed, belatedly regretting her generosity towards Millie. One thing was certain, however. If Millie believed she would be able to remain free of any further entanglements, she would be quickly disillusioned.

Two days later Dorcas received a letter from Edmund, who had already returned to Sandhurst. She recognized the handwriting and opened it with a strong sense of forboding:

> My dear Dorcas,
> The worst has happened. There is a child on the way – but the mother is not Prunella Gayford. To my surprise little Millicent Bayley confessed (under the influence of a few glasses of champers) that her sister Esme (who is married, would you believe?) is expecting Henry's child. It seems she has been seeing him on an occasional basis over the last few months and the Poppy woman knows nothing of the relationship! I'm sorry to be the bearer of such bad news...

'No you're not!' cried Dorcas, shocked and trembling. 'You're enjoying it!' She forced herself to read on:

> ...What a delicious tangle! Trust old Henry to make an awful mess of things and then pop off and leave it to others to

241

sort out ... A brother to be proud of, eh? Still, I look on the bright side. He makes me appear a thoroughly decent chap by comparison!

Dorcas sat down hurriedly and stared into space. 'Henry! You utter, *utter* swine!' she whispered. She had always suspected there might be another woman – she knew it was not uncommon among MPs who had a second home in London – but she had thought it best to pretend ignorance of any such affair. When she had once mooted the suspicion to her mother-in-law, Maria had told her that 'men had their needs' and pointed out that Henry was rarely at home with his wife and family. But an occasional woman as well as the Gayford creature! Whatever would Henry's mother say about that? Dorcas felt faint at the thought of having to show her Edmund's letter. She read on:

> I know no more details except the name Esme but a confrontation with the sister, Millicent, should produce all you need. She works as a dresser at Tapper's Supper Room, finishes about eleven o'clock. I'm off now to catch the train ...
>   In the most awful haste,
>   Edmund.

'Henry! How could you do this to me?' Dorcas felt a deep well of misery rise within her at this proof of the extent of her dead husband's infidelity. The familiar questions resurfaced to torment her. Had her whole marriage been a sham? Had all past twenty years meant nothing to him?

Further questions buzzed at her overburdened mind. Suppose her mother-in-law *did* insist on having the child in the family. She, Dorcas, would have to bring the child up. Fleetingly, the idea of another child appealed to her – but a love-child? A constant reminder of Henry's infidelity ... And how would her two sons take to the idea?

'Not well!' she muttered. Rising, she hurried to the sideboard and poured herself a sherry, drank it in two mouthfuls and poured another. She stood at the window, sipping her drink and trying to gather her wits. Somehow she must collect her thoughts before she went up to break the news to Maria. It was necessary to think matters through before subjecting herself to the older woman's strong will.

Today it would be her secret, she decided suddenly. Not a word to the boys or to Maria. She would pretend the letter arrived tomorrow. That decision gave her a little time and she relaxed slightly.

'Esme ... Who are you?' she whispered. 'I know you're married. Shame on you!'

Did Esme's husband know she was expecting another man's child, she wondered. Very awkward for her if she confessed to him. Hardly a happy household. But suppose the husband thought the child was his ... She narrowed her eyes. Maybe this problem would resolve itself. The first thing she must do was talk with Millicent, the dresser. She would tell Maria that tomorrow.

A faint smile touched her lips. 'You may think you've beaten me down, Henry, but don't be too sure. I think I shall go to London tomorrow to do a little shopping. I shall buy myself something new to wear. I shall stay overnight at a nice hotel and then pay a visit to Millicent.' She swallowed the last of the sherry and tossed her head. 'With a little luck I might just survive this!'

The following evening – Saturday – found a very chastened Millie attending to her Grecian ladies as they prepared to go on stage for the late performance. As they wriggled and tugged their way into the skin-tight, flesh-coloured body stockings, she moved from one to the other with her pins, fastening the drapes in place. Some preferred them draped over the one shoulder, hiding one breast but appearing to reveal the other with a seductive hint of nipple. Others chose a looped effect from both shoulders, which partly hid both breasts. Either way they were, without exception, fussy in the extreme, and Millie, still feeling the after-effects of her disastrous evening with Edmund, had little patience with them. Sick at heart over Edmund's duplicity, she nagged and grumbled until they complained.

'Ouch! Watch what you're doing with those

pins, Millie!'

'You're in a mean mood tonight, Mill! What's up?'

She couldn't tell anybody and Poppy, sub-dued in her turn by her recent awareness of Henry's betrayal, was also saying little. She and Millie had had a falling-out, though, as Millie protested, Poppy could hardly blame her for what Esme and Henry had done. Poppy, however, had felt like blaming some-body – *anybody* – and Millie was the only one readily available.

Once the women were lined up off stage for their entrance, Millie decided she could bear it no longer. She would go home while they were on stage. That way she would have a little time to herself. With any luck Poppy would go out with some of her friends for a late drink at the Hare and Hounds round the corner.

She had just stepped out on to the pave-ment when a woman approached her through the gathering fog.

'I'm looking for someone,' she told Millie nervously. 'Perhaps you can help me.'

Millie gave her a sharp look: small and dark, possibly in her late forties...

Before she could reply the woman said, 'I have to speak with Millicent Bayley and I'm told she works here.'

Frozen like a rabbit in the light, Millie's mind refused to function. 'I – That is–' she stammered. 'What's it about?'

'I can't discuss it with a third person but it

245

is very important.' She peered at Millie; even in the hazy gaslight she seemed to recognize Millie's confusion and at once jumped to the correct conclusion. 'Are you Millicent Bayley?'

Millie could only nod. In her present frail state she had no energy for deceit.

'Please,' the woman said. 'I have a hansom cab waiting across the road. If we could sit there and talk for a few moments...'

Millie put a hand to her head, which had been aching all day and now threatened to worsen. She glanced to either side as though hoping to be rescued, but the woman had taken hold of her arm as though to prevent her escape.

'I'm Dorcas Granger – Henry's wife,' she announced. 'I don't intend you any harm but...'

Millie's eyes widened. 'Mrs Henry...!'

'Yes. I'm sure you know that he died recently.' She was slowly urging Millie in the direction of the cab.

'I'm so sorry for your loss.' Millie knew how insincere she sounded. This woman meant more trouble, she thought helplessly.

When they reached the hansom they both climbed in, but Millie said shakily, 'I'm not going anywhere with you. Or with anyone else! Don't give the driver any instructions or I shall...'

Mrs Granger leaned forward. 'Driver, we shall be talking here for five or ten minutes. I shall make good your loss.'

'Yes, ma'am!'

Millie relaxed slightly. 'Why do you need to talk with me?'

'It's about your sister, Esme, of course. Perhaps you would be good enough to read this letter I've received from my brother-in-law, Edmund Granger.'

Millie cried, 'Oh no!' She saw it all immediately. She had told Edmund about her sister and he had passed it on to his family! Deprived of the hazy, alcohol-induced confusion, she was now horribly sober and aware of a crushing burden of guilt and responsibility. By her stupidity, she had made a bad situation much worse.

Mrs Granger said, 'The letter does Edmund no credit and he is less than charitable towards you. But that's the way he is.'

Millie read it and was deeply mortified. Edmund had betrayed her. He had made a fool of her. Worse, though – it was obvious that he had felt nothing for her. She said bleakly, 'I trusted him.'

'You are not the first, believe me! But I am not blaming you, Miss Bayley, for what your sister did. But I understand she is having my husband's child and that *does* concern me. It concerns our whole family. I must talk with your sister, but first I need to know the situation between her and her husband. Does he know the truth?'

Millie kept her mouth tightly closed, fearful of what would happen if she opened it. It seemed that anything she did or said could come back to haunt her. 'I can't–' she stammered. 'At least, I don't think I should–'

'Does he know?'

'Yes,' she whispered. 'He knows and he's willing to forgive her and bring the child up as his own.'

'Ah!'

'I can't say any more. Truly, I feel most disloyal to my sister. She will never forgive me.'

'I need to talk to her alone. Without her husband. If you will tell me where she lives, I will leave you in peace. You must see that I have an interest in my husband's child. I think I deserve a few minutes of her time after the great wrong she has done me. Miss Bayley, I have two sons and Henry's mother is still alive. We all have an interest.'

Millie leaned back. She felt as though she were drowning. This was all Esme's fault, so why did she, Millie, feel so horribly ashamed. She nodded tiredly. 'He's a bank manager,' she said. 'I visit Esme most Tuesday mornings and could take you to the house. I don't think she would be very happy if you turn up unannounced, but I could make the introduction and then leave. Esme is suffering from morning sickness and...'

'Is this her first child?' She gave no sign of sympathy for Esme's affliction, but then, Millie reflected, that was hardly surprising.

'Yes. She wants to keep it.'

Mrs Granger sighed. 'I'll stay on in town until Tuesday. Where shall we meet?'

They made the arrangements and then parted company. Millie watched the hansom rattle away and stood for some minutes alone in the darkness. Her heart was pounding from the exchange and she watched the MP's wife disappear into the fog with a sigh of relief. But almost at once a decrepit old man tottered by and whistled lewdly at her and, with a cry, she gathered up her skirts and ran all the way home.

It was ten o'clock the following morning and Esme was waiting for her sister to arrive. She regarded herself in the mirror, undecided how to appear. If she made too much effort to look normal, Millie might think her visits unnecessary. She brushed her hair with a few irresolute strokes of the brush and pulled it back into an untidy knot at the back of her head. There was no need to make herself look tired and wan – that came naturally.

'You look horrible!' she told herself. Millie, no doubt, would be blooming and full of her new, exciting life. It really was most unfair.

When the doorbell rang she found Millie on the step. Beyond her a hansom had pulled alongside the kerb and the horse was enjoying hay from its nosebag, which presumably meant that it was going to deposit a load of stinking manure on the road. Even the thought made her nauseous.

'Hello, Millie,' she said. 'It's kind of you to come.' She wondered why the cab had pulled up outside *their* house.

Millie quickly explained that the cab contained a visitor. 'It's Dorcas Granger, the wife of the man you called Wally. She insisted on speaking with you. I thought I might be able...'

Esme's jaw dropped. 'Mrs ... Oh no, Millie! How did she – I mean, who told her I–' She retreated inside the hallway, dragging Millie with her, and shut the door with a bang. Her heart began to race and she felt a nervous perspiration break out over her skin. 'I can't possibly talk to her. This is terrible! Send her away, Millie, for heaven's sake!'

Millie was shaking her head. 'You have to talk to her. It's the least you can do. You're having her husband's child and—'

They were interrupted by a firm knocking on the door.

Millie said, 'Let her in, Esme. The sooner you talk, the sooner she'll go back to Somerset.'

'Why me?'

'She wants to talk about the child. If you don't talk to her now, she's threatening to come back when Leo's here.'

'But how did she find out?'

'It's a long story, Esme. Just ask her in.'

Esme longed to slap her sister. She knew it was illogical, but Millie seemed to be one step ahead of her all the time these days and it was an uncomfortable feeling.

The knocking was repeated and before Esme realized what was happening, Millie had opened the door and a strange woman

250

had stepped into the hall.

'We have to talk, Mrs Walmsley,' she said quietly.

Esme stared at her. So this was the wife Wally had denied.

'Your husband told me he was unmarried,' she said defensively. 'He lied to me!'

For a moment the two women stared, each silently weighing up the other.

Millie said, 'Why don't you two sit in the parlour and I'll make a tray of tea?'

Afraid of being alone with the stranger, Esme made a grab for Millie's arm to restrain her, but too late. Millie had slipped away and Esme was forced to lead the way into the parlour.

As Esme sat down, she was trembling. 'There's nothing to talk about,' she stammered. 'My husband has forgiven me and ... he accepts the baby and...' She was gaining strength. 'We've told all our friends and they all think it's Leo's child, so I'm afraid you've had a wasted journey.'

The woman was looking down at her hands, which were folded in her lap, and seemed to be thinking. Although Esme realized that she was cast as the scarlet woman, she was heartened to see that she was prettier than Dorcas as well as younger. At least *something* was in her favour.

The woman looked up at last and steepled her hands, which were well endowed with expensive rings. Esme wondered if Leo would ever buy her such a gift. He could afford it now he was a manager. Maybe she would drop a hint...

Mrs Granger said, 'I'm only concerned with Henry's child. You must understand we are a well-established, close-knit family. The child is part of Henry and as such is part of the Granger family. Henry's mother is very proud and she hates the idea of Henry's child being brought up by strangers.'

'I won't be a stranger!' Indignation made Esme's protest a shriek. 'I'll be the baby's *mother*! How much closer could we be?' She wished now that she had taken more trouble with her appearance. This woman must be wondering what her husband had ever seen in Esme Walmsley. 'I don't want to upset you because I know how you must feel towards me, but I do want this baby. It may be the only child I ever have. We've waited several years without children and I began to think I might never have a child.'

'Perhaps if your husband knew of our interest, he would feel differently.'

Esme snapped to attention. 'Don't you try to browbeat me, Mrs Granger! Threats will not serve you well at all! There is no way you can prove that this child is not Leo's and I shall deny it.'

'But you have already confessed the truth to more than one person! Your sister told my brother-in-law and he wrote to tell me.'

'Millie told him?' Esme reeled. The knowledge of her sister's betrayal was like a physical blow.

'I'm afraid so, but you mustn't blame her. The initial fault lies squarely with you and Henry.'

Esme's mind raced. 'I could deny it! I could pretend I lied...'

'I understand you also told your husband the truth.'

Esme stared at her speechlessly. Millie had brought the world crashing down on her. She thought desperately. 'Maybe I lied to her – to Leo...'

'But why would you do that? Why would you hurt your husband with such a lie?' She sat up a little straighter. 'I have to tell you that we have spoken to our lawyers about the situation. It all depends on Henry's mother. I shall go home and report our conversation. She would have come herself but is bed-ridden with rheumatism.'

They both turned to the door as Millie reappeared with a tea tray and a plate of biscuits. Really, thought Esme crossly, there was no reason to make the wretched woman quite so welcome. Biscuits indeed. Why had Millie done this to her? She would never forgive her.

Millie said, 'I won't join you. I've a few jobs to do.'

That was true, thought Esme. The bed was unmade, the breakfast things were unwashed, there was a pile of washing to be ironed and Mrs Wetton wouldn't be in until after lunch.

Millie withdrew and Esme poured the tea; for a few moments they sipped in silence.

Mrs Granger said, 'Our children, two boys, were both well educated. We are concerned that this child—'

'That would be no business of yours!'

'We might be willing to help financially and we would certainly wish to maintain contact with the child. Until we have spoken with our lawyers—'

'Please don't bother to do any such thing. If you make any claim against my child, I shall deny everything and challenge you.'

'Your husband should be told of our offer, should we make one. He is going to incur all the expenses of bringing up a child and I can assure you it is no small sum. Or we could ask to have the child made a ward of court. So please don't be too hasty, Mrs Walmsley.'

'And don't you be too presumptuous, Mrs Granger!' Esme felt the colour mount in her face. A crumb of biscuit went down the wrong way and she coughed inelegantly. In desperation she said, 'I can't imagine that you could want to bring up your husband's love-child. No woman would.'

'Stranger things have happened, Mrs Walmsley. I did love my husband, whatever he might have told you and whatever he might have done.'

Esme struggled to contain her anger, fuelled as it was with fear. She stared fearfully at Henry's widow. The woman's self-control was enviable. Esme felt breathless with anxiety. This was all Millie's stupid fault. With an effort she stood up.

'I don't think this conversation is going anywhere useful,' she said as haughtily as she could manage. 'It seems a shame to keep the cab waiting. I think you should leave.'

Mrs Granger looked disconcerted. She put down her cup, dabbed her mouth with a handkerchief and stood up also. 'You will probably hear from our lawyer before the week is out,' she said. 'I'm sorry that you have been so uncooperative. It hasn't helped, has it?' She picked up her gloves and purse.

Esme hesitated, hoping to regain full control of the situation but not knowing how. The mention of a lawyer unnerved her because that meant Leo would have to know about this visit. Too late Esme wished she had been nicer to her visitor. She should have said she was sorry. She led the way in silence to the front door.

Mrs Granger said, 'Please thank your sister for her courtesy.' She swept out and down the steps to the waiting cab.

Esme watched her go with mixed feelings. The meeting had been a disaster – another disaster. She would have to tell Leo before the letter came from the lawyers. A cold dread settled in her already uneasy stomach. Suppose Leo wanted to give up the child...

Eleven

A little later, when Millie heard Leo's key turn in the lock, she felt the familiar rush of excitement at the knowledge that he was near. Annoyed with herself she counted to ten and then said quietly, 'He means nothing to you now.' The trouble was, that had been easy to say when she had had Edmund in her life, but now he too had betrayed her, she was in no mood to be strong. Added to which, she now had to tell him that Edmund was no longer in her life. The thought jarred. Would he gloat? Would he be truly sorry? Had he ever been pleased that her prospects had seemed so good? Or was he pretending? She had no way of knowing but...

He came into the kitchen smiling. 'I remembered this was your day here,' he told her. 'I left a few minutes early to...' He looked around. 'Where's Esme?'

'She felt very weak and – and shocked. She had a visitor. I'll tell you all about it.'

'A visitor?' Wary now, he allowed her to help him off with his coat, which he then carried to the hallstand.

'I'll explain while you're eating.'

'How does it happen that you have to break

all the bad news? Is she awake? Should I go up?'

'She's probably still sleeping,' Millie lied. 'I'll serve up in two minutes.'

She had cooked a beef pudding and now set to, cutting it into portions and adding cabbage and potatoes and generous gravy. At least she could break the news to him without a quarrel resulting from the information. Esme, she knew, would have ended up in tears and Leo would have lost patience with her.

As they ate, she began the story of the morning's encounter and had to remind Leo more than once that he could eat and listen at the same time.

He swallowed a mouthful of food and laid down his knife and fork. 'You're saying that they either want to help maintain the child or … or what, exactly?'

'Or maybe take it into their family. In other words, adopt the child and bring it up as theirs.'

'And the wife *wanted* to do this? I can hardly believe she could feel so magnanimous!'

'Eat, Leo!' she said again, although she had now laid down her own cutlery. 'It seems to be the mother-in-law who wants the child. She seems to be a matriarch of the old-fashioned kind. All-powerful. It's her grandchild, you see.'

Leo closed his eyes, his expression one of deep despair. 'Will we ever come to the end of this nightmare?' he asked. Opening his eyes

257

he regarded her soberly. 'I don't know how much longer I can put up with this, Millie. I don't have to ask if Esme might be willing to give up the child. That would be too much to hope for.'

In spite of her reservations, Millie reached out and patted his hand. 'She won't even consider it, and she has alienated poor Mrs Granger, who is not to blame for any of this. *Her* only mistake was in marrying Henry Granger! The truth is, Leo, I think she is probably a very nice person. I feel sorry for her – and for you, naturally. And for poor Esme who is being truly punished for her mistake.'

Leo pushed away his dinner. 'I can't eat,' he told her. 'Sorry, Millie. I dare say I shall have to talk to Esme when she condescends to wake up, but the way I see it there are two alternatives: either we agree to hand over the child completely and tell it nothing about its true mother, or we keep it and the Grangers have nothing to do with its maintenance. Anything in between would be unfair on the child...' He stood up suddenly.

Millie said, 'There's some stewed apples.'

He shook his head. 'There's something else I need to ask you, Millie. It's about this Edmund fellow. I have to tell you he worries me. That sort of—'

'That's over,' Millie muttered, not meeting his gaze. 'We had a – a difference of opinion and I – I ended it.' There was no way she could tell him how shabbily she'd been used.

258

It would be too humiliating.

'I'm really pleased to hear that, Millie. You know how I feel about you. I know I can't care for you myself – and that is my burden – but nor can I stand by and see you hurt. Not if I can prevent it.'

Millie fussed with the serviette and then rose and began to collect the plates. 'I know, Leo. We have got ourselves in a fine muddle but...' She wanted to say something hopeful about the future, but it seemed impossible.

He gave a short laugh. 'It's as though a pebble has been thrown into a pond and the ripples are widening. Now the Grangers are involved. Circles upon circles and no way to stop them. That damned Henry has a lot to answer for!'

Millie passed him with her pile of plates and said nothing. Leo had said it all.

Four days later Ned and his father walked along Carsley Road in thoughtful silence. It was no worse and no better than many streets in the heart of London – terraced houses, each with a basement reached by area steps. A few plane trees survived, but most had withered, ruined by unskilled pruning and lack of interest exacerbated by heavy soot pollution from the countless coal fires. The traffic, however, was not as heavy as in some of the surrounding streets and therefore the smell from the manure on the road was less.

Ned, aware of the deficiencies, said, 'Course, we'll move later when the money

259

comes in.'

'Oh aye, and when will that be?'

'Might move up in the firm – or get another job. I don't have to be a bailiff all my life, although I've good prospects where I am.'

His father shrugged. 'Nothing wrong with the job. Honest work ... What number is it?'

'Twelve. Up the other end.'

They moved apart to pass two ragged boys who were tussling on the ground, and immediately repeated the action to avoid an old woman with a small handcart laden with pieces of coal and twigs. From the sudden shrieks of protest that followed it seemed she had run the cart into the boys, but Ned and his father ignored their cries and walked on, their minds on more important matters.

'Here we are!' Ned said at last and produced a key from his pocket. 'Welcome to my humble abode!'

His father snorted. 'Give over, son! It's not yours yet and any rate you're only renting it!'

They went inside and found themselves in a dim hallway with a flight of bare stairs ahead.

Ned said, 'Chap upstairs is a German Jew. Watchmaker. Lives alone. Basement's a widow woman with three kids.' He opened a door on the left and they entered a bright room in desperate need of repair: skirting board frayed by damp, painted walls flaking, ceiling yellowed and stained and crumbling in the corners. There was a small grate. Nothing spectacular, but Ned saw it in his mind's eye and his spirits lifted. He waved a

260

hand. 'Touch it all up a bit. Pot of paint, new skirting, wash the ceiling, blacklead the grate. Be nice with a bit of a fire going.' He glanced at his father, hoping for approval, but Stan gave a cautious grunt that might have meant anything

There was a bedroom in a similar state and a scullery that overlooked a small yard.

Ned stared round the scullery with narrow-ed eyes as he pictured how it would be. 'Cold water on tap!' Ned told the older man. 'None of that trekking along the road to the stand-pipe with buckets and jugs! Shelves would have to come down and I'd put something decent up.'

Stanley said, 'I could do that for you'; then, in case he sounded too willing, quickly made a disparaging remark about the tiny yard with its outside privy. They went out through the back door and stood in the winter sunshine. At the end of the yard there was a fence with a gate that led into a narrow alley. This was for the access of the dustman. A large woman in the garden on their left was hanging up washing.

She removed a peg from her mouth and called a greeting. 'Moving in, are you?' she asked.

'Not me,' said Stanley.

'I will be, soon as I've smartened it up.' Ned returned the smile. This would be one of their neighbours. 'You lived here long?'

'Nearly five years. It's fairly quiet.' She shook out a shirt and pegged it to the line.

'Just me and my hubby since our boy joined the military. Married, are you?'

'Soon will be!' he laughed.

She picked up the washing basket and went indoors.

Ned looked at the balding grass and the ramshackle shed. 'Soon get this nice and trim. You reckon she'll like it?'

Stan nodded. 'Like as not. Women like things pretty. Your ma liked flowers. We had those tall things.'

'Hollyhocks! I remember staring up at them when I was a nipper.' He grinned suddenly and pointed to the grass. 'Room for a pram!'

'Get away! You're a bit young to start that sort of thing!' Stan nudged him with his elbow. 'So what's the deal with this place? You said you were getting it cheap.'

'Landlord's knocking half the rent off for the first year if I do it up. Piece of cake!' He tried not to look too pleased with himself.

'Does she know anything about this?'

Ned shook his head. 'Wouldn't want her to see it like this. You know women. She'd be bound to want to see it once she knew. When it's looking good, I'll bring her down here and pop the question. She won't be able to resist me!' He laughed.

His father sighed. 'Suppose she does?'

'She won't!' He was surprised by the question.

'But you haven't seen her for some time. She could have met someone else.'

The idea sent a shiver down Ned's spine.

'Not Millie!' The thought had crossed his mind, but he simply could not consider such a disaster. If he dwelt on that suspicion he would go mad. No. There was no other man on the horizon. 'She's busy, that's all.' He refused to consider the possibility that Millie might not marry him. 'What with that blooming sister of hers and the job at Tapper's.'

'So she hasn't – you know ... gone off you?'

'Course she hasn't!' He repressed his uneasy memories of their last meeting. 'She's a very independent sort of woman, you see. That's what I admire. One of the things, anyway. She's been stuck at home for years with her invalid father and now she wants to have ... a little freedom before she settles down. It's only natural.'

'Freedom?' Stanley, astonished, scratched his head. 'She's not one of these modern women, is she? Not demanding the vote? Nothing like that, I hope!'

Ned frowned. 'Don't rightly know. Never thought to ask.'

To change the subject, Stan asked him how he'd found the flat.

'I'd been sent to chivvy the old woman because she owed nineteen weeks' rent and the owner reckoned he'd been patient long enough. What did I find? She was dead from natural causes. Died in her sleep a few days earlier with the cat on the pillow beside her. The cat wasn't dead, of course, and the neighbour took it.'

'Poor old soul!'

Ned shrugged. 'You could say she died just in time. She'd have been turfed out on to the street and most likely ended up in the workhouse. Better to die in her own bed.'

Having seen the flat, Ned had seen the possibilities and had approached the landlord. Feeling very proud of himself, Ned was relying on Millie to be impressed. He was determined to keep the place a secret until it was ready; then he would bring Millie to see it and ask her to marry him.

He glanced at his father. 'So if you see her, say nothing about it. Not a word! Don't tell her where I am or what I'm doing. It has to be a complete surprise.'

Stan rolled his eyes. 'Bank on it, Ned. Your secret is safe with me!'

Unaware of the plans being made for her future, Millie continued with her life – working at Tapper's in the evenings and spending time each week with her sister, who seemed to be making little progress. The sickness continued, she had lost her appetite and was also becoming morose. Refusing to face the fact that she had brought the trouble upon herself, she blamed an unkind fate and saw herself as the victim of circumstances beyond her control. She was full of self-pity and there were times when Millie longed to shake her. But there were more times when she pitied her unhappy existence and she consulted with the doctor on more than one occasion.

'She is so listless, Doctor, and so restless at

night. I don't think it's good for her or the baby. Isn't there anything you can give her to lighten her mood? I can't bear to see her like this.'

The doctor offered various medicines and pick-me-ups, but nothing did any good. At last he suggested she drink a glass of stout at the end of each day; this did have the effect of helping Esme to sleep at night and Millie fancied she was a little stronger. She also gained a few pounds, which the doctor approved.

Leo was also causing Millie some concern. He tried to show an interest in his wife's progress, but Millie saw that he was simply going through the motions and was not convinced that he would ever reconcile himself to the child when it was born. What would happen then? Millie wondered. On one occasion she tried to talk to Poppy about the problems but was given short shrift.

'Don't bleat to me about your unhappy sister!' Poppy snapped. 'She has a good husband but she wasn't satisfied. She betrayed Leo, she betrayed Henry's wife and she betrayed me!' Seeing Millie's expression, she said, 'Well, didn't she? I was Henry's mistress. Nothing wrong with that. London must be full of mistresses. Knock on any door!' She tossed her head crossly. 'Dozens of men take a mistress. Even royalty! Henry the Eighth had a mistress as well as all his wives! Esme had no reason to stir the pot. If she's suffering now, it's only right after the way she behaved.'

Startled by this rebuke and uncertain of the logic of Poppy's argument, Millie decided never to mention her sister again or, if she did mention her, she would remember not to expect any sympathy. Now that Poppy had enough money to pay her own rent, Millie felt she was living on borrowed time and that at any moment Poppy might ask her to find somewhere else to live.

When the letter came from Maria Granger, Millie resisted the urge to share the contents with Poppy and hurried round to the bank to consult Leo. As soon as she was shown into his office she handed the envelope to him and sat down.

'I've received this letter from Henry Granger's mother,' she explained nervously. 'I'm not sure how to deal with it.'

'Granger's mother?' he echoed and began to read aloud:

Dear Miss Bayley,
    As you will know, I have learned from my son Edmund that your sister is expecting a child fathered by Henry, my other son. This child will be one of my grandchildren and as such I shall be most concerned about its welfare. I have discussed the matter with my daughter-in-law, who has agreed that we should adopt the child as soon as it is born.

Leo glanced up and Millie saw the hope in his eyes. He said, 'It would be one way out but...'

'But Esme will never agree!'

'I suppose not.'

'Would it save your marriage, Leo? If she *did* agree?'

'Ah! That's the question!' He shook his head. 'I doubt if anything can save it, Millie, but without this man's child it might just be bearable.' He continued to read:

I would like to talk to your sister but I am bedridden and unable to travel. I do not have her address but would appreciate it if you would pass on this letter to her so that she and her husband can consider the proposal. Perhaps they could travel down to Somerset to Harlene Hall to visit with our family. I can assure you that the child will be loved and treated as part of the family. Please ask your sister and her husband to give this matter serious thought as soon as possible. We would like to be in touch with our lawyers on the subject of the adoption.

Yours sincerely,
Maria Granger.

Leo held out the letter. 'Has Esme seen this?'

'Not yet.' Rejecting the letter, she said, 'You keep it. The contents are intended for you and Esme, not me.' She regarded him unhappily.

He smiled wanly. 'Poor little Millie. You don't deserve all this worry. It is none of your making, but you seem to be suffering as much as any of us! It's most unfair.' He took her hand in his. 'I'd do anything to undo the harm I've done you. All this misery for all of us. I blame myself.'

'Oh no, Leo! You can't—'

'But it all started when I turned my back on you and everything that has happened since has stemmed from that false move.' His voice shook. 'The guilt – knowing that I'm to blame ... It's a punishment. Oh Millie! Darling Millie! I can't bear this much longer!' He half-rose from his chair, drawing her hand closer and pressing it to his chest.

Alarmed by the turn of the conversation, Millie gently withdrew her hand, but his defeated expression was more than she could bear and for a long moment they stared at each other across the desk. Leo pushed back his chair and turned to come round the desk, but Millie took fright. She longed to hold him in her arms, but she dared not allow anything to develop between them. She must keep her feelings in check and Leo must be discouraged from thinking of her in a romantic light. Their lives had changed dramatically and there was no going back. She held up a warning hand and sat back on her chair. Leo hesitated and she saw the hurt in his eyes but forced herself to ignore it. When he had resumed his seat, she went on as though nothing untoward had happened.

'I thought perhaps you should see it first. Esme is so unresponsive these days and so easily upset. This won't help her, will it?'

It was not a question and they both knew it. The thought of parting with the child would send Esme into a state of hysteria. For a while he didn't answer as he fought with his emotions, but at last he was able to answer her.

'It won't.' He shrugged. 'The thought of motherhood is all that keeps her going. She talks of nothing else. Damn Henry Granger! I hate the very thought of him and I'm glad he's dead. I wish he had died a few months earlier! I wish I had killed him! He was a menace to women and that's the truth!' He rubbed his eyes wearily. 'Not that I'm much better!'

'Don't say that! You're not in the least like Henry Granger!'

Alarmed by his passionate outburst, Millie longed for the meeting to end, but they had come to no decision.

'Will you show Esme the letter?'

'No, because I know what her answer would be. And how can I go down to Somerset? How could I explain it to Esme?'

A silence fell between them, broken by a knock on the door. A young woman came in with a handful of letters for Leo to sign.

Leo took them from her and said, 'Thank you, Miss Levine.'

The young woman looked curiously at Millie, who wondered how much the staff at the bank knew of Leo's problems – if they knew anything. Maybe he had managed to keep his personal life private.

When the woman left them Leo said, 'Would *you* go down to see them, Millie? – as my emissary, if you like. It's a lot to ask, but you could explain it all – make them understand Esme's feelings.'

Millie hid her dismay. Go to Harlene Hall on such a mission? Could she cope with that? Her first instinct was to refuse. 'But you can write to them, Leo. You can put a good letter together.' She thought briefly of the wonderful letters he had once written to her but resolutely pushed the memory aside. 'Say Esme is unwell and you are unable to leave her.'

'Millie! A letter won't do. We both know it.' He leaned forward, his elbows on the desk, and met her eyes steadily. 'And aren't you the tiniest bit curious about the Grangers? And Harlene Hall? Aren't you curious about Maria Granger? I confess I am. She is obviously determined to be involved. She might want to see the child on occasions. She is related to it and we can't deny that. Esme may have to face up to that later on. It would help if we knew more about them.'

'But they are sure to put pressure on me, Leo,' she protested. 'They'll want me to persuade Esme to part with her baby and I can't do that. I won't!'

Leo, however, was not to be denied. Ten minutes later Millie left the bank and walked down the street, her head in a whirl. She had agreed to visit the Grangers at their home and to explain Esme's attitude towards the coming child. Leo would write and make all the arrangements and she would have to ask for a few days' absence from Tapper's. But as she walked, her stride grew more brisk and the frown left her face. She was still unhappy about deceiving her sister, but that was Leo's responsibility and if she was honest, she *was* curious about Henry Granger's family, especially Dorcas. She knew the 'other women' in Henry's life and it would be interesting to meet the rest.

It was gone two o'clock on the the sixteenth of December when Millie arrived at the door of Harlene Hall – a large, elegant building standing in extensive grounds. Impressed, she rang the bell and was greeted by a neatly dressed maid, who gave a small respectful bob and said, 'You're expected, Miss Bayley.'

Millie, her heart fluttering with nervous anticipation, followed her along a broad hallway and into a large expensively furnished drawing room. It was the sort of room she had never expected to find herself in and she tried not to be intimidated by her surroundings.

Dorcas rose to meet her, smiling nervously while one hand fiddled with a string of pearls.

'Miss Bayley,' she said. 'Thank you for coming all this way. I hope the train journey was reasonably comfortable. It's not my favourite form of transport. Do please sit down.'

Millie sat. So far she hadn't said a word. She had bought a new hat for the occasion and was wearing her best kid gloves, but she still felt out of place in the grand surroundings. Astonishing, she thought. Henry Granger had had all this yet was dissatisfied. He had found himself a mistress and then a second woman. She wondered how much Dorcas had known or guessed about her husband's life in London.

'I shall take you upstairs shortly to see my mother-in-law.' She leaned forward. 'I must tell you that adopting Henry's love-child is my mother-in-law's idea, not mine. She will do her best to persuade your sister that becoming part of the Granger family is in everyone's best interest.'

'But it would be you who brought the child up.'

'Exactly! Not that I am saying I wouldn't do it. If Maria makes up her mind, I wouldn't have any choice but...' She sighed. 'I have brought up my family and I now have to care for Henry's mother. In other words, Miss Bayley, I have a lot of responsibilities already. I could have wished Henry had not fathered another child, but it cannot be undone.'

She stopped for breath and Millie said, 'My sister, Esme, has always wanted a child, but for some reason it didn't happen. I have to tell you that this crisis has thrown her into a deep depression and the thought of becoming a mother is all that holds her together.'

'A deep depression!' Dorcas stared at her.

'My mother-in-law will not be pleased to hear that! Depression can be difficult to conquer. Is she fit enough to bring up the child? ... How about your sister's husband? Is he willing to relinquish the child?'

'He would be – but only if Esme is willing. He won't do anything to deepen the wedge between them. And it is a wedge. It has naturally caused tremendous problems for them both.'

A maid knocked and entered, carrying a tray with tea and biscuits which she set on a low table between Millie and Dorcas. For a few moments no one spoke while the maid poured the tea and then withdrew.

After a long, uncomfortable silence Dorcas said, 'I want to apologize about the way Edmund learned of the child. His behaviour towards you was unforgivable. He seemed to find it amusing, but I deplore his underhand tactics and so does his mother.'

Embarrassed, Millie didn't know how to reply and Dorcas continued: 'Edmund Granger is not a very nice man, Miss Bayley. In case you ever had any hopes in that direction, I suggest you think yourself fortunate that he is out of your life for ever. At least I hope he is. I have never found anything to admire in Edmund's character: selfish, devious, totally unscrupulous...!' Her face had hardened.

Millie thought that Henry had hardly been a saint but kept the notion to herself; at that moment the door burst open and a young man rushed into the room.

He had ginger hair and green eyes and was halfway to becoming a handsome man, although his nose was a little too narrow. Millie guessed him to be about seventeen years old. So this was one of Henry's sons, she thought.

'Lance! Can't you see I have a visitor?'

Would Esme's child look like that if it were a boy? Millie wondered. She tried to imagine a much younger Lance. He might have been a charming child.

Dorcas turned on him irritably. 'I asked you to stay out of here.'

'Sorry, Mama. I just wanted to let you know I need the trap. I'm going over to Brian's to shoot a few rabbits.' He cast a glance in Millie's direction and she felt immediately that he had dismissed her instantly as not worth his attention. She felt her face flush under the insult but said nothing. What could she say?

Dorcas said, 'That's fine, but rub down the horse when you get back. You left it for the groom last time and he wasn't too pleased!'

'It's his job!'

'Not after his working hours! And drop a brace of rabbits in for the Littons.'

He groaned. 'Not the Littons, Mama! They're so dreary and will insist on conversation. They still treat me like a child.' He adopted a strong local accent. ' 'Ow's school, Master Lance?' The boy rolled his eyes. 'As if they care one jot!'

Dorcas said, 'Just be nice to them.

274

They're—'

'...our tenants!' He groaned. 'I know!'

'Give them the rabbits! The husband's out of work with a broken arm and they're needy.' She waved an impatient hand and, with an exaggerated sigh, the boy withdrew.

Dorcas said, 'If you ever have a son, Miss Bayley, don't spoil him. It does them no favours...'

'I have no plans to marry.' Millie recalled how recently she had imagined a future for herself with Edmund, but that was all over.

With the other woman's encouragement she spoke about Esme's condition and Leo's feelings and finally Dorcas decided she should meet her mother-in-law. Millie glanced at the ornate ormolu clock on the mantelpiece and, seeing this, Dorcas said, 'There is no need to travel back this evening, Miss Bayley. We have plenty of room and can offer you a comfortable room and breakfast in the morning.'

Taken aback, Millie muttered something indecisive and the matter rested. She followed Dorcas along the corridor and up a wide oak staircase. The wall was hung with the portraits of past members of the Granger family. It was obvious there was money in the family – or had been in the past. The portraits showed young children on ponies, little boys with large hounds, women in quality clothes and stern-looking men holding leatherbound Bibles. At last she was shown into a large room, where an elderly women was

275

propped in a chair. A nurse was fussing around her but was immediately sent out.

'Mama, this is Miss Bayley, Esme Walmsley's sister.'

Millie looked at the old lady and found her daunting. She sat erect. Her grey hair, parted in the middle, was swept back into a chignon beneath the black lace cap. Her nightdress was hidden beneath a large silk shawl and a large rug covered her knees. For a long time she said nothing but subjected Millie to a fierce stare. Then she said, 'Sit down, please. We have to talk.'

Dorcas fetched a chair and, w' . an enigmatic glance at Millie, left the room.

Millie said, 'I'm sorry my sister was unable to come. Also her husband. He doesn't care to leave her alone while she is in this state.'

'State? What do you mean?'

'Rather depressed. It's all been very upsetting.'

'We, too, have been upset, Miss Bayley. Dorcas is being very strong, but she is naturally deeply hurt by events. Not that I didn't warn her. Any woman who marries a Granger is asking for trouble! They've always been the same.' She sighed. 'But we needn't waste time talking about Henry. His child is the problem. Dorcas is undecided but I am not. Dorcas is only a Granger by marriage, like me, but I go back further and I think like a Granger. I want the child, Miss Bayley. He will be a Granger and part of this family. I know the Walmsleys would care for the boy and I'm thankful it isn't Prunella Gayford who is with child – but we can do much better. The child's future is paramount, wouldn't you say?'

Pleased to be given a chance to speak, Millie said, 'I don't think the child would be happy with Dorcas as a mother if Dorcas wasn't willing. Esme, however, is determined never to part with the child.'

Maria smiled. 'I know Dorcas better than she knows herself!' she told Millie. 'She will think differently in a few months' time. Dorcas loved Henry despite his philandering ways and she misses him dreadfully. The child is all that remains of her husband and she will love it.'

'But surely it will remind her of Esme?'

Maria shook her head. 'It will remind her of Henry.' She tucked a stray lock of hair under her lace cap. 'Dorcas wanted more children – she longed for a girl – but fate decreed otherwise. She had three mis-carriages after the boys were born and the doctor warned against any more children. I can assure you that as time goes by my daughter-in-law will be as eager as I am to bring Henry's child to Harlene Hall.'

Millie was aware that Esme's wishes were not being taken into consideration. 'Esme wants a girl,' she said.

'It won't be. There is a dearth of girls in the family. I warned Dorcas, but she ignored me. She wanted a girl and was bitterly disappoint-ed both times.'

Millie decided she must make a stand. 'You need to understand, Mrs Granger, that Esme is afraid that she will never have another child. There have been no children so far. That is why she insists on keeping it, even though your son wanted her to...' She stopped in confusion.

Maria looked shaken by this inadvertent revelation. 'He wanted her to get rid of the child?'

Millie nodded. 'Perhaps we should keep that from your daughter-in-law,' she suggested, but Maria was obviously shaken.

'How could he?' she muttered, her eyes closed, her hands agitated. 'My own son!' Eventually she turned her attention to Millie again and said, 'What's that you say?'

Millie repeated it.

'Indeed we must. Dorcas would be beside herself to know that he...' She drew herself up with an effort. 'The boy will get an excellent education. He will ride, travel, will marry well. It would be selfish of them to deny him these opportunities. Has your sister considered all this?'

Millie hesitated. 'She doesn't know about your offer. Both Leo and I know that the thought that she might lose the child would seriously undermine her health, which isn't good at the moment.'

The old lady blinked in sudden consternation. 'What's wrong with her, Miss Bayley? She must have the best doctor you can find. We will willingly pay for her medical care.'

Millie explained that her sister was depressed and not eating well. 'The doctor is afraid she has some slight inflammation of the brain. That is why it may be unwise to tell her—'

Maria Granger interrupted her. 'You mentioned it earlier, but I hadn't realized the severity of the problem,' she said slowly. 'There is a very good man in Harley Street. I'll give you his name and you can send the bill straight to us. Mr Barnett – William Barnett. He and my husband were friends, although William was a good deal younger. A very good doctor indeed.'

Millie was beginning to feel anxious. It was obvious that Maria Granger had already made up her mind that Esme's child would become part of the family and Millie could understand her reasoning; but she also understood her sister and knew that, in her place, she would never give up her baby. What on earth was Leo going to say when she reported back to him? He might well be persuaded to side with Maria and that would create more problems and heartache.

As if reading her mind, Maria said, 'You must tell your sister my plans as soon as you get back to London. When she has recovered and is well enough to travel, she must come to Harlene Hall and meet the family. She will soon realize that her duty is to the boy and his future welfare.' She reached for a small hand-bell and rang it sharply. 'I shall write to your sister if you feel unable to talk to her about it.

279

One way or another she will learn of my plans.' She frowned. 'Where is that nurse? Ah! About time!'

The nurse came in and Millie wondered if this was a signal for her to leave, but the nurse hurried to the bedside table, poured medicine into a spoon and gave it to her patient. Maria screwed up her face with disgust and the nurse gave her a violet cachou to take away the taste.

When she had gone again, Maria said, 'You must stay the night. Too much travelling weakens the system, you know. All that jolting. Especially bad for women, I'm told. Rattles the skeleton and disturbs the inner organs.' She closed her eyes briefly; for a moment her face lost its stern expression and Millie was given a glimpse of the younger Maria, who must have been beautiful. She was aware of a sneaking admiration for the old woman who was determined to do well by her dead son's love-child.

But it was never going to happen. She knew that but kept her counsel. I'm only the messenger, she reminded herself – Leo's 'emissary'. She smiled faintly. She had had very little lunch – a slice of pie and an apple which she had carried in a small picnic hamper. The thought of a good meal and a comfortable bed was very seductive.

'I'll accept your kind offer to stay over-night,' she said. 'I admit I am rather tired.'

'Splendid!' To Millie's surprise, a smile finally brightened Maria's face. 'Tea will be served in twenty minutes,' she told Millie, 'and dinner is at seven. There is no need to change if you have brought nothing with you. No one will mind. Dorcas will lend you a nightdress. I'm sure she will enjoy some company. We are very far from London here and have few visitors. Dare I say it – Dorcas will welcome some gossip!'

Five minutes later, Millie left her in the care of the nurse, who was settling her down for an afternoon nap, and made her way down-stairs. So there was a human face to the old lady, she mused. That was a relief. Perhaps the Grangers were not quite as cold and calculating as she had feared.

Twelve

Millie travelled back the next morning with her head full of new anxieties. One anxiety, however, had been dispelled. She now knew that the Granger family were well intentioned and would, if given the chance, make a happy home for Esme's child. She had half-hoped that she would dislike them and would be able to say so. Now, however, she had no option but to be truthful. Dinner the previous evening had been a surprisingly cheerful affair; even Lance had exhibited good manners towards her and seemed surprisingly eager to have a young brother – or sister.

Before catching her train back to London, Millie had been invited to walk in the nearby woods with Dorcas and the two black labradors. The weather was cold but there was a wintry sun and they moved briskly through the wood, skirting the large trees, their feet rustling through a thick layer of autumn leaves. Millie was entranced, amazed at the peaceful scene, which was only disturbed by the antics of the dogs.

Their conversation had been easier than Millie had expected, for Dorcas had shown an interest in her and she had found herself confiding in her about her friendship with Ned Warren and her job at Tapper's. To her surprise, Dorcas had envied her her life, confessing that, for children, life at Harlene Hall was ideal, but that for a woman it could be 'deadly dull' at times; and life at Tapper's sounded exciting! She also referred to Ned on one occasion as 'that charming young man of yours', which rather surprised Millie and gave her something to think about on the journey home.

But for most of the journey back to London Millie rehearsed how she would describe her stay with the Grangers. Leo might well feel that the child's adoption by the Grangers would be a better solution, but she had made up her mind that, once she had passed on the information, she wanted nothing more to do with the problem. The decisions were up to Leo and he could no longer expect her to act on his behalf.

The church clock had just struck four; Millie's thoughts were still miles away when she let herself into the flat and was startled to hear shrieks of laughter. Obviously Poppy had company. Pulling off her gloves and unbuttoning her coat, she called, 'Poppy! I'm back!' and moved into the drawing room. There was no sign of anyone, but a trail of clothes led to the bedroom door. Embarrassed, Millie hesitated. Should she call out again or put on her coat and creep away? Before she could decide the bedroom door opened and a young man came into the room. His upper body was bare, but the rest was covered by army breeches with dangling braces. His feet were bare, his sandy hair was tousled, but he was nice-looking and he carried an empty champagne bottle.

For a moment they stared at each other in shock. Millie retreated a few steps.

He began to laugh at her consternation and turned to call over his shoulder. 'Poppy! We have another young woman here. Shall I ask her to join us?'

There was a shriek from the bedroom and Millie retreated further, her face burning. 'Please!' she murmured. 'I'm not stopping. I just called in to – to collect...' To collect *what*? Millie's mind was a blank.

He said, 'Oh dear! We've made her blush! Never seen a man with his braces down?' He winked. 'I'm sure this won't be the last time!'

She was frozen with embarrassment

Poppy came out with a sheet wrapped round her. Her eyes were bright and her hair hung loosely curled around her smooth shoulders. In a word, she looked radiant. Millie thought, Whatever she's doing, it suits her!

Poppy hiccuped then put a hand to her mouth in mock dismay. 'Millie, meet Clive! Clive, meet Millie! Trust you to turn up like a bad penny.'

'I'm sorry! Really I didn't think. I was just eager to tell you all about...'

Clive said, 'Don't run away, poppet! I've no aversion to *two* women!' He turned to Poppy.

284

'You didn't tell me about this little darling! That was naughty of you!'

Little darling! Millie cringed. She wondered how long Poppy had known the man. She had never mentioned anyone called Clive.

Poppy grinned at him and said, 'You were looking for the second bottle! Go get it!' She smiled at Millie. 'I thought you'd go straight to your sister's. Sorry if we startled you. Clive's a friend of the dreadful Edmund, who thought, quite rightly, that we'd like each other.' She raised her eyebrows. 'And we do! So ... could you possibly lose yourself for a couple of hours? He's got to get back to Sandhurst this evening, so we haven't got much time.'

'Of course. I'm so sorry. I'll go round to Esme's.' Millie backed into the hallway and reached for her coat and gloves.

Poppy disappeared back into the bedroom, but Clive, carrying a bottle of champagne, followed Millie to the door. As she reached for the lock, he pulled her towards him with his free hand and pushed her against the wall.

Taken by surprise and crushed by his weight, Millie felt breathless and her attempted protest came out as a hoarse cry, which made him laugh.

He whispered, 'I'd like you to stay! A three-some could be exciting.' His free hand was sliding down her body.

Millie struggled to free herself, but she was trapped. Leaning forward, he kissed her on the mouth, then put a finger to his lips and whispered, 'Not a word!'

Poppy shouted, 'Come on, Clive! I'm thirsty!'

'Duty calls!' he whispered and drew back, releasing her.

Outside the door, Millie fled down the stairs on trembling legs, pulling on her coat as she went and cursing her luck. She had interrupted their love-making! Would Poppy ever forgive her? And as for Clive ... and that illicit kiss! Her cheeks burned at the thought of it; but then guilt filled her as she admitted to herself that it *had* been exciting. Had she betrayed Poppy by keeping the kiss a secret? Should she have called Clive's bluff by calling for Poppy to 'rescue' her? Poppy might well have assumed it was Millie's fault and accused her of flirting with him. Clive might even had made that his excuse! No. Much better to say nothing and forget the whole incident.

She thought suddenly of Dorcas hankering for the excitements of life in London and reflected, 'You don't know how lucky you are, Dorcas! Make the most of your peaceful existence. London can be a little too exciting at times!'

Halfway to The Laurels, Millie changed her mind. She wanted to speak with Leo before she saw Esme, but she had no desire to endure another session at the bank. That particular conversation must wait, she decided. For a moment she hesitated, trying to calm her feelings. Was she welcome anywhere? she wondered unhappily. Perhaps Ned would be pleased to see her. Impulsively she changed direction and made her way to Stanley Warren's workshop in the hope of seeing Ned. Since their last meeting she had felt guilty about the lies she had told – pretending that she wanted to be independent and so on, when the truth was that she had been stupidly infatuated with Edmund Granger. Perhaps 'making a fool of herself with Edmund Granger' would be a more honest description. Now she wondered if Ned had met anyone else while they were apart. It would serve her right if he had. There had never been a real understanding between them.

What had Dorcas called Ned? She frowned. 'That charming young man of yours'. *Her* young man? Was that how others saw the relationship? Perhaps that was how Ned had seen it.

'Oh Ned! I'm sorry!' she whispered.

He had certainly talked of marriage but in an indirect way. Had she misunderstood, or did he really want to marry her? And if so, did he still want to, or had she frightened him away by her talk of independence? More to the point, did *she* want to marry *him*? Could she ever be happy with anyone but Leo?

She found Stanley busy in his workshop, bent over his bench, planing a narrow length of wood. When he caught sight of her in the doorway, he stopped and stepped in front of his work. 'It's nothing,' he said quickly. 'Just a

– a bit of skirting board for – for someone. A customer.' His smile was unnaturally bright.

Hiding her surprise, she said, 'How are you? I've been away visiting friends in Somerset.'

'Zummerzet?' He laughed. 'I've heard of it, but blessed if I know where it is.'

'The south-west.'

'Ah! That's it then. Nice is it?'

'Very pleasant. Is Ned about?'

'...He's at work.'

'D'you know when he'll be finished?'

'No. No idea.'

He looked nervous, she thought. 'I thought – I'd like to see him, maybe this evening.'

He didn't meet her gaze. 'Not this evening. No. He's busy all evening.'

Millie's heart sank. It sounded as though he had been told to say that. It sounded *rehearsed*. 'I see.' She hesitated.

He said, 'So how's the freedom going?'

'Pardon?'

'Ned was saying how you're one of those modern women. You like your own freedom. Is that what Somerset was? Freedom?'

'Freedom?' Confused, she tried to figure out what he meant.

He said, 'After the vote, are you? Is that it?'

He didn't sound hostile, just nervous. Suddenly she remembered the excuses she had made. Obviously Ned had repeated them to his father. Millie cursed her stupidity. Maybe Ned didn't like modern women and she had alienated him. She opened her mouth to explain what she had meant, but Stanley was

288

once more busy with his plane.

She said, 'Maybe I could see him tomorrow evening, before I go to Tapper's.'

Stan avoided her gaze. 'Happen he'll be busy again,' he muttered. 'I reckon he'll be busy most evenings.'

Millie felt as though he had slapped her. Poor Ned. He was obviously very hurt; his feelings for her had undergone a change and his father wasn't prepared to talk about it. Probably he, too, was annoyed with her. Maybe he had never thought her a suitable woman for Ned and was glad to see the back of her.

Demoralized, she said, 'Goodbye,' and he muttered something without looking at her. Crushed, she retreated. Her heart was heavy as she wandered aimlessly along the pavement. It was plain that she had offended Ned and he didn't want to meet her again. Well, she could hardly blame him. Aware the fault was hers for treating him so casually Millie tried to convince herself that there were plenty more fish in the sea, but the hurt didn't lessen and the pain was increased by knowing that she had hurt Ned. She felt badly about the way she had treated him and her self-esteem plummeted painfully. Making her way into the park, she sat on one of the seats, wrestling with her conscience. Should she write to him and apologize? It might not make any difference, but it was the least she could do ...

Half an hour passed while she watched the

other inhabitants of the park come and go. With Ned beside her, people-watching had been fun, but today she sat alone and envied the young couples arm in arm, and the nannies with their prams reminded her of married life and babies and made her feel wretched and unloved.

For the next twenty minutes she was sunk in self-pity, but eventually her natural resilience won. Her mood brightened and she told herself that 'something would turn up'. She didn't know what, but she rallied a little and determined to accept what had happened and move on.

'No more regrets!' she whispered. 'What's done's done!'

Less than half an hour since, she had been called a little darling by a complete stranger! So she must be reasonably attractive and with luck would meet someone else.

'So there is no need to panic!' she muttered. She thought about Dorcas and then about Esme and thought how much more fortunate she was than either of them. She was unencumbered and all her future was before her. When an elderly lady wandered past with a tubby mongrel on a lead, Millie gave her such a cheerful smile that she promptly sat herself on the seat next to Millie and recounted her husband's recent death in uncomfortable detail.

When she finally wandered off again, Millie decided she had given Clive time to leave Poppy's flat. She was entitled to go back: she paid her rent to Poppy. Arguing herself into a positive frame of mind, she set off with her head held high; but as she turned the corner and headed for the park gates, she missed Ned's warm and friendly presence beside her and her eyes glistened with unshed tears.

All day Wednesday Millie fretted over her unhappy position. The suspicion was growing that she was probably no longer welcome as Poppy's flat-mate now that Poppy was recovering from Henry's death and a new admirer had appeared on the horizon. Also, Millie's financial contribution to the rent was no longer needed, since Henry had left Poppy well provided for. It was now nearly Christmas and Poppy had made several references to friends she planned to invite, and that made it obvious that Millie's sofa would be required.

She was coming to the conclusion that she had been wise to accept Leo's invitation to spend a few days with him and Esme at The Laurels over the Christmas period, but what was she to do after that? She did not want to lose Poppy's friendship; she did not feel able to stay on there, but nor did she want to return to The Laurels permanently. She certainly did not want to give up her job as a dresser at Tapper's, as this was her sole means of support and the only thing that allowed her some independence.

Two days later she was still brooding on her problem as she bent her head over the sewing machine in the confined space of the ladies' dressing room at Tapper's. It was quarter to eight and in the supper room the evening was well under way. The lively tunes of the first hour had given way to softer melodies, which allowed the diners to talk to each other in between mouthfuls of the day's special, which was stewed eels and boiled potatoes followed by steamed treacle pudding and custard.

The costume lady was away for three days, nursing her sick father, and the job of all minor repairs now fell to Millie. Fabric tears, bursting seams and missing buttons all came her way as well as her normal duties; but she had been promised an extra three shillings and, although she was rushed off her feet, she had taken on the extra work gladly. She had Christmas presents to buy. In the past she had had time to make these, but now lack of time forced her to buy them. She had bought Esme a pair of white cotton gloves for the summer and for Leo she had chosen a travel book about Italy. Poppy would receive a silk rose to wear on her best dress and Millie was now wondering whether or not she should buy something for Ned. It would be sad if he *had* discarded her, but if he did still consider himself a friend, it would be awkward if he sent her a present and she had nothing for him. She confided this dilemma to fifty-year-old Jessie, a large woman with a sweet face who currently sang a duet with her husband early in the evening.

Jessie frowned. 'Buy him something cheap

and wait to see if he gives you anything. If he does, you can give him his whatever-it-is.'

Millie carefully snipped the thread and pulled the blouse gingerly from the machine. It was hardly the neatest repair, but from a distance no one would notice.

'I'd make it something edible,' Jessie advised. 'Like a box of Turkish delight. I love Turkish delight ... Then, if you don't have to give it, you can eat it yourself.' She turned back to her mirror and tweaked her curls. 'Lordy! I can see a grey hair!'She winced as she pulled it out. 'I give my father pipe-cleaners.' She was wearing a low-cut dress of dark-green bombazine, which revealed a great deal of her generously powdered bosom, and held an ornate fan that she claimed brought her luck and continued bookings. 'So do you fancy him? This fellow?'

Millie returned the blouse to its hanger and was aware of a deep need to share her feelings with someone. 'Yes I do but ... I met someone else and for a time ... Well, I neglected Ned. That's his name. Then the other man...' She sighed. 'He let me down badly.'

'But you still like him – this Ned?'

'Yes, but I think he's found someone else. I can't blame him.' She swallowed, remembering the hurt she had inflicted so carelessly.

'Found someone else? That's quick, that is. Maybe he never did love you.'

Before Millie could recover from this terrible suggestion there was a knock on the door. It was the conjuror – a thin man with a

293

mournful expression and a drooping moustache. He wore grey serge trousers, a crumpled shirt and a waistcoat that seemed made for a larger man. He held out a black coat with a red lining which was full of interior pockets of varying sizes.

'I'm looking for the costume lady.'

'That's me for the moment.' Millie smiled at him. 'What can I do for you?'

'I hide stuff in these pockets,' he explained, 'but one of them has got a hole in it. Bloomin' awkward it is too. Lost a white mouse last week.'

Jessie shuddered. 'Can't your wife do it?'

'She's passed on.' His face crumpled.

Millie said quickly, 'I'll stitch it for you. It won't take long. You can collect it in ten minutes.'

He thanked her and departed before she could change her mind. Jessie watched disapprovingly as Millie worked on the red silk pocket.

Jessie looked thoughtful. 'He probably never had a wife.'

'Jessie! You've got a nasty, suspicious mind.'

Talking about wives reminded Millie of the conversation that had been interrupted. She said, 'Ned talked about marrying me but I – I thought he was joking.'

'Cheer up!' Jessie leaned forward and patted her knee. 'You can get him back. If he's a decent chap, he'll forgive and forget. If he won't, then maybe he's not as nice as you thought!' She laughed. 'My Harold asked me

294

six times before I said yes!'

Millie regarded her doubtfully. 'But are you glad you accepted him?'

'Course I am! Happy as pigs in muck, we are. Hardly a cross word.' A boy put his head round the door: 'Jessie Turley – three minutes, please!'

Jessie slid carefully from the stool and gave a final glance at her reflection. She pressed her lips together and fluttered her eyelashes. 'My public is clamouring for me!' she mocked and with a grin was gone. Millie heard her footsteps retreating in the direction of the stage.

Nearly two hours later Millie left the Grecian ladies undressing and, her work over, made her way along the passage that led to the stage door. As she passed the stage-doorkeeper's office, he put his head outside and said, 'Young chap was here a while back, looking for you. I said you was busy and told him to come back later.'

Millie's heart leaped. 'Did he give his name?'

'I didn't ask – but he might still be out there, waiting.'

Outside, the usual crowd were huddled inside their coats and scarves, but there was no sign of Ned and Millie's hope faded. He had given up and gone home. Her chance to make amends had slipped away; but at least he had come to find her, which must be a good sign. She was about to turn away when someone touched her shoulder and she turned to find Leo beside her.

'Leo!' She thought immediately that disappointment rang in her voice, but he seemed not to have noticed. 'It's not Esme, is it? She's not...'

'Nothing's wrong. Not exactly, Millie; but I want to walk you home. May I?'

'Certainly.' She gave a last glance round to make sure that if Ned *had* come looking for her, he had now gone, then set out homeward with Leo beside her. After a moment he slipped his arm through hers and she bit back the protest.

'I just wanted to say how much I'm looking forward to Christmas ... because you'll be back home with us. I've missed you so much, Millie. You will never know just how empty the house is without you.'

Millie said nothing.

'Esme is no better,' he offered, after an awkward silence. 'I keep trying to imagine what it will be like when the child arrives. I want to feel generous and supportive, but I don't and the nearer it gets ... And Esme is quite hysterical at times and is very unwilling to let the Grangers know when the baby is born. She's terrified they will somehow take the child. Make a legal claim somehow. You must try to reassure her, Millie.'

'I'll do my best, but I promised to tell them, Leo, and I will. They do have a right to know that much.' She glanced up at him as they passed one of the street lights. By the flickering gaslight she saw just how tired and drawn he looked. 'Are you eating properly?' she asked. 'You look thinner than I remember.'

'I'm not eating or sleeping and I'm struggling to keep up with my work.' He turned to look at her. 'The truth is, I no longer care for Esme and am almost at my wits' end without you, Millie. I don't know how I'm going to carry on and that's the bitter truth. I'm no use to Esme. I can't help her. Or myself. I can't face the future, Millie.' His voice shook. 'Yesterday I thought...' He closed his eyes briefly. 'I came to the conclusion I might as well end it all.'

Millie stopped abruptly, shocked and afraid. 'Leo! You can't say such a thing! End it all? You can't mean it!'

They stood in the darkness, staring at each other. Millie was stunned by his admission. Never in her worst moments had she ever imagined such a thing. Leo taking his own life? It was monstrous. She put up a hand to touch his face and found it wet with tears. 'Oh Leo!' She threw her arms around him as though she might physically protect him from himself. 'That's unthinkable! God in heaven! You must promise me you will never do such a thing. Promise me, Leo!'

But he remained silent, wrapped up in his misery, and for a long moment they clung fearfully together. Neither saw Ned, who was hurrying to catch up with them and who turned back without a word.

★ ★ ★

The following day, Millie hurried round in the early afternoon to see Esme's condition for herself. She was in two minds about alerting Esme to Leo's state of mind, assuming that perhaps, wrapped up in her own hysteria, Esme was unaware of her husband's desperation.

Knowing that Millie was going to call in, Esme had made an effort. She had washed and dressed and told Millie proudly that she had prepared a simple meal for Leo when he came home at midday.

'Don't you always prepare a meal for him?'

Esme pouted. 'How can I when I feel so weak? This beastly sickness! He often has bread and cheese or a slice of cold pie. He doesn't starve himself. If you felt as ill as I do, you'd be more understanding.'

On the surface Esme appeared reasonably normal, but Millie fancied she saw tell-tale signs in the nervous twisting of her fingers and the slightly breathless way she spoke. Glancing round the room, Millie also noted the vase of dead flowers and the ashes in the grate. How on earth was her sister going to care for a child when, in spite of her defiant words, it was obvious that she was barely managing to cope with the bare essentials of running a home? Millie began to see the situation in its entirety and found it deeply worrying. How exactly could matters improve if neither Leo nor Esme had the will to make changes? Hiding her dismay, she said briskly, 'Now what can I do to help?'

Leo had bought a small Christmas tree and Esme asked her to decorate it. As she draped it with ribbons and hung it with tiny stars, she encouraged her sister to share her woes.

'Leo tells me I'm becoming hysterical, but that's not true,' Esme insisted crossly. 'I'm able to rest and I can relax at home. Leo's the one who's under a strain because of his work. He worries about me for no good reason and tells the doctor I need something to calm me down. He's the one who needs help.' As she spoke, her hands clenched in her lap and there was something a little feverish in her eyes. 'He didn't have to go running to you yesterday. I don't *need* you – although it's good that you're here,' she added hastily, 'and I'm looking forward to Christmas.'

'I thought you were going to hire a nurse or someone to help you in the house.'

'Leo wanted to but I forbade it!' Her chin jutted. 'I don't want someone fussing round me all day. It would drive me crazy. Leo just wanted it for his own sake – to make life easier for *him*. And you weren't much help – determined to abandon me and "have a life of your own"!' Her tone made it clear that she would bear this particular grudge for a long time.

Trying to avoid the guilt this provoked, Millie bit back angry words and concentrated on the small fairy doll that was going to top the tree. She said, 'Is the doctor satisfied with your progress?'

Esme shrugged. 'He says I must rest in bed

299

whenever I feel weary, so I'm in bed most of the time and I'm *bored*! No one to talk to all day. And Leo keeps insisting that we have to inform the Grangers when the baby arrives.'

'We do.' Millie glanced at her anxiously. 'I agreed to it. You sent me down there to do what I could and I thought it fair. Naturally they will be interested. I told you, Esme: they are decent people.'

'Well-meaning do-gooders!'

'No!'

She stood back to admire her handiwork and Esme took the opportunity to change the subject by asking Millie about her work at Tapper's.

Millie described the previous evening, but it was clear that Esme wasn't listening – that there was something weighing on her mind. She seemed to be miles away, her expression dark, unhappiness etched into her features. Millie watched her uneasily from the corner of her eye until suddenly Esme said brightly, 'So, Millie, do you still see that young bailiff?' She forced a crooked smile. 'Ed Somebody?'

'Ned Warren, you mean.' Taken by surprise, Millie fell back on a lie. 'From time to time. He's very busy at the moment ... and so am I.' Her eyes narrowed. 'Are you all right, Esme?'

'Certainly! What makes you ask?' Her tone was defensive, but her lower lip trembled.

'You look so pale and...'

'My head aches abominably. I woke up with it. It happens a lot lately.'

To avoid upsetting her, Millie offered to make a pot of tea and escaped to the kitchen; she busied herself with the crockery while the kettle returned to the boil. She felt deeply sorry for Esme with her list of ailments and wondered how it would have been if the child had been Leo's. Would it have made any difference? Millie knew very little about pregnancies. She wondered if it were possible that Esme's guilt was exacerbating her problems; or if the worry of the Grangers' involvement had a bearing on her mental health. She could see why Leo was depressed, but Esme also deserved sympathy and it seemed Leo was unable to give it.

Deeply troubled she returned with the tray, but on re-entering the room was immediately alarmed to find Esme in floods of tears. Quickly setting down the tray she rushed to put a comforting arm round Esme's shoulder but it did no good. As Esme sobbed uncontrollably she muttered a jumble of words that made no sense. Seconds later she began to shake; then her eyes rolled back in her head and with a cry she collapsed and fell back in the chair unconscious.

'Esme!' Desperately Millie tried to rouse her. She patted her face, shouted at her and slapped her hands, but to no avail. She wanted the doctor but was afraid to leave Esme alone. Had this attack been triggered by the pregnancy? Or had Esme had a fit of some kind? Was this the hysteria Leo had hinted at?

Worse still was the thought that Esme might

die. In a panic, Millie decided she must first alert Leo and leave him to call the doctor. Leo must come home from the bank at once. This was definitely an emergency.

She shook Esme again and was relieved to see her eyelids flutter.

'Where ... What are you...?' Esme was recovering consciousness and Millie whispered a prayer of thanks. As soon as Esme was wide awake Millie fetched a quilt from the bedroom and wrapped it warmly around her sister, tucking the edges down into the chair.

'I won't be more than a minute or two,' Millie told her.

She went outside and found someone to take Leo the message.

Thankfully, Millie returned to the parlour and helped a very confused Esme to sip her tea. Gradually a faint colour seeped into her face and not long afterwards Leo arrived followed quickly by the doctor.

Millie waited in the kitchen until the doctor left. She watched Leo carry his wife up the stairs to the bedroom and was surprised to find the usual pang of envy missing. Was she at long last free of her consuming passion for Leo? The thought was a sobering one. How could the love she had felt for Leo throughout all those years be fading? Could that happen to true love? As she stared out of the window into the small back garden, the gloomy shadows cast by the familiar shrubs looked sinister. With a slight shudder Millie glanced upwards, but brooding cumulus clouds did nothing to lighten the sombre atmosphere and added to her growing fear. Suppose Esme had died! She would for ever have blamed herself for withholding help and friendship when her sister most needed them.

She reached up to close the curtains against the winter evening and, frowning, pushed the fear from her mind; instead, she pondered the unwelcome notion that she had fallen out of love with Leo. From what Leo had said the previous night he had not lost his love for *her*, so what did that say about the depth of her own emotions? Sighing, she turned as Leo came back into the room.

'The doctor's worried about her,' he said, dropping wearily into a chair and rubbing his eyes. 'The headaches are a bad sign – something to do with the pressure of her blood. And the nausea should be easing by now. She needs iron and he suggests spinach and other dark-green vegetables, but you know how Esme hates them. I asked him to give her a tonic instead.'

'What about the child?'

He shrugged. 'He says all is well ... so far. I got the impression that he was trying to be cheerful for our benefit, but underneath I sensed his disquiet.'

Millie came to a decision: 'I'll come back for a while, if you think I can make a difference, but...'

'Millie! You're an angel!' His expression brightened at once.

'But only if I can keep my job at Tapper's.'

Leo protested, as she knew he would, that she would be overworked and would become ill in her turn, but she resisted his arguments. In her heart she saw her return as a surrender, but Esme was her sister and she couldn't stand by and see her health deteriorate more. After further discussion it was agreed and Millie breathed a sigh of relief. She would move her possessions out of Poppy's flat and resume her residence at The Laurels but – and it was a big 'but' – she would be beholden to no one, would come and go as she pleased and would not give up her financial independence.

Two days later Millie was surprised and delighted to find Ned Warren waiting in the rain for her when she left Tapper's. His coat collar was turned up, his shoulders were hunched and water dripped from his hair.

'Ned! It's so good to see you.' She fumbled to open her umbrella and drew him beneath it. 'I thought – that is...'

'I'm sorry it's been so long.' He pulled her under the big black umbrella but made no attempt to kiss her. 'Have you missed me?'

'Most certainly I have!' She wanted to kiss him but was afraid of a rebuff. In the dim light from the nearest gas lamp it was difficult to see his expression.

At that moment Jessie emerged from the stage door and Millie introduced them. Jessie had no umbrella and was off in search of a taxi, but she gave Millie a large wink before she splashed away, her head down against the rain.

Ned said, 'Only when I came Saturday I nearly missed you, and then I saw you with Leo Walmsley and I wondered ... what exactly was going on.'

From his accusing tone of voice Millie realized at once that he had seen her embrace Leo. 'Ned! That was nothing. That hug. He was in the depth of despair – talking about ending his life!'

'Ending his life! You mean *killing* himself? But why?'

Millie hesitated. 'They have problems, Ned. Esme is deeply depressed and the doctor is worried. I was so sorry for him. That's all it was. The stage-doorkeeper told me a young man was waiting and I hoped it was you, but then Leo turned up so...'

'The chap said I was too early, so I went away and came back later on.'

'I came round to see you one day, but your father – he seemed to be warning me that you weren't interested any more. That you wouldn't want to see me.'

'I was busy.'

'Too busy to see me?'

He hesitated. 'Yes. I'm sorry. I was doing something for us – for you and me. Tomorrow I'll show you what it is.'

Millie noticed that his voice had lost some of its coldness. He slid an arm round her waist and at last she felt able to kiss him. For a moment they clung together and Millie's relief was intense. He hadn't abandoned her.

They began to make their way back to Poppy's flat, splashing through the dark puddles and ignoring the heavy rain. When they reached it, they huddled together, not wanting to be apart and Millie wished she had a flat of her own so that she could invite Ned inside for a cup of cocoa.

She said, 'You're soaked, Ned. Take my umbrella and—'

'No need. It doesn't bother me. Millie, I have to see you tomorrow. I want you to meet me at this address.' He pulled a piece of paper from his pocket and thrust it into her hand. 'I want you to meet me there at ten o'clock in the morning. You *must* be there, Millie. Will you promise?'

'I will but ... Where *is* this place? I mean, why do I...?'

Laughing, he pulled her close and kissed her. 'It's a surprise, Millie. Just *be* there!'

Before she could question him further he turned and ran back the way he had come. Millie watched until he was out of sight, then, with a light heart, lowered the umbrella and went in.

At five past ten Millie was ushered into the hallway of number 12, Carsley Road. The smell of new paint told her that it had been newly decorated a warm ochre and the wooden stairs had been scrubbed clean.

'Who lives here?' she asked, her voice low.

Instead of answering he led her into the

306

front room, where a small fire burned in the grate. There was no furniture except for a brass coal scuttle, newly polished, and a rug in front of the fire. It was bright and cheerful and the large bow window let in the sunlight.

Ned waved his hand. 'A few sticks of furniture. I thought you might like to help me choose some.'

'Me? But whose...?'

'A woman's touch. You know. It's for a friend of mine. Come and see the kitchen.'

Puzzled, she followed him into the small back room, which looked out over a tiny yard. The stove gleamed dully from a recent application of blacklead and a small table stood in splendid isolation in the centre of the floor. The window sparkled.

He said, 'It needs curtains. What do you think?'

'Yes, it does.'

'I mean what colour do you fancy?'

Millie looked at him suspiciously. 'Is this *your* flat, Ned?'

'No. It's ours, Millie.' His voice shook slightly. 'At least it's ours if you'll have me. That is, it's ours...' Seeing the shock in her eyes, Ned swallowed hard. 'You have to say yes, Millie! I – I did it for you. For us. I mean, I want us to live in it as man and wife.'

Millie felt faint with shock and joy. 'Man and wife? Oh Ned!' They stared at each other in a kind of wonder. 'I do say yes,' she stammered. 'I *will* marry you, Ned!'

Briefly he closed his eyes and his lips moved

in a silent prayer of thanks, and then he opened them and took Millie into his arms in a fierce embrace.

For Millie the next hour passed in a haze of excitement laced with unbelievable happiness. She was going to marry Ned. It was rather sudden, but it felt completely right and she didn't have a moment's doubt that they would be happy. They wandered the rooms, eagerly discussing the furniture and making plans for their future. At ten past eleven Stan turned up and was delighted by the news. He kissed Millie and congratulated his son.

'Now you know why Ned was so busy,' he told her. 'I helped here and there, but he did most of it single-handed. Worked his guts out, you might say. You should have seen it before he started. A proper dump!'

Ned explained that as soon as they had a few bits of furniture he would move in. By the time they were married it would be finished.

The wedding was set for early May so that Millie could stay with Esme until her child was born. Only then could she leave with an easy conscience. It suited Ned well enough, for he had plans for the garden and also wanted to do some overtime, if there was any, so that he could amass a few savings.

Before they left, Ernst Muller, the elderly German from upstairs, came down to introduce himself. He was a tall, sad man with dark eyes and a small beard, and he moved like someone troubled by rheumatism. On

hearing the good news, however, he brightened at once and warmly congratulated Ned
and Millie on their coming marriage.

'You vill be very happy in ziss house,' he
assured them. 'I tell you. Ziss is a happy
house!'

Millie, her hand in Ned's, gave him a bril-
liant smile. She didn't doubt him for a
moment.

Thirteen

20 April 1892

After Christmas winter came in earnest, with heavy snowfalls that softened the landscape but turned the roads into muddy slush. When it melted, the cold winds arrived and, to Millie's relief, Leo insisted that she take a taxi to and from Tapper's and he paid for it himself. It seemed that spring would never come. Gradually the weather improved, but still the weeks passed slowly for all three of them.

Esme became increasingly depressed and irritable, as her pregnancy continued to be problematic and the doctor was a regular visitor. Leo, dismayed by his wife's moods, became withdrawn, saying little and immersing himself in a book whenever he could. It was, Millie realized, his way of escaping the grim realities, but it meant that she had little in the way of companionship and began to rely heavily on her evenings at Tapper's and her time spent with Ned, which she felt were all that kept her sane.

When Esme's first contraction came, three

days earlier than expected, Millie was in the bedroom with her while downstairs in the kitchen Mrs Wetton was finishing off the ironing.

It was Wednesday, the twentieth of April and Esme had just struggled back to bed after her morning wash and a half-hearted attempt to clean her teeth. Millie had just helped her into a clean nightdress when Esme let out a groan and doubled up.

'Is it cramp again?' Millie asked.

For a moment Esme made no reply but continued to clutch her abdomen. At last she straightened up, her face white. 'It's a different pain. I – I think it's the baby!' she whispered.

Millie felt a moment of pure panic, which was replaced almost immediately by excitement and a rush of hope. Maybe the baby would change everything and miraculously bring Esme and Leo together again. She reined in her enthusiasm. First things first. Her first duty was to her sister and, seeing Esme's anguished expression, she forced herself to smile and to speak calmly.

'How wonderful! This is what we've all been waiting for.' She stepped forward, threw her arms round Esme and kissed her. 'Now you get back into bed while I get a message to Leo and—'

'I don't want Leo here!' Esme moved cautiously towards the bed and clambered in. 'He'll make me nervous! Tell him if you must, but ask him to stay at work. *Please*, Millie!'

Millie nodded. 'But I must also send Mrs Wetton for the midwife.'

Bette Sargent had been recommended by the doctor and had already visited the house on two occasions. She was a plump, comfortable woman, untidy but jolly. Millie thought her somewhat casual in her approach to the coming birth but knew that the doctor found her entirely acceptable. She and Esme seemed to get along well enough and Millie assumed that the coming baby was creating a bond of some kind between them. Maybe mother and midwife always found common ground.

Mrs Wetton, highly excited, was despatched to the midwife's house – which was three streets away – with a message that contractions had started. Leo was tied up with a client but a similar message was left for him and Millie, feeling strangely privileged, settled down to await events. She had resisted the instinct to telephone the Grangers, preferring to wait until the baby was born and she could tell them a few details. She knew very little about childbirth, although the doctor had sketched in the basic details for her in the unlikely event that she might somehow be forced to deal with the birth alone – a prospect that terrified her.

She was dismayed by the amount of pain her sister was experiencing and wondered how Esme could bear it. Nothing, it seemed, could prepare a woman for the agony and trauma of the birth of a first child. A knock at the door announced the return of Mrs Wetton with the midwife and Millie hovered in the kitchen while the first examination took place upstairs.

Mrs Wetton made a pot of tea for four. 'Don't you worry about your sister, Miss Bayley,' she said. 'It's no laughing matter, I grant you, but pain's a funny thing. The minute it ends and you're holding your little one, you forget it. If you didn't, you'd only ever have one kid! And if men had to have them, we probably wouldn't have any!'

In spite of her encouraging words Millie found it hard to bear the screams that came from upstairs, but when she ventured into the bedroom an hour later, Mrs Sargent smiled reassuringly. 'The water's have broken!' she said. 'A bit earlier than expected for a first-born but...'

'But quite normal?'

Mrs Sargent shrugged. 'Every birth is different,' she told Millie. 'Nothing to worry about.'

'Does it mean the baby will come early?' She hoped it would for her sister's sake.

Another shrug. 'We'll have to wait and see! You'll be an aunt before too long.'

Millie glanced down at Esme and squeezed her hand. 'All's going well then,' she said with an encouraging smile.

Esme tried to return the smile, but there was a sheen of perspiration on her face and the hair clung damply to her forehead. There was a haunted look in her eyes as she anticipated the next contraction.

She said, 'Leo was delighted when he heard the news. I told him the baby might already be born by the time he gets home.' This wasn't true, but did it matter if it made Esme happier?

Mrs Sargent pulled a wry face. 'That was a bit hopeful. First babies take their time.' She was relaxing in a chair beside the bed, knitting something that looked like a shawl. Seeing Millie's gaze, she held it up for inspection. 'Shawl for my grandson. Due in a month's time.' She explained that she had three daughters and five grandchildren. 'I don't get time to do much knitting, so I give each one a shawl and that's the end.'

An hour later it seemed to Millie's inexperienced eyes that Esme was no nearer the end of her struggle and she made her excuses and went downstairs. Mrs Wetton had gone home and Millie took refuge in the familiar warmth of the kitchen, where she huddled on a chair by the stove. One day, she thought with a smile, she would be in Esme's position but with *Ned*'s baby on the way. For Ned she would willingly go through the agonies of childbirth to give him the family he craved. Her smile broadened. In just over four weeks she and Ned would be married and she would move into number 12, Carsley Road to begin her new life.

But for Esme, her troubles might not be over. If only this were Leo's child and not Henry Granger's ... Her thoughts wandered to the Granger family. Soon Millie would be writing with the news. She thought of widowed Dorcas, her autocratic mother and the two sons. The child would mean something significant to all of them. These thoughts led to Edmund, their fateful ride through Rotten Row and her own gullibility.

'Stupid. *Stupid!*' she muttered.

If only she had kept the truth from Edmund, the Grangers need never have been involved. She would never forgive herself for that. Thinking of Edmund brought her naturally to memories of Clive and she shuddered. As the unpleasant memories began to take over, she pushed them firmly to the back of her mind. Those days were over. She jumped to her feet. Inactivity was no use to her, she decided, and, finding a tin of polish and some dusters, she hurried into the parlour and began to work on the furniture.

The baby – a girl – was finally delivered at half past one the following morning and not a moment too soon, in Millie's opinion. After a long and difficult labour Esme's face was flushed and her eyes glazed with exhaustion. She gave her child a hurried kiss then fell into an uneasy sleep while the midwife went about her work undeterred, cutting the cord, washing the child and tidying the bedroom. Millie offered to help, but Mrs Sargent insisted she could do it quicker herself and, to prove it, was soon out of the house and on her way home.

Leo had moved into the spare room for a few days to allow mother and baby a little space. At least that was his explanation and no one had challenged it.

For an hour in the big bedroom Millie sat beside her sleeping sister and watched Henry Granger's little daughter as she dozed fitfully in her small wooden crib. The baby reminded Millie of Lance Granger – small, with fine ginger hair and delicate features. Fascinated, Millie studied the small nose and rosebud mouth and the tiny fingers so tightly clenched.

'Welcome, little Flora,' she whispered, stroking the downy hair.

After much discussion they had decided to name a girl after Aunt Flora. Esme had confided that she wanted the name Henrietta, after the child's father; but Millie, shocked, had persuaded her to abandon the idea, arguing that another permanent reminder to Leo of his wife's infidelity was out of the question.

Flora fidgeted in her sleep and Millie smiled down at her, trying to imagine the life she would have. Esme would adore her, but how would poor Leo feel about her? Perhaps he would grow to love her. If he didn't...

She pulled herself up sharply. There was no point in imagining the worst. They must live one day at a time and, hopefully, with patience and goodwill on all sides, the problems would solve themselves.

'I love you, Flora,' she told the sleeping

child, 'and your mama loves you. Your great-aunt Flora will be delighted with you.'

Tomorrow Esme would write to Aunt Flora and Millie would write to the Grangers.

'The Grangers!' she muttered. That was another thorny problem that would have to be solved. Millie sighed. The future for Esme and her husband was not going to be easy, but Ned had told Millie not to let *their* problems spoil her own happiness and she knew he was right. Now she reminded herself about the dress she had bought for the wedding – a simple skirt and jacket of soft cream silk and shoes to match. As soon as Esme was on her feet again they would go shopping for her and Millie knew that the prospect of a shopping trip, after so many months feeling ungainly and awkward, was something her sister was desperately looking forward to. In her mind's eye she saw herself and Ned standing together at the altar, making their wedding vows, and Ned carrying her over the threshold of their flat. They had invited Ernst Muller and Mrs Potts from the basement and Stan and Aunt Flora would also be there.

In a more cheerful frame of mind Millie finally tore herself away and tiptoed back to her own room and into bed, where she slept soundly, unaware that her optimism was about to be severely challenged.

At first it seemed that the baby's arrival was helping to dispel some of the gloom. Esme, transformed by the presence of her baby, quickly mastered the art of breastfeeding and little Flora was a contented baby. Leo professed a polite interest in the child, which satisfied Esme, although Millie saw through his half-hearted enthusiasm and wondered if it would last. The first hint of trouble came three days later, when Esme complained that her right leg hurt.

'It's my calf,' she told Millie. 'It's quite tender when I touch it and it ached so much I was awake half the night.'

Alarmed, Millie felt the need for advice, but Mrs Sargent was busy with another confinement, so they called in the doctor, who examined the leg and found it slightly swollen above the knee. This, he confided to Millie, was a worrying complication.

His voice heavy with anxiety, he explained that on occasions during childbirth, a clot of blood could settle in the leg. 'For various reasons, Mrs Walmsley has been almost bed-ridden for too long. The clot causes the leg to swell and can travel up into a major vein. We call it an embolism, but there is no need to alarm your sister. There are steps we can take to dissolve it.'

Millie nodded. 'I won't tell Mr Walmsley either. He will only—'

He glanced up sharply. 'On the contrary, he *should* be informed. This can be very serious, Miss Bayley.'

Thoroughly frightened, Millie stared at him, but he avoided her gaze, busying himself

318

with the contents of his black bag.

Twenty-four hours later the leg was severely swollen and Esme was in a lot of pain. At twenty to four, as Millie walked the baby up and down after her feed, Esme gave a sudden cry. Millie turned towards her and saw that she was doubled up in pain and her face was chalk-white. With a cry of agony Esme stiffened. She stared at Millie with terrified eyes and then slowly fell sideways with one arm dangling over the edge of the bed. Millie returned the baby to her cot and rushed to her sister's side.

'Esme! *Esme!*' she shouted. 'Speak to me! Oh God!' Frantically she waited for Esme to regain consciousness, but she remained still and silent. Gently, her heart racing, Millie lifted her up and laid her back against the pillows.

As though aware of the tension, Flora began to whimper, but Millie barely noticed. She was holding her sister's wrist and waiting for a pulse which didn't come. Frozen with shock, she waited. This couldn't be happening. Esme *must* open her eyes – or make a small sound. Anything to prove that she was still alive.

'Esme! You can't – you have to open your eyes!'

Fifteen minutes later she drew all the curtains at the front of the house to indicate a death. Baby Flora's mother would never open her eyes again.

★　★　★

319

Later that evening the house had fallen silent behind the drawn curtains. Leo and Millie sat at the kitchen table, dazed and numb with grief, and tried to come to terms with their loss. Millie's eyes were red from weeping and her hands were constantly in motion, wiping away tears, fidgeting nervously with her locket or pushing back a stray strand of hair. Leo's eyes were dark with grief and the shock of loss.

Millie broke the silence: 'I should have noticed what was happening...'

'Stop it, Millie!' Leo lifted his head wearily. 'You can't blame yourself. The doctor said there was no way anyone could have foreseen it. It was a pulmonary embolism and they are always fatal. It happens.'

'But I didn't help, did I? Perhaps if—'

'Don't you think I've been thinking along those same lines, Millie? If I'd been more caring ... If I'd taken more interest ... If the baby had been mine ... So many "ifs".' He covered his face with his hands and groaned.

Millie could think of nothing to say. She couldn't help him. She was overwhelmed by the conviction that her own happiness and forthcoming marriage had made her selfishly unobservant. The sudden nature of the tragedy had shattered her peace of mind and now a large question mark hung over her plans. Leo had been left with another man's child to bring up and Millie knew that the strain would be too much to bear. Few men could survive such an unkind twist of fate and Leo had never been strong emotionally.

She said, 'The doctor will find a nurse for her, but later you'll need a kind-hearted woman to care for her – and for you. You might...'

But Leo had turned to her with shocked expression. 'A kind-hearted woman? What on earth...? I thought *you* would stay with me. Esme is gone and now you and I can be together. Isn't this what we have always wanted? – just to be together. We can bring up the child. I could bear it if you were with me, Millie. I think Esme might approve if she is looking down on us. You and me and her child.'

Stunned by the suggestion, Millie struggled for words. Did he expect her to give up her life with Ned? It had never occurred to her and now she was shocked in her turn.

She stammered, 'But what about Ned? He's expecting to marry me in a few weeks' time. We love each other, Leo. Everything's arranged.'

He stared at her in disbelief. 'You don't seem to understand, Millie. He knew he was only second best...'

'Second best? No! Ned was never that!'

'My dear, he *was*! You agreed to marry Ned Warren because you and I could never be together. But now we can. Fate has intervened. You will have little Flora to bring up. We'll bring her up as ours ... and we will have each other. We cannot marry, but officially you can be my housekeeper. It happens all the time. Please, Millie!' He reached for her hand and clasped it tightly. 'I can't believe you will let me down. I need you, Millie. Without you I shall die. Understand that, Millie. I shall simply give up and die.'

Confused and desperate, Millie nodded, trying to put her thoughts in order. Was this where her duty lay? 'I don't know, Leo. I can't do this to Ned. He adores me – and I love him.'

Leo drew back, startled, and frowned. 'Are you saying you don't love me, Millie?'

'No. I'm saying that I still love you *in a way*, but...'

'Millie! You told me when I fell for Esme that you would never love anyone else! I thought that at least *you* would stand by me. I *need* you, Millie!'

Millie regarded him steadily. I needed you then, she thought, but you deserted me for Esme. There was no bitterness in her heart and no sense of retaliation. She was simply acknowledging that she owed him nothing. 'Time has passed since then, Leo. I was very young and now I love Ned and am promised to him. I can't and won't desert him.' She took a deep breath. This was the moment to make matters entirely clear to him. 'I don't want to devote the rest of my life to you and Esme's child. I deserve more than that, Leo.'

'So you intend to desert me?' He pushed back his chair and sprang to his feet.

Staring at her with a mixture of anger and fear, he struggled for words then shook his head in frustration. Without another word he rushed from the room and she heard him open and then slam the front door. The noise woke the baby, who began to cry, and Millie hurried upstairs; but within minutes Flora had gone back to sleep, a tiny fist pressed against her mouth. Millie knelt beside the crib and watched her, fascinated as usual. This was Esme's child, the baby she had wanted for so long. How ironic that the baby's birth had brought about her death. For a moment she wondered if she had been too hasty. Was this God's way of making it possible for her to live with Leo and have a child? Could Leo be right about that?

'But I want to marry Ned!' she whispered. 'I want to have my own child – more than one, in fact. I want to be with Ned and give him a family.'

Ten minutes later she went downstairs. Glancing at the clock, she saw that it was just after ten and now she began to worry about Leo. He had looked so desperate when he left the house. Her first instinct was to go in search of him, but she could hardly leave the baby alone in the house – and where would she look for him? He could be anywhere.

Exhausted by the traumas of the past few days Millie fell heavily into a chair and waited. She tried telling herself that Leo was a grown man and it was not her job to look after him, but it still felt wrong to go to bed without knowing that he was safely home. As the minutes became hours, she began to think fearfully that perhaps he *had* been pushed to the end of his endurance. Perhaps she should go to the police ... but they would laugh at her. He had only been gone a matter of hours. With a sigh she made up the stove and fetched a shawl. With her dead sister in the hospital morgue and a motherless baby asleep upstairs, Millie thought bitterly that it surely must be one of the darkest nights of her life.

When Millie awoke next morning, cramped from her sleep in the chair, it was five to eight. She listened for sounds from the baby and, hearing nothing, hurried upstairs. A glance into the main bedroom showed her that Leo had not returned. Baby Flora was wide awake. Quickly Millie washed and pulled on the black dress she had worn to her father's funeral then returned to the baby. She was about to scoop her from the crib when she heard the front door open and shut and ran downstairs to greet Leo. He looked haggard, his clothes crumpled, his hair dishevelled, his face unshaven.

He held up his hand to ward off her reproaches. 'Don't, Millie! I know I've been a thoughtless idiot. You must have been worried.'

'I've hardly slept, Leo! What were you thinking of?' In spite of her relief at seeing him alive and well she was unable to hold back her anger. 'You left me alone here – wondering if you had thrown yourself into

324

the Thames! How could you? Don't you think I have enough on my plate without...'

He stopped her by stepping forward and throwing his arms round her. His kiss was fierce and his stubble scratched her face as she tried to pull back.

It was difficult enough, for her instinct was to return the kiss by way of consolation, but that was out of the question.

'No, Leo!' she gasped. 'You know we can't do this.'

He released her immediately. 'I'm sorry. That was selfish of me. Forgive me.' She nodded and told him to go upstairs and sleep, but he shook his head.

'I've walked the streets and done a lot of hard thinking. I can't run away any longer. The doctor will be calling with the death certificate and there are arrangements to be made for the funeral. I'll wash, shave and change my clothes. You'll see, Millie: I'm not as useless as you imagine.'

Millie washed and fed the baby and as she held the small warm bundle in her arms, she began to have doubts. This lovely little girl deserved all the love Esme would have given her and for a few intense moments Millie felt torn between her two futures. Should she stay with Leo and Flora? Could she face a loveless existence – because that was what it would mean. If she and Leo were secret lovers, she might have a child and the inevitable scandal would be disastrous for all of them. Sighing, she kissed Flora and returned her to the crib

325

just as Mrs Sargent arrived to check up on her progress. Leo appeared, looking tired but respectable, and Millie left them to their discussion. With a heavy heart she made herself concentrate on the various household tasks that needed to be done.

She was longing to see Ned and tell him what had happened, but there had been no opportunity. More than anything she longed to be with him and to feel safe. In her present state of mind it seemed impossible that she would ever be happy again. The loss of her sister would shadow everything, and the wedding to which she had been looking forward would now be a more sombre occasion without Esme. It might even have to be postponed because the family was in mourning.

She had also promised Leo that she would write to the Grangers and break the bad news. After a hurried breakfast of scrambled eggs, which was shared with Leo and Mrs Sargent, Leo set off for the funeral director's office; Millie saw Mrs Sargent out and sat down to write the letter. She had written only five lines when there was a knock at the front door. To her dismay she stared into the anguished face of Dorcas Granger.

'The curtains!' Dorcas cried, a hand on her heart. 'Please, *please* don't tell me Henry's baby has died. I don't think we could bear it.'

'It's not the baby. I was writing to you when you knocked.' Millie opened the door and Dorcas stepped inside. 'It's the mother. It's Esme.' Fresh tears spilled from her eyes and after a moment's hesitation, Dorcas put her arms round her.

'Your sister? Oh, my dear girl! How simply dreadful!'

Millie led the way into the parlour and invited her visitor to sit down while she alerted Mrs Wetton to the need for tea and biscuits. Dorcas, to her credit, looked genuinely shocked by the news and listened attentively to the details of the tragedy.

'What can I say?' she asked. 'I'm so sorry. And what a cruel twist of fate. I know how much your sister longed for the baby. Is it another boy?'

'A girl! They have called her Flora after an aunt.'

Dorcas brightened. 'A girl! That's wonderful!'

Millie nodded. 'But let's go up and see little Flora while we wait for the tea. Her father – I mean Leo – will be back eventually. He's gone to arrange the funeral.'

Dorcas took Millie's hand. 'All your joy turned to grief. It's so unfair. I know my mother would want me to express her regrets also.' As she followed Millie up the stairs, she said, 'How has your brother-in-law reacted to Flora? It's not unusual for the father to blame the child for the wife's death. And in the difficult circumstances...'

Millie paused on the landing. Unwilling to betray Leo, she said, 'He's in a state of shock, as you can imagine. I think he's very confused and wretched at the moment.'

'You must have your hands full. I can still remember Henry's death. There seemed to be too few hours in the day to deal with everything.'

Millie was silenced by this reminder. How painful the events must have been for Dorcas and her family. At least Esme's death was not about to promote rumour and cruel gossip.

As they went up the stairs, Millie said, 'I'm getting married in a few weeks' time.'

'Miss Bayley! How wonderful for you.'

'I haven't had a chance yet to talk to my fiancé. He doesn't even know Esme's dead.' She shrugged helplessly.

They walked into the bedroom and found Flora fast asleep. She looked perfect, and Millie saw tears shining in Dorcas's eyes as she looked down at her husband's legacy.

'She's beautiful,' Dorcas whispered. 'Incredible. The image of Lance when he was born! The same ginger hair. Maria will be so thrilled when I tell her.' She swallowed hard. 'How could something so wonderful come out of something so...' Raising a hand quickly to her mouth she stifled the rest of the sentence, but Millie guessed that she had almost said 'sordid', and her next words confirmed that her guess was correct. 'Miss Bayley, I'm so sorry. I didn't mean ... That was so stupid of me!'

Millie flew to Esme's defence. 'It was wrong, but Esme genuinely thought she loved him. Maybe she did. She thought he was free to marry her.'

Dorcas rolled her eyes. 'Poor Esme. And poor, foolish Henry. I don't doubt he loved her *at the time*! He could never resist an attractive woman, but he didn't always treat them well. The news of the pregnancy must have terrified him.' She sighed and shook her head. 'God have mercy on Henry's women! Me, the Gayford woman, Esme, his poor mother Maria ... and even you, Miss Bayley.'

'Me?' Millie blinked. 'I can assure you...'

Dorcas managed a faint smile. 'Not in that way, but haven't you been dealing with the after-effects for months and trying to undo all the damage? You have been drawn into Henry's net just as surely as the rest of us!'

They drank tea together and talked for the best part of an hour until Flora began to cry and then Millie brought her down and handed her to Dorcas. She warmed some milk and left Dorcas to spoon the milk into the tiny mouth.

Leo returned and was taken aback by the news that Flora and Dorcas were together in the parlour. He stood in the middle of the kitchen and regarded Millie with horror. 'What's she doing here? Who invited her?'

'Nobody did, but she couldn't wait to see the baby. She has travelled up from Somerset on Maria's orders! By rights she should have been Flora's mother.'

'I can't see her. I wouldn't know what to say to her.' He was already halfway out of the door, but Millie caught hold of his sleeve.

329

'Wait, Leo. You must speak to her. It's only civil.'

'Civil? Her husband seduced my wife!'

'Esme must have been willing, Leo. She was in love, remember.'

'She thought she was!' His eyes narrowed with the beginnings of anger.

'You *thought* you loved Esme, as I recall!' Millie snapped. She refused to lower her gaze and at last he let out a long breath.

'I'll see her. Five minutes, that's all!'

Millie watched him walk stiff-necked from the kitchen. He went into the parlour and shut the door firmly to let Millie know she wasn't wanted.

'That suits me!' she muttered. Being one of Henry's women had no appeal for her and she longed to escape. She felt desperately weary and tearful and on impulse she hurried up the passage, pulled on her jacket and went out. She needed to be with her beloved Ned.

When she returned several hours later, she found Leo sitting in the kitchen with his head in his hands. When he looked up, she saw that he had been weeping.

'She's gone, Millie, and you mustn't blame me.'

Millie groaned inwardly. They had quarrelled. She should never have left them. She unbuttoned her gloves. 'What did you say to her? You must have known she was in a delicate state. Poor Dorcas.'

'Not Dorcas. I mean the baby. Flora.'

Millie frowned. What on earth was he saying?

He repeated: 'The baby's gone, Millie. It was...'

'Dorcas stole the baby? Oh God! I never would have—'

'No, Millie. She took her with my blessing. I gave her the baby. She wants to adopt it. She begged me and – and I thought it best.'

Millie sat down heavily and tried to take it in. 'Flora has gone?'

'I knew you wouldn't agree so I said—'

'Oh Leo! What would Esme think? You gave away her child!'

'It's what Dorcas wanted.'

Millie shook her head. 'No! She came to *see* the child. She wanted to see it, that's all.'

'But that's because she didn't know what had happened. When she knew Esme was dead and had time to think about it, she saw that I was not the right person to bring up the baby. Sweet as she was, the child was nothing to me. She was everything to Dorcas. Flora was Henry's child and Dorcas has always wanted a girl.' He rubbed his face tiredly. 'Their lawyer will be in touch. I've given my word, Millie, and I won't go back on it.'

His logic was irrefutable and Millie wavered. Almost reluctantly, she was beginning to see it all from the point of view of Dorcas Granger and reluctantly admitted to herself that Leo spoke the truth. Far better for Flora to grow up where she was loved and cherished by her own family than be brought up by a reluctant Leo as a constant reminder of Esme's infidelity.

He said, 'I know you won't forgive me, but one day, before too long, you'll have a child of your own. Yours and Ned's. Somehow I have to pick up the pieces and go on with my life. That's what Dorcas said.'

Millie whispered, 'Flora is my niece!'

He looked at her eagerly. 'Dorcas said she would ask you to be her godmother and you could see her whenever you wished. You haven't lost her, Millie.'

'But I'll miss her. I loved her.' Her voice shook.

'But not enough to stay with me and bring her up as ours.' His voice was full of reproach. 'You made your choice, Millie. You chose Ned.'

Still deeply shocked, Millie thought of the tiny child asleep in the crib and burst into tears of anguish. Leo came round the table, pulled her to her feet, held her close and murmured soft words of consolation. Somewhere deep in her heart Millie knew that he was holding her for the very last time.

Two years later, Millie and Ned stood in the sunshine on the lawn at Harlene Hall and watched young Flora running across the grass after a red felt ball on a string which Lance was pulling. Finally he allowed her to catch up with it and she gathered it to her with a peal of laughter. The young man was smiling and the little girl laughed up at him.

Her eyes were as green as his.

Dorcas smiled at Millie. 'He adores her,' she said. 'Both boys did, but especially Lance. I was astonished. I thought they might resent her.'

Millie held her own child in her arms – a boy of fifteen months named Robert Stanley after his grandfather. He had the same dark curls as Ned but his eyes were brown. Now he struggled impatiently to free himself and she set him down on the grass. Robert had only just learned to walk and still preferred to crawl everywhere at great speed.

Today was the twenty-first of April – Flora's second birthday. The Grangers often invited Millie and Ned to stay with them and they all enjoyed the visits. Although Maria was adamant that they would never tell Flora about Esme and Henry, they wanted Millie to see her grow up and to reassure her that the little girl was happy.

As Robert set off towards Flora, Ned said proudly, 'He'll be having a little brother or sister before too long!' and winked at Millie.

Dorcas cried, 'Really? Congratulations.'

Millie said, 'Leo sends his best wishes. Did I tell you he was courting? Her name's Dorothea Levine and she works at the same bank, so they are having to be very discreet. But we like her, don't we, Ned?'

He nodded. 'He went through a bad time but she's done him a power of good.' He touched Millie's arm. 'Maria is calling to you.'

'Oh! Is she?' Millie turned and waved to the old lady who had just been carried out from the house and settled in her favourite chair. A card table was set beside her with a glass of lemonade. Millie walked across to talk to her as the cook came towards them, carrying the birthday cake.

Millie stood beside Maria and Dorcas paused as she passed. She whispered, 'Here we are again! Three of Henry's women! Four if you count Flora! I wish he could see how we have all survived the storm.'

Except for poor Esme, Millie amended silently. For a moment she thought wistfully of her sister but said nothing to spoil the moment. Poppy, another of his women, had married Clive and moved away. With a glance heavenward, Millie hoped Esme might also be looking down on them to admire her beautiful daughter.

Sometimes in the darkness of a wakeful night, Millie wondered about Henry Granger. How little she had guessed, when she had seen him in Tapper's Supper Room, that he would change so many lives, in so many ways, for ever.